CROSSING THE CONTINENT

Also by Michel Tremblay

Chronicles of the Plateau Mont-Royal

CROSSING THE CONTINENT

A Novel

MICHEL TREMBLAY

Translated by Sheila Fischman

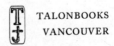

TALONBOOKS
VANCOUVER

Talonbooks
P.O. Box 2076, Vancouver, British Columbia, Canada v6b 3s3
www.talonbooks.com

Typeset in Adobe Caslon and printed and bound in Canada.
Printed on 100% post-consumer recycled paper.
First printing: 2011

The publisher gratefully acknowledges the financial support of the Canada Council for the Arts; the Government of Canada through the Book Publishing Industry Development Program; and the Province of British Columbia through the British Columbia Arts Council for our publishing activities.

La traversée du continent by Michel Tremblay was first published in French in 2007 by Leméac Éditeur and Actes Sud. We acknowledge the financial support of the Government of Canada through the National Translation Program for Book Publishing, for our publishing activities.

LIBRARY AND ARCHIVES CANADA CATALOGUING IN PUBLICATION

Tremblay, Michel, 1942–

[Traversée du continent. English]
Crossing the continent / Michel Tremblay ;
translated by Sheila Fischman.

Translation of: La traversée du continent.
ISBN 978-0-88922-676-0

I. Fischman, Sheila II. Title.
III. Title: Traversée du continent. English.

PS8539.R47T6813 2011   C843'.54   C2011-902481-0

This is a work of fiction. The names
of some characters are real, but
everything else is made up.

— M. T.

For Lise Bergevin, who has been asking me for ages for a novel about Nana's childhood

*Him do I hate even as the gates of hell who says
one thing while he hides another in his heart.*
— HOMER
The Iliad, translated by SAMUEL BUTLER, 1898

*To write is to make the dead rise from their
graves and to pull them along into the light.*
— ROBERT LALONDE
Espèces en voie de disparition

*Imagining something is better than
remembering something.*
— JOHN IRVING
The World According to Garp

1

THE HOUSE IN THE MIDDLE OF NOWHERE

They took shelter on the veranda that surrounds the house on three sides. Grandpa Méo had built it a few years ago, to keep them – Rhéauna, the eldest; Béa, who was younger; and Alice, the youngest – from getting lost in the endless fields that file past to the horizon, where it's so easy to lose your way toward the end of summer when the corn is high. And for a promenade in the evening with his wife on his arm, without having to worry about the mud or the dust from the dirt road that leads to the main route. They cover ten times, twenty times the length of the wooden veranda from end to end and stop when Joséphine declares that she's too tired to go on, when they both know that it's Méo whose legs aren't what they used to be. The neighbours think the addition to the house is useless and even more, pretentious, but if they'd known how much pleasure it gives Joséphine and Méo on their long walk every night they might change their opinion.

The two little girls are sitting on the top step of the big white-painted staircase, their knees squeezed together, and they've placed their precious paper bags between them. Alice is having her nap in their room and she will discover her surprise bag on her pillow when she wakes up. The girls suspect that it won't be much of a surprise today because money has been scarce for some time and the exotic fruits – oranges, for instance, or the legendary pineapples they had tasted, howling with happiness, a few years before – have disappeared from the Sunday afternoon menus with no hope that they will come back. Grandma Joséphine had practically apologized when she took the three tiny bags from the cupboard where she'd hidden them. But the two girls had laid on their enthusiasm a little too thickly and Grandma seemed satisfied. No one was fooled, but their Sunday afternoon was saved from monotony.

Before opening them, they try to guess what might be inside the two brown paper bags.

Béa scratches her knee where a mosquito bite is blooming into a big red spot that's been causing her a good deal of pain since morning because she's been scratching it so much. A vicious circle that has been driving them all crazy since the beginning of summer. Although Grandma has been telling them not to scratch, that it will be gone in half an hour if they tough it out, but they can't help themselves, especially Grandpa who all his life has sported the most spectacular and nastiest sores. So they scratch their itches with their fingernails, emitting long sighs of relief, even if it means that a few minutes later it will all begin again, worse than before. Even Grandma doesn't follow her own advice: she complains a little too often about how her arthritis is so painful that she has to massage her bones, her excuse for scratching herself ... Her three granddaughters and her husband laugh a little and she tells them, with a shrug and a smile of bad faith at the corners of her lips, that they can't imagine how painful arthritis is. Meanwhile, Béa's knee is a pitiful sight and Rhéauna expects a crying jag before the day is over. Béa is more lethargic, but for some unknown reason, not so patient than the rest of them.

"Anyway, it can't be candy, the bag doesn't weigh enough."

Rhéauna shrugs.

"I don't care what it is as long as it's something to eat."

Béa lets out that laugh of hers that so often sends flocks of crows up from the fields. This time it's a rabbit that scampers off, ears flat, muzzle quivering.

"Don't worry, we can eat it. Grandma knows us."

Her sister hefts the bag again.

"Could be, but I don't think it's very filling ... It hardly weighs a thing!"

On that she's mistaken. Béa is the first to open her bag, as usual, and is instantly ecstatic.

"Peanuts in the shell! We haven't had those for ages!"

Grandma had found a huge bag of peanuts in the shell on

display out front of the general store the day before and, despite the exorbitant price, thought she'd make the children happy by purchasing a handful for their Sunday afternoon snack. Peanuts are a rare commodity in Maria, Saskatchewan, in this year of the Lord 1913, and she wondered how the bag had ended up on Monsieur Connells's steps. She knew that peanuts came from the southern United States, Georgia or the Carolinas, anyway, a good long train trip and, during her lifetime, she had seen them only rarely.

Béa thrusts her hand into her bag, takes out a peanut and pops it open with her thumb and forefinger.

"Just think, Grandma pretended she was sorry when she gave it to us. She really got us. What a surprise!"

Rhéauna's mouth is already full.

"It's so good, it's so good, it's yummy!"

Béa taps her arm.

"Don't talk with your mouth full."

"Look who's talking! You could've waited to swallow before you said that."

The next few minutes are pure delight. Happy, they laugh, bodies offered to the sun, mouths full of the sweetish taste of the peanuts which they chewed for as long as possible before they swallowed. To make it last.

The last peanut is gone and Rhéauna looks at her sister who hasn't finished masticating.

"You fixed it so you'd finish after me!"

Béa gives her a big smile.

"Grandma says so all the time, Nana. You eat too fast."

It's true. She likes to eat and when her plate arrives she has trouble containing herself: all those wonderful things to eat, often fatty because they don't skimp on butter in the house, they attract her and she's not satisfied until she fills her mouth, emphasizing the pleasure she feels at the combination of tastes with little exclamations of bliss that amuse the rest of the family. Especially eight-year-old Alice who thinks that she's the funniest thing on earth with her clucks like an excited turkey and her sighs of contentment.

"And Grandma always says you make everybody wait because you don't eat fast enough."

Which is also true. It sometimes seems that Béa deliberately chews for too long as if to test the family's patience. But she claims it's because she likes to swallow her food after she's extracted all the juice, and they've decided to believe her.

But Rhéauna doesn't think she's been beaten. She takes a peanut shell from her bag, rubs it a little with her forefinger to remove the stiff little hairs attached to it and pops it in her mouth. She knows that Béa is too scornful to take up the challenge, ensuring herself of an easy victory that's still fairly agreeable. So she starts to chew with little murmurs of appreciation as if she'd just put a delicious candy in her mouth, one of the ones she and Béa liked best, a honeymoon or a peppermint heart.

"Anyway, you can't boast about winning today! It's my turn, I'm going to finish way after you!"

Béa gapes at her for several long seconds before replying:

"You'd have to give me a brand-new dollar with the King of England's picture on it to make me eat that and I wouldn't eat it. It doesn't count, you'll find out when you eat things you aren't supposed to. You're cheating, Nana. What's in your mouth isn't even real food!"

Rhéauna goes on with her painful mastication. It tastes terrible. Like a rough piece of wood with no juice. It breaks between her teeth with an unpleasant sound instead of soaking with saliva, it scrapes her tongue, it sticks to the roof of her mouth and she'll have to chew for hours before she can swallow it. And she's not sure that she can ... Also, it doesn't even taste like peanuts, it tastes like the bark of a tree. Just the thought that she is chewing a piece of bark turns her stomach. Only pride keeps her from spitting it to the bottom of the steps, where the ants would be thrilled with the unexpected feast. The girls have discovered any number of spat-out candies crawling with ants that try to dissect and then transport them to their nest. In fact, one of their sister Alice's favourite games is to find what she calls "alive candies," then sit and watch the nervous little bugs, studying them for hours without tiring.

Meanwhile, Béa turns away, pinching her nose.

"If you're going to throw up, smarty-pants, go do it inside the house. I don't feel like having Grandma make me help you clean up your mess!"

But there's no question of Rhéauna losing face. Béa won't have the satisfaction of seeing her grimace as she spits out the pulp of wet peanut shell. So she persists, chews, swallows the bit of liquid that tastes like the devil, without flinching, sitting stiffly on the top step, maybe staring a little but with forehead high and heart pounding: she has just asked herself what would happen if by bad luck peanut shells turned out to be poisonous.

Because it often happens that the two of them are like communicating vessels, always thinking the same things at the same time even though they aren't twins, Rhéauna is not surprised when her sister says barely a few seconds after the thought had crossed her mind:

"I think I read somewhere that peanut shells are poisonous."

Rhéauna smiles despite the more and more disgusting taste that fills her mouth.

"If you're trying to scare me you're wasting your time."

"I just said it so you'll know."

"Yeah, sure ..."

"Sometimes it's even fatal."

"If it were fatal you'd have stopped me before I put it in my mouth, Béa. You're my sister."

Béa moves very close to her. Rhéauna can smell peanuts on her breath, an odour so wonderful it makes her want to spit out the horror that she's masticating.

"Who says I'd've stopped you from eating your shell even if I knew it was fatal?"

"Come on, Béa, you wouldn't have let me die ..."

"Oh, no? That's what you think."

Tears, fat and generous and numerous, are there before Rhéauna can hold them back. A few seconds later, they've wet her face and neck. Béa also possesses the loathsome power to always come up with the words that will burn, aiming every time at the place that hurts most, and she's happy to use it on the whole family, her grandparents as much as her two sisters. It's not spiteful, it's her way of defending herself and everyone knows it; Grandma Joséphine has explained it more than once. But it's painful and it's sometimes hard to forgive her for what she's said. Afterward, of course, she claims she didn't mean it …

Rhéauna knows very well that Béa would never let her die, not poisoned by a peanut shell or any other way, but the mere thought that she can actually claim the opposite so she'll think that she hasn't lost the ridiculous bet overwhelms her though she doesn't know why, and she realizes that she can't hold back the goddamn tears that must delight Béa, despite the impassive face she shows.

She wipes her eyes, her cheeks, her neck on the sleeve of her crushed cherry-red dress that she likes so much. Even that is going to be ruined!

"Nana, your dress is going to be covered with snot."

Rhéauna is on her feet in less than a second and she points to her sister after spitting out what she had in her mouth, the better to enunciate:

"You're taking revenge, aren't you? You're taking revenge because for once I won! You're always like that! You can't accept not winning. You always have to put in your two cents' worth or else you make us pay for not letting you have your way. Have you any idea how bad what I put in my mouth was? You could've let me win for once! It doesn't cost much to make people happy once in a while."

Without wasting a second, and apparently to defy her sister, Béa pounces on her own bag of peanut shells, takes a handful, stuffs it in her mouth and starts to chew. Now she's the one talking with her mouth full.

"You can cry all night, Nana, but you still won't win!"

Rhéauna watches her chew for a good moment before she replies.

"Maybe peanut shells aren't poisonous but I hope you choke on them!"

She leans toward her sister. Their noses nearly touch.

"Can you imagine what it's like to choke on a handful of little pieces of dry wood that won't go down when you try to swallow them! Eh? It sticks in your throat, you can't breathe, you turn really bright red, your eyes pop out of your head, your tongue gets thick and then you haven't got any more breath and you die, with a death rattle like a poisoned rat!"

Béa is already spitting out the peanut shells, then she raises her head, a nasty smile on her lips.

"Anyway I still won!"

Supper was tinged with a glumness that surprised Joséphine. Usually there's no lack of subjects for conversation around the table – three little girls aged eight, nine and ten have things to say – but that night she senses an animosity between the two older ones that she can't explain. Something she didn't witness must have happened that afternoon, and all her attempts to pierce the mystery of their serious expressions and furious looks are in vain. No doubt, it's some trivial matter between two idle children trying to pick a quarrel, a fight over nothing. She's used to settling some of those every week. This time, though, it's going on, their foreheads stay creased, their mouths bitter, when usually Nana and Béa are reconciled over a generous helping of shepherd's pie or beef stew. They both like to eat – even though Rhéauna is constantly denying the evidence – and usually a good hot meal can tone down their turbulent little-girls' quarrels. They forget that a few hours earlier they were pulling the other's hair and calling each other names and the conversation, made up of minor anecdotes from country schools or small-town rumours that can't be checked, picks up where they'd left it at the meal before this.

Even Alice realizes that something is wrong. She swallows her stuffed cabbage while she watches her sisters, each one in turn, trying to figure out what could have happened between them for such a silence to fall over what is usually the liveliest meal of the day. They are the ones who usually make conversation and she drinks in their words, thinking to herself that she can't wait to be as old as they are and have so many interesting things to say.

But less fearful than her grandmother, she gets right to the point:

"You aren't talking very much."

Béa lifts her nose from her plate.

"We aren't talking at all, there's a difference."

"How come you aren't talking at all?"

This time it's Béa who replies. With her mouth full.

"Because we haven't got anything to say! We aren't like some people I know, we don't talk when we've nothing to say ..."

Joséphine allows herself to intervene because Béa is too unfair. Alice is the quietest member of the family and no one can accuse her of being a chatterbox.

"Béa, don't accuse your sister of what you deserve to be blamed for! And I've told you a thousand times, don't talk with your mouth full!"

Now, for the first time in ages, since she was very little, in fact, when it was all she could come up with if she couldn't think of anything to say, Béa sticks out her tongue at her grandmother, a tongue still covered with overcooked cabbage and greasy pork. It's ugly, it's rude – everyone agrees, herself first – and a kind of indignant amazement falls over the dining-room table. Forks stay frozen between plates and mouths, Grandma's shoulders are shuddering and Grandpa, who usually hears nothing and sees nothing at the table because women's conversations bore him, shoots a look filled with such anger that Béa swallows a mouthful that goes down the wrong way and she chokes.

Rhéauna leans over her.

"I told you you'd choke."

Méo slaps the table, just once. The four women hunch their shoulders, dreading one of the rare but terrifying fits of rage by this overly patient man who has a hard time controlling himself when he gives in to anger. But he says nothing, merely gives Béa a filthy look.

"I'm sorry, Grandma. I won't do it again."

Joséphine wipes her face with her apron which she'd forgotten to remove before taking her place at the table.

"I don't know what's the matter with you two tonight but you're scaring me ..."

Méo gets up, walks around the table, leans over Béa and grabs her plate in an exaggerated gesture.

"If your grandmother's food makes you stick your tongue out, you can do without."

He takes the plate to the sink after pouring its contents into the garbage.

The meal is over. Stomachs are knotted, no one wants dessert, the table is cleared in seconds. Méo stands next to his wife, who is clearing the table.

"What's got into them this time?"

She gives him a desperate look.

"Who knows? Maybe they can sense what's coming ..."

He puts his arm around her waist the way he used to, draws her toward him.

"Oh, come on. How would they know?"

"They can't, Méo, but children sense things ... They must feel that something's coming. I can't do it, Méo, I can't do it."

He kisses her behind the ear. That was how he'd seduced her forty years earlier when their country did not exist yet and they were nomads, he was in any case, looking for a place to settle. Before they were won over by the vast Saskatchewan prairies, the extravagant sunsets and the possibilities of tremendous harvests thanks to the rich and fertile soil. Before that small parcel of land in the middle of nowhere, in a landscape with no horizon that had always belonged to a people of whom they were the proud descendants and had finally come back to them. Before the house that Méo had built with his own hands for the sons his wife hadn't given him because she'd had four daughters – Ernestine, Titite, Maria and Rose whom they never saw as a matter of fact because they were scattered all across the continent. The Desrosiers "diaspora." Which is the only fancy word he knows – he found it in a newspaper article about Jews and Cajuns – and he often says it when he talks about his family.

"I'll tell Nana you want to talk to her ..."

She brings her hand to her heart.

"How can I do it, Méo? How can I do it? Don't go. I'll look after it ... It's my role to look after it."

He kisses her, on the mouth this time, a wily type who has no other argument.

"You've got through so many other things, Joséphine ..."

She can't hold back a sob. And he doesn't try to soothe her.

"Not like that, Méo! Usually it's the others who decide to leave."

"Open your windows, poor things, before you suffocate!"

It's too hot in the girls' room. In mid-August, the nights are cool and they're afraid of getting sick because they are sensitive to the cold, that she can understand, but there's a limit! They are feigning sleep, Béa actually mimicking – badly – a gentle snore, so their grandmother opens the window herself, grumbling. Immediately the wind sweeps into the room, lifting the white lace curtain that the little girls often pretend is a ghost come from the depths of the prairies to chop them into little bits and eat them raw. It's cold, it's damp, it already smells of the autumn that's on its way but it's healthy, too, if you cover up. She's told them hundreds of times …

"Sure it gets chilly and damp early around now, but it's cool, fresh air and it's good for you! Béa, I know you aren't asleep. Get yourself under the covers before you catch your death of cold!"

Béa obeys without opening her eyes, as if she were moving in her sleep.

"Don't try, I know you don't walk in your sleep!"

Joséphine sits on the edge of Rhéauna's bed.

"Don't you pretend you're asleep, Nana. I don't believe you either."

Rhéauna opens her eyes, looks at her grandmother who, how strange, avoids making eye contact. That's new. Generally she kisses them, one after the other, pulls up their covers and wishes them good night, looking at them with a kind of concentration filled with goodness and love that turns their hearts upside down. This time, nothing like that.

"I have to talk to you, Nana."

The tone is serious, the voice hesitant. Rhéauna understands at once that it won't be a pleasant conversation and that she'll have to avoid it. So as not to suffer. She is surprised to think such a thing and she frowns as she does when she can't find the solution to an arithmetic problem. Suffer? Where did that come from all of a sudden? Just because her grandmother wants to talk to her …

"Why do you want to talk to me, Grandma? I didn't do anything. Béa started it …"

Her grandmother cuts her off with unusual abruptness which worries Rhéauna even more.

"It's got nothing to do with what happened at supper, sweetheart. Now come with Grandma. She'll make you a nice cup of cocoa."

Cocoa? At this hour of the night? Béa and Alice open their eyes, raise their heads from their pillows. Their grandmother, sometimes accompanied by their grandfather, tucks them in every night and, often, it's one of the most agreeable moments of the day. But this is the first time she's pulled one of them out of bed, just like that, at a time when they're supposed to be asleep. They suspect that something serious is brewing, although they are envying Rhéauna, lucky her, who has permission to get up, go downstairs and settle down over a nice, hot cup of cocoa!

"Can't you talk to me here?"

Joséphine bends her head slightly, smoothes the beige-and-blue blanket, clears her throat.

"No. I have to talk to you by yourself …"

"Do you think I did something bad?"

"Of course not. But I have to tell you something very important."

This definitely doesn't augur well and all of a sudden the two youngest stop envying their older sister. Experience has taught them that "something important" always means "something horrible." They watch their grandmother and their big sister leave the room, both of them worried for reasons they can't identify, and they consider themselves lucky that they can stay warm breathing good fresh air, even if it's cold, while some strange conversation is going on in the kitchen. If they were more courageous and if it weren't so cold they would slip onto the upstairs landing and try to hear bits of what's said down below. They sense, though, that it will be better to stay safe in their bed. Safe from what? Knowing that they won't be able to get back to sleep, they exchange a worried look. The moon has just appeared between the clouds, the light that bathes their room is an unhealthy blue. The ghost of something threatening glides into the room and starts to prowl around their beds. They are scared.

✗

Joséphine has heated the milk, saying nothing. And Rhéauna, who could use a comforting word, watches her, silent, too. She suspects that in the next few minutes her life is about to change. In her head, the mind of a ten-year-old child who is intelligent and full of life, everything is orderly, regulated, compartmentalized, both feelings and everyday actions. That's what reassures her most of all, and this surprising break in the order of things is a sign, she's sure of it, that something dramatic is about to happen. To her. To her who barely five minutes earlier was trying to concoct some way to take revenge on her sister Béa and pay her back. Is that why she's going to be punished? Because revenge, the mere idea of revenge, is a mortal sin worthy of a visit from her grandmother to her room practically in the middle of the night to give her some bad news? That's it, she knows it, she's going to get some bad news after she's finished that darn cocoa. If she refused it, if she pushed aside the cup, would it make any difference? If she got back into bed right away, could she divert the course of events to avoid the calamity that's liable to appear at any moment? A calamity! That's it! It's a calamity that her grandmother is going to tell her about!

"I don't want any cocoa, Grandma …"

Her grandmother does not turn around to answer her.

"I'll just make one for me then."

Rhéauna gathers her courage and hurls herself into the void with her eyes shut.

"It isn't very nice, Grandma, I mean what you're going to tell me, is it?"

Joséphine has leaned against the stove as she continues to stir the cocoa in the pan.

"Yes, Rhéauna, it's something nice. Very nice, even."

"So why is your face so sad?"

"Because for me it won't be very nice …"

She sits down close to her granddaughter, runs her hand through her hair that's so beautiful, black and shiny like that of her ancestors. The hair of the Cree people, rich and glossy as ebony.

"The good news, Nana, is that your mother wants to see you."

An enormous burst of happiness shakes Rhéauna who is on her feet at once, forgetting all the negative thoughts that have been stabbing her for several minutes.

"Mama's coming to see us!"

Her grandmother takes a sip that she finds too hot and blows on the liquid so she won't burn herself with the next one.

"No, sweetheart, it's you who's going to join her."

At first, Rhéauna doesn't understand. Or arranges not to understand. She hasn't seen her mother for years. Among the very few and vague memories of her, she sees an agitated woman with unsettled moods, very funny when she's feeling good but capable of being easily angered and unfair at the slightest opportunity – because she's tired, she claims – a whirlwind of energy that nothing can break down and that's hard to follow day by day. All that is so far away! In both time and space. Her early childhood she had spent at the other end of the continent, in a country called the United States, in a state known as Rhode Island, in a city on the seaside called Providence. But her memories are like a vast pool of troubled water where a few vague images float. The sea, when she thinks of it, is above all a smell. Of salt and humidity. Here in Saskatchewan, the humidity is different from that at the seaside and it never smells of salt water. There's no salt water anywhere, just prairies, flat and monotonous, whose movements, however, sometimes resemble those of the great Atlantic Ocean that rocked her first years. The same swell, calm or furious, but made up of fields of hay or corn instead of real waves that break on the beach. And around here, the only beach is the road that runs along the cornfield, and not one wave ever comes there to die. Instead of kelp flung up by the sea there are only abandoned birds' nests and spilled cobs of corn trampled by malevolent children.

The horizon is as far away, as flat as it is here, but without being liquid. And the dangers hidden there are different, but according to her grandparents, just as devastating. You can't drown in a field of grain but you can get lost.

And now four or five years after getting rid of her and her two sisters, her mother is calling her from the other end of the world. What for? Why doesn't she come here? Why does she not take the trouble to cross the continent herself and visit them if she misses her daughters so badly?

Her grandmother has often explained, especially when huge packages – full of useless things that made the three girls happy – arrived from Providence at Christmas or their birthdays, that if their mother had sent them to Saskatchewan to her own mother it was because life in Rhode Island was too harsh, and her job in a cotton mill drained her energy and she wouldn't have been able to raise her three children as she wanted, especially since her husband had been lost at sea during a heavy storm. Their father, whose only legacy was a weird name, Rathier, dead at sea. At least that was how their mother explained his absence. The girls were too small to remember him, however, and Rhéauna often dreamed of a giant sailor who watched over her when she had problems or when she was afraid of the monsters lurking in their bedroom closet, who also smelled of salt water. And of fish, because apparently he'd been an excellent deep-sea fisherman who often stayed out in huge boats for months in search of big fish, and no one understood how they stayed afloat: the boats were made of metal and everyone knows that metal doesn't float! She also tried sometimes to imagine the accent he must have because he was French from France and he talked very differently from all the French Canadians who'd taken refuge in the United States at the turn of the twentieth century, to try to fight poverty by working in the American cotton mills. The Frenchman from France had fallen in love with a Cree from Saskatchewan and that had led to what it led to ... And now the whirlwind of vague memories, exotic smells, vague images and a foreign accent came back all at once to haunt her in the middle of the night, in the month of August, just as she was about to get ready for the new school year! Her routine was going to be changed, her life disrupted, just because her mother wanted to see her?

"In Providence? I'm going to Providence in Rhode Island in the United States?"

"No, your mother's back in Canada. She's moved to Montreal. That's not quite as far as Providence ... It's in the province of Quebec, you know. I've often talked to you about the province of Quebec."

Rhéauna has no interest in the province of Quebec, even though her grandmother has always described it as a kind of earthly paradise for those who, like them, here in Maria, have chosen to speak French in an English-speaking country that doesn't want them and looks down on them. In Saskatchewan, it's hard, every day is a struggle; in Quebec, or so they say, it's easier because there are more people who speak French ...

"What about my sisters?"

"Your sisters will join you later."

"What do you mean, join me? Aren't I just going to visit my mother?"

And it is there, she can sense it, that the crux of the mystery, the heart of the calamity that will land on her at any moment, is hidden. Oh, she knows what it is, she has guessed it, and she'd like to flatten her hands over her grandmother's mouth to keep her from uttering the next sentence. But that wouldn't change a thing. Even if they're not expressed, the facts are still the same. She is condemned. To cross the continent. Just once. In one direction. Her mother had entrusted them to their grandmother, promising to come back for them someday, she remembers that very well – tears, kisses, oaths – now that day has arrived, even if she and her sisters finally doubted their mother's intentions, and she has to accept it.

No.

She's not obliged to accept it.

Her grandmother must have read the determination in her

eyes because suddenly she takes her hand and strokes it as if to console her.

"You don't want to see your mother again?"

"I want to see my mother again, here, in Maria, with everybody, not in Montreal. She was supposed to come and get us, wasn't she? Why does she just want to see me? Why aren't my sisters coming?"

"I told you, your sisters are going to join you later on ..."

"I don't believe you."

"Nana, I forbid you to use that tone of voice with me!"

"It isn't you I don't believe, it's her ... If she says she wants to see all three of us how come I'm the only one that's going?"

"Because you're the oldest ... Because she wants ... I don't know ... maybe she wants to test it to see if she can bring up children."

"She already showed us that she can't, didn't she?"

"Nana, don't talk about your mother like that! She's a very brave woman ... And stop arguing as if you were an adult! You're still a child, and you're going to do as you're told."

Immediately she regrets her words and gets up to hold Rhéauna against her belly that's so welcoming, witness to numerous confessions, wet from countless tears and smeared with the snot of overly sensitive children.

"That means I'm never, ever coming back here, doesn't it?"

"I don't know, sweetheart."

"What will I do? How will I be able to live without you and Grandpa?"

"Maybe we'll be able to come and visit you now and then ..."

"Promise?"

"Of course, I promise."

Rhéauna looks up. Her eyes are dry and that worries her grandmother.

"I don't believe you."

"You know very well that all I can promise you is to do everything I can to let us see each other ..."

"That doesn't mean anything."

"What it means is that at least I'm going to try, Rhéauna. That's the best I can do."

"When do I leave?"

"Fairly soon … Some time next week …"

"On the train?"

"Yes."

"It's a long ways away."

"It's all arranged. You'll make three stops and, at each of them, one of your grandfather's sisters will be waiting for you or else one of your second cousins. Your great-aunt Régina in Regina, your great-aunt Bebette in Winnipeg and your second cousin Ti-Lou in Ottawa."

"Aunt Régina isn't very nice."

"She's had a hard life."

"That's no reason to be mean like her."

"You'll just spend one night at her house. Same as with the others. Between trains."

"How long will it take me to get to Montreal?"

"Three or four days I imagine."

"I'm going to spend three or four days all by myself on the train?"

"Don't be afraid, everything will work out. There'll be people to look after you on each train, that's their job, they're paid to do it. And I'll give you a piece of paper with your name on it and your address and the phone number of the general store written on it. Nothing's going to happen to you. Nothing. I'd've liked to go with you, I'd have liked to see Maria again, but I have to stay here to look after the others."

Rhéauna grabs her grandmother's cup and takes a long gulp. It's warm and sweet and it makes her feel better.

"Don't let me go, Grandma."

"If I don't let you go it will start all over again later on. She's your mother, Rhéauna, she decides …"

"No. You're my mother."

The little girl looks up at Joséphine's troubled face. The grandmother could think of nothing to reply, especially not a protest.

"Keep me with you. Keep us with you. I don't want to go to Montreal. I don't want any province of Quebec. I don't want my mother."

"Don't say that. You mustn't say that."

"I don't want my mother and that's that."

She runs out of the kitchen and Joséphine hears her noisily climb the stairs as she does when she's mad or has just been punished.

Joséphine has been expecting this moment for so long, she has already suffered so badly that she can't show her pain, can't express it as she would like. She feels it, yes, but from very far away, buried in a corner of herself so remote that she can't dig it out and transform it into words, into tears, into curses. She stands there in the middle of the kitchen for a long moment, suffocating. She had entertained the hope that she would keep her three grandchildren forever because their mother would never be able to make both ends meet where she was, in Providence, or because she realized that she wasn't cut out to be a mother. All that time she had played at being their real mother, no doubt she'd become that – and now came the moment of separation. A punishment? Because she'd believed that she could think of them as hers without saying too much about their real mother or dangling the hope of seeing her someday? A usurper receiving her punishment, that's what she will become.

She sets her cup on the edge of the brand-new sink that Méo has just put in under the pump, runs some water. For a long time. It's cold. It comes directly from far down in the earth. It hurts. It feels good.

"Aren't you asleep? Go back to bed!"

It feels even colder in the bedroom. The nighttime dampness has seeped in everywhere and the air seems wet. Rhéauna shuts the window and races back to her bed.

Béa hasn't moved. She merely looks at her sister and frowns. Two very black marbles in the dark. Intimidating. Béa is impressive when she's serious. Rhéauna lifts the blanket, climbs into bed next to her sister. She is shaking but now it's not from cold.

"I know you didn't get into my bed to warm up my place, Béa ..."

Béa presses herself against her, puts her arm around her sister's waist.

"What happened? What did Grandma say?"

Rhéauna's sigh is not an ordinary sigh. Béa knows her sister's sighs, which are often sighs of exasperation. Because of her. Because of what she does, what she says. But this one, deeper, longer, ends with a kind of trembling close to a sob that is new, as if it were stretching out because, in fact, it didn't want to end. But maybe it will never end either. Because Béa suspects that she will hear it in her head for the rest of her life: first she'll remember that endless trembling, the expression of something that's impossible to say, a sigh that she heaves without realizing it, and then what will have followed, terrible news that will have turned their lives upside down. Suddenly she doesn't want to hear the news, but it's too late, she has asked for it and, soon, her sister will tell her. At the end of the endless sigh.

Rhéauna turns her head, looks her straight in the eye.

"Let me cry a little first. Afterward, in a little while, when I've finished, I'll tell you everything ..."

But she doesn't have time to cry: Alice has just got into bed with them. She inches her way between her two sisters and huddles up next to Rhéauna.

"Can't you get to sleep either, Alice?"

The youngest, most-vulnerable member of the family has a tiny, fluty little voice when she is worried. Her grandmother says that it's the voice of a mouse in a trap.

"I don't want to be the last one to find out what's going on, as usual."

The three of them huddle together. If it were because of a storm they would laugh at their fear, at the same time complaining about the narrowness of the bed, about the smells that come from it, but this is a serious moment and they need to be crowded together like this. They need this exchange of warmth to get through the minutes that will follow.

And when the story comes, in little murmured admissions, in delicate touches because Rhéauna wants to spare her two sisters, not rush too much, they are galvanized by the horror of the looming separation, of the loss of the grandparents they adore, of the journey to be taken, first by Rhéauna, then by the other two – a whole continent to cross, it's unimaginable – and above all by this new life they don't want with a woman they don't know in a strange and distant city when they're so happy here in Maria, hidden and protected in the middle of nowhere.

For once, Monsieur Connells, who owns the general store, greeted them with open arms. He has been advised of their visit and knows that today Joséphine will have money to spend. A lot of money. It's not every day that you have to put together a whole new wardrobe for a child and he rubs his hands at the thought of the dollars – ten? twenty? *thirty?* – that will land in the drawer of his cash register.

Word soon made the rounds of Maria that the eldest of the Rathier girls, grandchildren of Méo and Joséphine Desrosiers, was going to join her mother in Montreal. Comments, good and bad, quickly follow. Some of the nastiest claim that the little girl's mother, Maria, is a prostitute in Providence and a floozy in Montreal because that's all she knows how to do; others claim that she is going to be a servant in some rich person's house in Outremont, a fancy part of the city, and that she'll drag her daughter into the same trade to make more money; others, finally, believe the story that Joséphine has been telling forever because they have also seen relatives leave their country for the eastern United States to try to make a better living. They all take pity on the child who is going to be thrown, without being consulted, into a dangerous adventure from which it's impossible to imagine how it will end and that will unfurl in a world that no one knows in Maria. To travel across Canada by train like that, all alone, is dangerous, isn't it? And all those strangers you travel with. Men on their own who may be looking for prey …

Joséphine has turned a deaf ear on all those negative considerations since last week but it's beginning to get on her nerves and it is here, at the general store, that she has decided to put an end to the ridiculous gossip and rude remarks. After all, it's the best place in Maria to start a rumour that you want everyone to know. More than on the steps of the Sainte-Maria-de-Saskatchewan church, because here there's no holding back. They're not in the presence of God or, even more, his representative, curé Bibeau, who screens everything, censors and slashes away at everything and, from the steps of his church on Sunday morning, transmits a version of the news that he himself has expurgated, that he imposes as the only possible truth, shouting and gesticulating broadly. Despite her deep piety, Joséphine has always been wary of him, and fears that if she ever decided to confide in him, he would always side with the most ill intentioned, the most depraved and that he would push for a disgusting portrait of her daughter and her granddaughter, supposedly to set an example. Or to illustrate his theory that no one should leave Maria, especially not to go east where there are so many opportunities to lose their souls. The opportunity would be too good, he would most likely take advantage of it to discourage his parishioners from moving away from his influence.

Maria is an anomaly in Saskatchewan. A small Francophone, Catholic enclave surrounded by Anglophone Protestants, lost in the middle of prairies so vast they seem infinite and forgotten by all because of that difference, it has withdrawn into itself and come to believe that it is a world complete, well defined, governed by unchanging laws dispensed by one man: the curé. A narrow and simple-minded way of thinking, encouraged by this somewhat despotic but in fact sincere priest, that ultimately made it a place impossible to live in, under its false appearance of a neat and tidy countryside and a picturesque village. Although knowing that they would be shouted down by the majority of Maria's inhabitants, those who have the courage to leave know that they've made the right choice and never return. Some inhabitants in their early twenties, among those who are starting to look beyond the limits of the village, actually envy Rhéauna – in hushed tones of course – and wish her great happiness at the other end of the country. Even as the daughter of a prostitute or a maid in the house of a rich family. And when word started to get around that she would soon be joined by her two younger sisters, they applauded at the thought that a complete family from Maria was going to get rid of its overly tight ties to this village at the end of the world and cooped up in its solitude. The grandparents are too old. They could tolerate neither the journey nor living so far away, but the three girls have the unheard-of good luck to experience the vast world and the most liberal of the young villagers envy them.

Monsieur Connells has brought out the prettiest things he had for a little girl Rhéauna's age, spread them out across the wide varnished counter – white stockings, bloomers and other underwear, dresses, coats, gloves, shoes, little straw hats. The shelf for "Little Girls 4 to 10" has been cleaned out and the storekeeper hopes he'll sell Joséphine Desrosiers everything he has in Rhéauna's size. He has even taken out the Eaton's catalogue, in case ... For shoes, for instance, of which he doesn't have many to choose from.

Rhéauna, who's been silent and reserved ever since she learned that she was leaving, peers at it all with a glum look. At any other time, she would jump for joy and shriek with excitement before so many nice clothes, but this sudden abundance of riches – you have to be rich to afford a whole new wardrobe all at once – leaves her cold despite her grandmother's encouraging words.

"Yes, it's pretty, Grandma, really pretty ..."

She feels the softness of the bright-red winter coat, the lightness of the pale-green organdy dress, but says nothing. Joséphine turns her head away to hide her annoyance.

"Just try a little, Nana. Monsieur Connells knows quality, and he's brought out all his nicest things for you. The clothes you wear here wouldn't be right for Montreal. You'd look poor, and your mother sent me a good-sized cheque so I could buy clothes for you ... Just try, Nana!"

Rhéauna looks down, runs her hand over a scarf so soft that it feels like silk.

"I know all that, Grandma. But you'll never see me in those clothes. Did you think about that?"

Joséphine bows her head, brings her hand to her heart.

"What you wear doesn't matter to me, sweetheart, you should

know that ... And the day you leave you'll be wearing all new clothes so I'll be able to see you in some of them ..."

Monsieur Connells coughs into his hand and takes out from behind the counter what he considers to be his pièce de résistance: a pair of winter boots so fine, so light, so soft they'd be unthinkable in a place like Maria, but that Rhéauna will certainly be able to wear in Montreal where as everybody knows the wooden sidewalks are scraped every day and there is less snow than here. They even say – though no one really believes it – that whole winters can go by there without snow!

"I don't know why those boots have ended up here. You couldn't wear them in Maria. But when I knew you were going to Montreal, Nana, I thought about you right away ..."

Joséphine fingers and hefts the boots.

"These boots are for a woman, Monsieur Connells. They're way too big for her."

"Then she can give them to her mother! Your daughter Maria, we used to call her Maria from Maria when we were little, remember, she'll certainly be glad to get such a fine present from her daughter ..."

"We don't know her tastes, Monsieur Connells and, even more, we don't know her shoe size!"

When she leaves the general store, she has on the same clothes as when she went inside. She did agree to try on a few items – the pale-green dress, for instance, that cost the earth – but she refused to put on the straw hat or the pretty, crocheted white gloves as Monsieur Connells had suggested:

"Children usually like it, Nana, wearing clothes that've just been bought for them ... You'll be pretty in them, why won't you try them on?"

"They're clothes to wear on a trip ..."

"You won't wear them just on your trip. You'll go on wearing them in Morial ..."

"That's just it. I don't want to look here the way I'll look in Montreal!"

Her grandmother hasn't said anything. She simply paid – with crisp new bills, fresh from the bank – pursing her lips. She feels that Rhéauna is gradually moving away from her, from her sisters, too. From everyone, in fact. As if she were getting ready for the separation piecemeal instead of waiting for the final cut. Maybe to reduce her suffering. Joséphine, who wants to fuss over her before she leaves, to spoil her, to stuff her full of all her favourite things to eat – who knows what she'll be able to eat there, with a mother who goes to work, in a city where fresh food may be rare – doesn't know how to react. She is used to simple situations, to problems that require common sense, and the helplessness of her granddaughter who will soon be separated from everything she knows and sent to the end of the world has her flustered. When her daughter Maria left, it was quite the opposite: she had chosen to go away. She couldn't wait to hop on the train, to leave for good what she called a hole in the middle of the cornfield and finally be free. Now, though, she can find neither the words nor the actions to console Rhéauna. She has tried to talk with her, but the obstinate little girl told her that everything was fine, that she understood the situation and couldn't wait to see her mother again. She hadn't said though that she was anxious to leave.

Joséphine would need advice for handling this grave problem, she knows that. But where can she go? Not to the presbytery, certainly, where she would find only unwillingness to understand and ignorance. Yes, ignorance. The booming fat man is an ignoramus of the worst kind and she'd never ask him for advice. The school mistress maybe; she seems to appreciate Rhéauna's intelligence and acuteness. Meanwhile, the tension in the house is going up and everyone is miserable. Alice, already skinny, has stopped eating and Béa gawks at her sister as if she doesn't recognize her. As for Méo, his misery can be read in the furrows of new wrinkles on his forehead.

The other night he'd said to her:

"We're going to lose them one by one, Joséphine. As if they were dying one after the other. We don't deserve that …"

The purchases paid for, she picks up the packages – a number of brown paper bags, a few boxes – and follows her granddaughter who has already left the store, head down, making the little bell fastened to the door jingle.

It's a cool, late-August day. It smells like the beginning of the harvests and the children are already talking about going back to school. Rhéauna thinks about the school she will attend in Montreal, a gigantic red-brick box like all the schools in big cities, so she's heard, where hundreds of pupils are crowded in, whereas she is used to a tiny country school where she knows everybody. She has trouble picturing herself in a class of thirty pupils – *thirty* students, there aren't that many in the whole school in Maria! – with as classmates children who'll think that she has every flaw in the world because she comes from far away and they'll laugh at her Saskatchewan accent. (A few years ago, a visitor from the city of Quebec detected in the inhabitants of Maria a slight English accent, which everyone saw as an insult.)

A new life, a new mother, a new school full of strangers ... On the front steps of the general store, she is overcome by an urge to cry. She'd like to plunk the packages she's carrying on the floor, sit on the top step and give in to the sobs and angry cries that she's been holding back ever since she learned that she will be going away. But no. Not in front of her grandmother. Her grandmother has to think that she's strong. She's not sure that Joséphine is taken in by the role of the reasonable little girl that Rhéauna has decided to play until her departure – because of the looks she has intercepted and her frowns when they talked about the journey, because of the expression of doubt that she reads in her grandmother's eyes when she insists that all is well, but would never admit, to anyone, how unhappy she is.

The buggy is waiting for them at the door. Devil, the family horse who doesn't live up to his name, is placidly munching the apple that Méo just put in his mouth. Méo himself is taking the sun as he smokes his pipe, which today smells sweetly of vanilla. He has decided to treat himself to the package of vanilla tobacco he's been coveting for weeks. It's good, it tastes like dessert and it numbs a little the pain that he's been feeling ever since he learned that his granddaughter is going away. Old age, yes, fine, he's accepted it for ages, it's in the order of things, it happens to everybody; but the departure of a source of joy and pride like Rhéauna, of a child you hadn't expected, who arrived without warning in your existence at an age when you thought you'd brought up all the children life had to give you – this cruel separation after five years of a family life transformed by the presence of three turbulent, funny, exasperating little girls, the loneliness of a solitude for two that awaits him and Joséphine in the silence imposed on a house accustomed to cries, to laughter, to high-pitched voices – will be the end of him, he knows it. And it is death, hidden very nearby, snickering, unyielding, that awaits him. He wants to go first. Or at the same time as Joséphine. Because a day without her is unthinkable. Even more than a day without Rhéauna, without Béa, without Alice.

When Alice arrived in Maria, she was only three years old. She doesn't know her mother at all, has no memory of her: why should she pick up and join her at the other end of the world? Blood ties? Just because of blood ties? Ties of affection then? Worried nights because fever has struck a little girl with no resistance, the first steps, the first words, the first start of the new school year, the first communion, the first adult sorrow in a child who is too young to know an adult sorrow? Rhéauna, who skips rope in front of the house chanting, "One, two, three, alairy / My first name is Mary / If you think it's necessary / Look it up in the dictionary"; Béa who wolfs down her serving of pigs'-feet stew and congratulates her grandmother for being the best cook on the planet; Alice and her dolly, Geneviève de Brabant, whom she drags everywhere because it's the prettiest thing she's ever seen! His daughter Maria has never known any of that and she dares to beg to have her children back after she has abandoned, yes, abandoned them so she can earn a few dollars in a cotton mill where life is certainly no more enjoyable than it is deep in the prairies! It's fine to repatriate three little girls who've already been brought up, but will she know what to do with them? After the homecoming kisses and the attempts at self-justification, what will she be able to do with these three girls she doesn't know? These dark thoughts ruin somewhat the sugary taste of tobacco and suddenly Méo wishes he could erase the last weeks, go back to the beginning of August when life was so sweet and so simple. Well, almost. Because life on the prairies is never sweet or simple.

He helps his wife and his granddaughter to lift their packages into the buggy, gets them comfortably settled on the leather bench.

Devil has finished his apple and now turns his head in the hope he'll be given a second. No. Another time. Méo clicks his tongue twice. The horse recognizes the starting signal, moves away from the general store, prances across the village.

Rhéauna has leaned her head against the back of her seat without watching the landscape pass by as she usually does. Worried, her grandmother bends over her.

"You haven't got a headache, have you?"

46

Rhéauna opens her eyes. Makes a slight, sad little smile.

"No, but I was wondering …"

"What?"

The little girl looks at her grandmother, knitting her brow.

"Why does Mama absolutely want you to buy clothes for me here? Wouldn't it have been easier to wait till Montreal? The clothes must be a lot nicer, a lot more stylish in Montreal, mustn't they? And I wouldn't have had as much baggage to cart all the way there."

Joséphine has asked herself the same question several times and she's not too sure that she has found the right answer.

"I don't know … Maybe she knew you were going to be staying with all kinds of people and she wanted you to be pretty … Especially for your aunt Régina who's so critical …"

"Aren't my clothes from here nice enough for Grandpa's sisters?"

"Maybe that's what she thinks."

"Was she ashamed of her clothes when she was in Maria?"

Joséphine lifts her bangs which have fallen over one eye.

"When your mother was in Maria, Rhéauna, she was ashamed of everything."

"Was she ashamed of you?"

"I said everything. That means us, too."

Joséphine feels a pang as she thinks back to the terrible scene her daughter had put on just before she left thirteen years earlier, in the cursèd year 1900. Her fierce determination, her need for freedom in a village that could only stifle her because she felt so confined here, her desire for vast horizons from which every trace of grain – goddamn corn, goddamn wheat – would have disappeared; the ocean as far as the eye could see with real tides and real surf; dangerous water instead of the exasperating calm of the fields of oats. On one hand Joséphine, who wondered who it was, in her family or Méo's, that had passed on to Maria her need to be away from her birthplace – to resume wandering after years of an intentionally sedentary life; on the other hand, the other Maria, ready to pounce, for whom leaving meant survival. With no possibility of compromise between them, no comprehension either. The mother had dreamed of peace and quiet, of stillness, and she'd found them; the daughter swore by the vagabond life and adventure.

But as her mother had predicted, Maria soon paid the price of freedom. She'd become a prisoner of the water as she had been of the land. Because you had to earn your living to survive. As much there as here. And the cotton mills of Rhode Island – the goal of her journey, the promise of quick money, the easy life of big cities with people less narrow-minded and more fun than the walking dead you met in Maria – in the end did not represent at all the deliverance she dreamed of. All the same, though, maybe she had managed to get rid of the suffocation that she felt in Saskatchewan, which would have killed her if she'd stayed in Maria. At least that was what her mother hoped, though she had never been aware of any sign of freedom or happiness in her daughter's letters. Even with that Simon Rathier, a stranger she had married on a whim, who'd given her three children before he disappeared in a storm. But when all's said and done, maybe Maria simply had no talent for happiness.

And when they arrived by train from Regina, those three poor, little, trembling, hungry things from whom Maria had been obliged to separate because she couldn't provide for them, their grandmother had understood the desperation of her child who was too proud to come back and hide herself away in the hamlet where she'd been born but who didn't want her children to suffer from her own hardship and her obvious deficiencies.

And now the oldest was going to retrace part of the same path, once again without asking for it.

Rhéauna looked away to watch the wind play in the tassels of the corn.

"Anyway, I hope she won't be ashamed of me ..."

Joséphine pats her hand, brings it to her lips, kisses it.

"No one will ever be ashamed of you, Rhéauna. Never."

On the eve of her departure, Rhéauna becomes guilty of one thing that from time immemorial has been forbidden in Maria – her grandparents are uncompromising on the matter – and that she dreams about nearly every night when the weather is mild. All the children in the village talk about it, but no one since Maria Desrosiers, it seems, and therefore since the end of the last century, has dared to do it, even the biggest show-offs among the boys. Because it's dangerous. According to the old folks anyway who can back up their fears with horrible stories about children with their throats slit, slashed open or made unrecognizable because they'd tried too hard to defend themselves. Against what? Ghosts or wild animals from the beyond or from deep in the prairies, stemming from their religion or that of their Cree ancestors. What matters are the atrophied limbs, the chewed-up faces and the lives ruined because someone dared to disobey his parents. On fine summer days then, all the children dream of becoming the first human being since Maria Desrosiers to break that law and survive.

That night though, you can't say it is mild. The beautiful July nights are far behind, nearly forgotten, the cold damp weather has come early. A chilly little wind is playing in the corn, and the owl that lives in the barn is hooting in a sinister way almost non-stop. At any other time, Rhéauna would have thought he was warning them about the presence of nocturnal creatures – delicious bats with their unpredictable flight patterns, for instance, the wind's favourite food; a predator in search of fat hens; or sinuous, hypo-critical snakes – but this time she's sure that he is mourning her departure. No, not sure, she knows that isn't so. The owl doesn't even know that she exists; but the thought that even nature is lamenting the final separation that will take place tomorrow mor-ning feels good and, with her elbows resting on the windowsill, she lets herself imagine that Maria, its nature as well as its inhabitants, will never get over her disappearance.

But this waking dream, though fairly satisfying, isn't enough. She has just one chance to prove to everyone that she is the bravest or that all the stories about injured children, she is beginning to suspect, are only there to scare the youngsters, force them to be obedient, and she decides to take that chance, to play with fire, to risk everything. If she emerges from the adventure crippled or disfigured, her mother will be the only guilty party and will have to content herself with seeing a monster disembark from the train at Windsor Station. It will be her tough luck.

Rhéauna doesn't take the time to think, she doesn't want to fall into the ridiculous terror that characterized her whole childhood and she gets dressed, taking every possible precaution to avoid waking her two sisters. Who may not be sleeping either, come to think of it. What is she to do if they decide to follow her? Send them back to bed? Encourage them to come with her? But both stay motionless and Rhéauna, relieved, tiptoes out of the bedroom.

She is about to make herself guilty of the unspeakable, the forbidden, the unthinkable: she is about to step into the field in front of the house to listen to the corn grow!

According to legend, when the Great Manitou had finished drawing Saskatchewan with a piece of charcoal – a few strokes for a flat horizon, an elevation or two to break the monotony, a group of clouds in the sky because they're pretty – He thought that it was very empty so He created grain. For colour and movement. Wheat, oats, rye and other grasses appeared then and, finally, the majestic sweet corn that can attain eight feet at the end of August and, with the help of the wind, can imitate the sound of the sea so well that it is hard to tell them apart though He has never known the sea. Then He populated it all with plains animals, with fat, mouth-watering fowl, with hideous creeping things, too, earthworms and snakes of all kinds – the worms to aerate the soil, the snakes to control the population of small animals – before He decided to make the first human being. A Cree, of course. To reign and keep watch, to organize and safeguard. The legend does not say whether the first Cree was a farmer, if he immediately understood the importance of the grain or discovered the sweet taste of corn and its nutritional virtues right away, but tradition has it that, from the outset, he had devoted boundless veneration to it, quickly elevating it to the rank of myth, his first one and, perhaps the most important, that he had even invented a legend maintaining that when the Great Manitou finished creating Saskatchewan ... So it's a legend that bites its tail and therefore can't be verified. Like any good self-respecting legend.

The same legend also claims that, for some reason or other, the Great Manitou forbade humans to listen to the corn growing, though it makes a terrible racket at night. They are allowed to listen to the crackling and whistling sounds as long as they're not in the middle of a field – if they're walking along a road with their family, for instance, or smoking a pipe on their own front steps to drive away the mosquitoes after supper. They aren't allowed to go down the steps, cross the road and walk into the cornfield with the intention of listening to it grow. Especially adults. Why? Some, rebels and hotheads, like Maria Desrosiers, claim that it's a story made up to stop the young folks from going into the cornfields to do what is forbidden outside them. If they're wrong, as generations of curés have maintained, the true reason has never been known. And no one tries to find it any more. That's it, that's all. No need to think about it, just obey. Other stories, even darker and more grim have been tacked on over the years: the stinky creature Boulamite who smells like mothballs and bites the feet of children caught wandering in the cornfields after nightfall; the boogeyman, Bonhomme Sept-Heures, who carries on his back a big burlap sack in which he keeps the heads of naughty children and – this is the slightly secret version that is only revealed to those on the verge of adolescence – the fairy Mortal Sin herself and her promises of licentiousness without punishment. Sceptics claim that it's the meeting place for religion imported from Europe and the more natural, less twisted one of Saskatchewan's original population. And that it was there that the Christian god replaced the Great Manitou. Permanently. Never, according to them, had the god of the Cree displayed such bad taste as to make up stories in which what is natural isn't and what is not is. For the Cree, nature and religion are one; for the Europeans, nature was pagan, lawless, and had to be renounced as much as possible and, above all, separated from religion. Why? Other legends. Countless. Inexplicable. Endless.

The legend then had become a double-headed creature with two different origins, the second one eventually winning out over the first as Europeans and their descendants settled the prairies, driving the Cree off their land. And that is the one that is believed in Maria, Saskatchewan, now in the early years of the twentieth century. The one that Rhéauna Rathier, daughter of Maria Desrosiers, is going to disobey. Twenty years after her mother.

Muffled up in the winter parka that she dug out of the big cedar chest and that reeks of mothballs – in fact, that is what attracts stinky Boulamite in the fall, apparently – Rhéauna hurries across the little road that separates her from the cornfield. What has she got to lose, after all? When all is said and done, in her present state, death, no matter how atrocious, would be welcome. She inches her way through corn nearly twice her height, strides through the chilly, humid night. She pulls her parka tight so her body won't lose any heat. What strikes her first is the strong smell of humus that the recent heavy rains have watered and of ripe grain ready to be cut, threshed, winnowed, plucked, stored. Or in the case of corn, eaten, just as it is, hot, with butter and salt. Her mouth is watering and she smiles in the dimness. If only her grandparents could see her. Or her sisters. To think about eating corn at a time like this!

She strides ahead, pushing aside the stalks that are in her way. She tries to go in as straight a line as possible, to avoid getting lost. In the daytime, it's fairly easy; if she gets lost because she has gone in a circle without realizing it, she can simply call out and Grandpa will be there. But now, in the middle of the night, it's not the time to turn to the left or the right if she wants to find her way. She looks at the sky. Dear God, it's so beautiful! She doesn't know how to read the stars as some people in the village claim they can do, to explain the past and predict the future armed only with the position in the sky of certain planets at your birth and their location at the present time. Nor could she use the stars as a guide and find her way again, like her father, the master mariner, though he did lose his way on the ocean. And perished, the idiot.

But to hear the corn grow she'd have to stop walking and prick up her ears, wouldn't she? She makes too much noise with her fall boots and she's the one who makes the cornstalks crackle as she pushes them aside to advance. To stretch out on the ground as in winter when she and her sisters make angels in the snow with wings unfurled? No, the ground is probably too wet and she doesn't want to come down with a cold. To die, yes, that would be fine to save herself from exile, but not a bad head cold, they're too horrible ... She stops under the starry vault, grabs two or three stalks bodily and shuts her eyes. What will she hear first? The much-anticipated crackling, as dry as the crack of a whip when an inch or two of a corn plant shoots out of the earth all at once, according to legend, or the arrival of creatures of the night that have smelled her, who've come now to eat her up and at this moment may be slithering through the tall corn so they can burn her feet or cut off her head? She smiles again. This time, though, it's a tiny little smile. It's funny, here, in the midst of danger, when she should be shaking with fear, she feels instead as if a kind of peace has fallen over her. Does it mean that danger, at the very heart of itself, no longer exists? So that when you are far removed from it, it makes an impression while in its presence, when you ought to be shaking, crying and asking for a favour, you think that it's ridiculous?

She waits. Two minutes. Five. Nothing. Oh, the wind is there. It's always present on the prairies, but she knows it well and manages to disregard it. No, what she is waiting for is a good loud crackle, just one, just to say that it exists, that corn really does grow with a sound like a loud crack of a whip and always at night.

Then comes the thought that the corn, in the end, is perhaps perfectly ripe, that it has finished growing, that it's too late to hear it come out of the ground.

But suddenly, joy of joys, there's a huge crackling sound. It's not the sound of footsteps, or an animal's call, or the wind in the corn, it is the genuine crackling of something huge that is emerging from the earth, pushing with all its might, of a creature in full growth that wants to live, to declare its presence, an expression of nature exploding with life, and Rhéauna gives a shout of joy. She's heard it! She's heard the corn grow and no animal, no baleful creature, has struck her down and devoured her alive, or carried her off like a trophy to deep inside some hiding place.

She doesn't wait to hear it again, she has heard what she wanted to hear; she turns around and gets back on the road without losing her way. She would like to plant herself in the middle of the little dirt road and howl her happiness. But she has to control herself, reveal nothing to anyone and go away as her mother had done, convinced that legends are just legends and the whole wide world less dangerous than she'd thought. She still doesn't want to go but at least she's no longer afraid.

✕

She finds both her sisters lying in her bed. Eyes wide open. Seemingly worried, even terrified by what she has just done. Alice raises her head as soon as Rhéauna shuts the door behind her.

"You went out in the corn, didn't you?"

Béa leans on her right elbow.

"Did you see Boulamite?"

"Did you see Bonhomme Sept-Heures?"

"Frogs?"

"Snakes?"

"Ghosts?"

"Are you dead?"

Rhéauna bursts out laughing, she can't help it. She bursts out laughing and elbows them aside so they'll make room for her in the bed. At last, something warm! Alice shrieks because her big sister's feet have just brushed against her leg. They can hear Grandpa's voice in the bedroom next to them.

"What's going on? I heard the stairs creak, now you're yelling in the middle of the night! Am I going to have to get up?"

The three girls, who know what it means if their grandfather gets up when everyone is in bed and supposed to be asleep, calm down immediately.

"It was me, Grandpa, I went downstairs to get a drink of water."

"Okay, but make sure you don't have to get up to pee, Nana! I don't want this to go on all night, this fooling around! If your glass of water makes you want to pee, use the chamber pot!"

Concerned all the same, despite her sister's laughter, Alice repeats her question:

"You aren't dead, Nana, are you?"

Rhéauna turns around, hugs her, plants a kiss on her temple.

"No, I'm not dead and, if it makes you feel any better, I can tell you I'm more alive than ever …"

They spend the whole last night in the same bed. And they don't sleep much. Now and then a little snore goes up in the bedroom when Alice or Béa falls asleep briefly, abruptly for little moments that are more like a loss of consciousness than what their grandmother calls sleepyheadedness, but Rhéauna stays awake. She'll sleep on the train to Regina, even though the trip is fairly short.

She describes for them her foray into the cornfield, the lies they've been told all their lives, the beauty of the sky when you are deep inside the pitch-dark, the exhilaration of the wind that sways the tremendous stalks and ruffles your hair; she talks as well about her departure the next morning, about their separation, which shouldn't be very long, about their departure, too, imminent and so unsettling, she knows that, but they'll have to see it as the beginning of a great adventure, though she herself is not convinced. She goes so far as to predict that they'll be happy with their mother in that province full of possibilities where the people who talk French are the great majority in a city that they say is huge and already filled with cars, whereas here in Maria there are only two; that has at least ten nickelodeons if not more, and streetcars and buses and electricity everywhere. In the end she is caught up in her own story and lets herself imagine Montreal in the summer, Montreal in the winter, its long right-angled streets, car horns even in the middle of the night, and the unbelievable smell that escapes from the doors of the numerous restaurants, too many to count, so they say. And the mountain right in the middle of the city, because there is a mountain, a real mountain, in the very heart of Montreal! An enormous playground that will be the opposite of the boring prairie where nothing ever happens. She arranges things so that she doesn't have to think about the red-brick schools and the mean little girls from the cities who'll make short work of the poor Rathier sisters, come from the depths of the prairies, talking with an accent you could cut with a knife and helpless in the face of big-city sophistication. She repeats the word *sophistication* in her head; she has just learned it and she thinks it's the most beautiful word in the French language. Or at least one of the most complicated ones she knows.

Which stops her from lingering on the thought of the imminent absence of their grandparents from their lives.

And the presence of this mother they don't even know.

All the unshed tears begin to flow. Luckily, her sisters don't see them, they've just gone to sleep, somewhat reassured, whereas her heart is beating wildly. She doesn't want to leave. There are still two hours before her grandmother will come to wake her. Perhaps she will die in the course of those two hours or, if she doesn't sleep, maybe the time won't pass, maybe the moment for getting up and dressing in her new clothes simply won't come. Or the train will be derailed as it pulls into Maria Station tomorrow morning. And she falls asleep in spite of herself.

At dawn, Joséphine finds the three little girls entwined in Rhéauna's bed, like three motherless kittens. And finally, she, too, allows herself to cry.

Her shoes are too small, her hat scrapes her forehead and her coat – which her grandmother has bought two sizes too large so it will last for several years – floats on her back. Looking at herself in the mirror just before she leaves her room, she tells herself that at least it won't be so hard for her to leave as it will be shameful to show herself like this in public. They will have to cross the whole village to get to the station, and she would like it if no one sees her decked out as she is in clothes that don't suit her, in colours that are ridiculous for a little girl from the country. She is going to leave a crowd that's not sorrowful but joyous. And the final memory of her in Maria will be of a scarecrow that looks disgraceful but is dressed in new clothes and waves goodbye to a crowd that is laughing at her.

Her sisters don't laugh, though, when they catch sight of her. They gawk at her and nudge one another. Béa feels that she has to tell her sister she's beautiful but Alice merely stuffs her thumb in her mouth, a bad habit she's barely been cured of. Rhéauna tells herself that it's the first change brought on by her leaving: her sister Alice is a baby again!

All five are on the veranda, somewhat stiff, formal and silent. The buggy is waiting at the bottom of the steps. And for once, Méo has decorated Devil who looks dashing with his straw hat that Rhéauna envies him because he looks so good in it. Her grandfather takes the pipe out of his mouth, hits it against his heel to empty it though he knows that he should have done it on the road, where Joséphine won't have to sweep it up, grumbling about how bad it smells.

"You're as pretty as a princess, sweetheart! Do you know that?"

Rhéauna makes a face, one of her ugliest, that makes her sisters laugh – what a relief! – and makes a little bow that could pass for a curtsey if you didn't realize that she's being ironic.

"Yeah, sure. A princess in a poor people's fairy tale! Cinderella of Saskatchewan! Snow White of the Prairies!"

Joséphine chooses to find it funny and swats her bum to make her come down the steps.

"Your coat is red, Nana. You forgot Little Red Riding Hood."

"Little Red Riding Hood wasn't a princess, Grandma."

Her grandmother looks her straight in the eyes.

"No, but she knew how to stand up for herself."

"Okay. The Little Red Riding Hood of the village of Maria. I wonder what kind of Big Bad Wolf I'll meet on the train!"

She knows that she's hit the mark because what worries her grandmother most in this whole adventure is the four train trips she will have to make before she gets to Montreal.

"Nothing's going to happen to you, sweetheart."

She drapes a little midnight-blue velvet purse around her neck – it clashes a little with the red coat – that is held in place by a leather strap.

"Everything's in there, Nana. Your name and address and the phone number for the general store, the numbers of the three people you're going to stay with and even the one in Montreal for your mother, who's got her own private number, lucky her. Your train ticket. Some money. You can't get lost. Someone will look after you on every train. They're used to carrying children travelling by themselves. Did you put your favourite books in a bag like I told you? It's going to be long, especially between Winnipeg and Ottawa, you'll need something to do …"

She's rambling; she's said it all a hundred times these past few days but she can't think of anything else: the fine words of appeasement that she prepares at night when her husband thinks she's asleep, the words of consolation that come so easily when Rhéauna isn't there – all get stuck in her throat just when her granddaughter needs them most, and she could kick herself.

Rhéauna gives one last apple to Devil who, knowing nothing about the drama going on around him, chews with obvious enjoyment, cranes his neck to pick up from the beaten earth the pieces that have got away from him. When he's finished swallowing the sweet flesh, he turns his head a little in the hope that another apple will suddenly appear from the little girl's pocket. But everyone is already in the buggy and he hears the click of Méo's tongue. He doesn't hurry the horse, no switch will stroke his flank, so he advances slowly, lazily, like on a Sunday afternoon when the ride is only a ride and there's no important race at the end.

Rhéauna has turned around on her seat. She is watching the house move away, swaying a little because the buggy isn't all that stable. After a few hundred paces, she starts to slip into the cornstalks too quickly, because of the gentle slope the buggy follows at this pace. The staircase disappears first, then the veranda. Never again will she walk there after nightfall, eating a slice of bread and ketchup or drinking the last glass of milk of the day. She won't hear the laughter or the shouts of her sisters, the not-at-all-severe warnings of their grandparents. The tips of the corn hide the bottom of the door, climb, conceal the knob and the little square window. The wind creates a kind of swell that blurs the whole front of the house behind a living curtain of grain. The roof, all that's left is the roof, which disappears in turn, as if the house has just sunk forever into the fertile soil of Saskatchewan.

Never. Never will she see this house again.

She turns her head. All the others are watching her. They are reading her mind, she knows that. They have followed attentively everything that she has just experienced and none of them has the power to console her.

She undoes the collar of her coat.

"Sure I know that fall is coming, but this is just August."

That's all that is said between the house and the door of the little country railway station.

Even when the people from Maria, some of them on their

doorsteps, others gathered in front of the general store, wave their hands or big white handkerchiefs by way of farewell.

Farewells. That's what they are. Farewells.

But at least no one's laughing at her.

According to Joséphine, the train station in Maria looks like a badly wrapped pound of butter that's been left outside on the prairie. Short and squat and sickly yellow, with no personality and, worst of all, poorly kept up, it turns its back on the village as if it wants to be forgotten and greets just two trains a day – the one from Prince Albert on its way to Saskatoon and the one from Saskatoon on its way to Prince Albert. Monsieur Sanschagrin, a retired Mountie, plays the dual role of station master and ticket agent. Grumpy and suffering from a perpetual cold, he never smiles, never says *Bon voyage* to people who are leaving or *Welcome* to those who are arriving, and rushes the unfortunate people who show up to buy their tickets at the last moment when he's supposed to be on the platform with his little flag and his whistle because the train is about to pull into the station. If they want to go beyond Saskatoon – to Alberta in the west or Manitoba in the east – they have to be there an hour early: Chief Sanschagrin, as he likes to be called, writes slowly and doesn't really understand the Canadian Pacific Railway schedule. It's too complicated and the print is too small. Oh, he'd like to have an assistant – aside from old man Sylvestre who's supposed to clean the station but spends most of his time smoking his pipe and looking out at the fields of wheat – a young fellow he'd allow to sell the tickets, but the young people in Maria, all of them farmers' sons, aren't interested in sitting behind a ticket window all day long, waiting for the two trains to pull in, when the wide-open spaces call to them and he's there all by his lonesome, as he says to anyone willing to listen, running the whole station.

It's another twenty minutes before the arrival of the train from Prince Albert that will take Rhéauna to Saskatoon and then Regina, to her aunt Régina's, her grandfather's youngest sister, a strict and taciturn woman who has always terrified the little girl. The whole family is sitting on the big wooden bench that runs along a good part of the station wall opposite Gate One – the only gate – that opens onto Platform One – the only one.

They are sitting very upright, the girls' hands on their knees the way their grandmother has taught them, Méo stuffing his pipe after trying to send a friendly sign to Monsieur Sanschagrin who has not responded – oh, it's all very well to forge ties over a glass of gin at the general store on a winter night, but here, we work! – and Joséphine is lost in thought. They could exchange heart-rending farewells; in fact, they need to, but when the moment comes they can't do it, all five are glued to their bench, silent and glum. Each one in turn looks at the big clock that hangs above the ticket window. It's nearly time. Monsieur Sanschagrin has stepped out of his cage and donned his station master's cap. Before he steps onto the platform, just as he's about to bring his whistle to his mouth, he turns toward the line of Desrosiers who look at him as if he were an executioner and shouts at the top of his lungs though there are only five people in the station:

"All aboard! *Prochain arrêt Saskatoon*, next stop Saskatoon! Alllll aboooard!"

Her grandmother hugged her tight, unable to say a word; her grandfather swallowed his tears; only her sisters let themselves go and cried, copiously. With her big suitcase beside her, she herself hasn't moved, her lips quivering slightly but not too much. Strangely enough, no goodbyes have been exchanged though both grandparents and granddaughter know that they'll probably never see one another again. Don't say things. Avoid them or arrange so that they don't exist. A calculated chill instead of outpourings, though they are necessary.

She did not turn around when she climbed into the buggy so she hasn't seen the dejection in the eyes of Joséphine and Méo from whom one-third of what is left of their reason for living is being taken away this morning while they wait for the rest to be cut off. Will the other two leave on the same day or will they have to live twice more through this intolerable scene that should be taking place amid heartbreaking sorrow and cries but is actually happening in a terrifying silence? Will they be able to bear three departures, three times on the same train?

When Monsieur Sanschagrin's whistle echoed in the early morning chill, Rhéauna held out her ticket to the tall man with a moustache who had just asked her if she was Rhéauna Rathier due to leave for Saskatoon, Regina, Winnipeg, Ottawa and Montreal. He spoke each name in a resonant voice as if they were all exotic destinations on the other side of the world. The door of the car closed with a gruesome bang, she ran to the first window, pressed her nose against the glass and then, as the train was starting to move, her sisters and her grandparents on the wooden platform waved desperately, she allowed herself to weep, to cry, to pound her fist. She wished that the other four wouldn't see her collapse, that she could wait for the train to pull away from the station before she gave in to her sorrow, but she couldn't help it, she didn't want to go away, to cross Canada or visit her two aunts and her second cousin, then lose her way in the big city, Montreal, with the mother she had stopped loving so long ago. She wanted to stop everything – the train that was picking up speed, the course of her life that was branching off in a direction she hadn't chosen, the nightmare that was starting here, this morning, that perhaps would never end. She thought about jumping off the train, at the risk of breaking her neck, or pulling the alarm bell to stop it. Or throwing herself at the tall, moustached man, who was looking at her wide-eyed, to punch him and beg him to give her back her family. She thought about dying or, rather, that's what death was: a definitive departure for an unknown destination. Alone. In a moving prison. With no hope of a change.

This time it's the entire village of Maria that seems to be swallowed up by the fields of wheat. And rye. And oats. And corn. The steeple of the church of Sainte-Maria-de-Saskatchewan floats for a moment above a square that's greener than the rest, of wheat that's not yet fully mature though it will soon be haying time, then it, too, will drown in the waves of grain and disappear for good. Never again will she see that either. She will talk about it all her life, she will describe the colours, the smells, the horror of bush-fires like the one last summer, the beauty of summer sunsets and the northern lights in winter over the vast plains, the tears that will come to her eyes whenever she imagines her grandmother bending over her wood stove where a pot of beef and vegetables is simmering, or her grandfather rocking on his veranda and smoking his smelly pipe, or Devil chewing diligently on a juicy red apple. That's all over now. She takes out her handkerchief, wipes away her tears, settles into her leather seat and looks out, shattered, at the endless plain that is running at full speed on either side of the train.

DREAM ON THE TRAIN TO REGINA

She is all alone in a large empty room. Three tall doors painted white stand in front of her. That look out, she's sure, on three other empty rooms that also … From the first door comes an old lady, tiny and dried up, who tells her that it's too hot to wear all those clothes, she should take off her coat. Which she does. Then the lady starts repeating, non-stop: "That's better, eh, a lot better like that, not so hot, you won't be so hot, it's a lot better for you," while she dons the coat and buttons it with calculated slowness, then smoothes it to enjoy the softness of the wool. It's too small for her, she's all dressed up, she looks crazy, but Rhéauna doesn't feel like laughing. She wants her coat. Because fall is coming. And it's cold in Montreal, especially on Mount Royal. She's going to need her red coat and she holds out her arms toward the old lady who has just stolen it from her and is now acting as if nothing has happened. From the second door emerges a kind of little girl at least sixty years old who hops like a frog; she is pudgy and red-faced, and too good-humoured to be sincere. It's not kindness that Rhéauna reads in her eyes, it's malice. "You'd better take a bath, you're all dirty, what you need is a good bath, come and take a good bath, Auntie's going to lend you a lovely swimsuit …" Since when does a person wear a swimsuit to take a bath? But she obeys, takes off all her clothes, gets into the black woollen bathing costume that will likely be very cold when it's wet. "You're so pretty like that! Now go and get washed …" And the sixty-year-old little girl folds Rhéauna's clothes as she drapes them over the back of a chair that has just appeared because she needed it for Rhéauna's folded clothes. And the lady who emerges through the third door, a blonde, whereas her two sisters — her sisters? are they sisters? impossible, she's too young! – have hair as black as a raven, has just one leg. She is breathtakingly beautiful but she has just one leg and she has to hop over to Rhéauna. "For heaven's sake, since when do you wear a swimsuit to take a bath? Take that off, you get naked when you want to wash! How do you reach yourself when you've got a bathing suit on? Rhéauna understands, blushes. She has never talked about such matters with her grandmother and she has always managed to "reach" herself with the soap and she hasn't had to talk about it with anybody. She doesn't want to take off her swimsuit but she can't help it and she sees herself, yes, she sees herself pull it off regardless, transformed by forces that she doesn't understand, that have taken hold of her body and are making her undress, just like that, in front of a stranger who has just one leg and seems to be enjoying herself. Now Rhéauna is naked in front of the three women, the one with a coat that's too small, the one who looks like an old little girl, the one who is a peroxide blonde and has just one leg. Each of the three raises an arm and says in unison: "You go next door to take a bath. Go take your bath next door." Rhéauna is cold, she's ashamed, she tries to hide herself with her hands that are too small, she steps toward the door – because now there is only one – and pushes it open.

She finds herself back on a gleaming hardwood floor lit by an electric system of a kind she's never seen; it is blinding, intimidating, more powerful than daylight. She shields her eyes with one hand and realizes that she is on a stage in a theatre. She has never seen a theatre but this is how she imagines them from the descriptions of Grandpa Méo, who boasts willingly and often of having once visited the Pantages Vaudeville in Edmonton, where he saw scantily dressed women wiggle their behinds in a very pretty way: a big stage of varnished wood, blindingly lit, a great dark space filled with rows of red seats, you become aware of them when your hand shields your *eyes. What can she be doing there? After all she's not going to take her bath on a stage in front of … men like her grandfather who've paid to watch her take her bath! But there's no one in the house. Yes, there, in the fourth row, right in the middle, a fourth lady whom she can't really see clearly because she is so far away. The only spectator in a vast theatre. The lady gets up, takes off her gloves which are very long, much longer than hers or Grandma Joséphine's. It takes time, Rhéauna is cold, she realizes that she's been trembling for a while now. The lady holds out her arms, smiles. The rest of her person is hazy, but not her smile. "Right, now show me what you can do!"*

She wakes with a start. One of her fairy-tale books is on her lap. Was that a dream? She has the impression, though, that she had read the dream, that it was written in the same style as her fairy tales, with words that keep coming back all the time, words that lull you and sometimes put you to sleep … She has already forgotten what the dream was made of, if it was one, but she is left with an impression of discomfort that makes her heart beat like a terror-stricken bird. She looks outside. A city is coming near. Saskatoon. She's not going to stop there, she has to stay on the train, which will just make a quick stop. Then the trip to Regina will be a little longer. One of her aunts, great-aunts rather, will be waiting for her on the platform in Regina. Her aunt Régina. Her great-aunt Régina. Régina from Regina. That's right, now she's starting to think as she did in her dream.

2

RÉGINA-COELI

There's no one waiting for her at the station in Regina.

If her aunt is late, she must have a good reason. Rhéauna sits on a bench that's made not of wood like the one in the station in Maria but of cold, hard metal, and looks around her. She has never seen such an impressive building – she doesn't remember passing through here five years ago, she was too young – her worry is somewhat alleviated by the crowds of travellers, the whistles of trains pulling into or out of the station, the announcements of departures and arrivals that emerge from invisible loudspeakers. The actual building is overwhelming, like a church but bigger. The church of Sainte-Maria-de-Saskatchewan would easily fit under the metal vault with its exposed beams. Even the steeple wouldn't reach the ceiling. A little dazed she rests her feet on her suitcase to show that it is hers and that no one should approach it. She looks at the big clock above the ticket windows. She has been waiting for nearly fifteen minutes. If her aunt Régina doesn't come, what is she supposed to do all alone in a big city? But she'll come. After all, she can't have forgotten her.

The little girl is hungry. During the stop in Saskatoon, she'd wolfed down the sandwich Grandma Joséphine had fixed for her. It was good. A thick chicken sandwich. Along with a handful of radishes. And a slice of raspberry pie. But that was quite a while ago. Her stomach is making unpleasant growling sounds and, on top of it all, she's thirsty. She did spot a water fountain near the ladies' bathroom, but she didn't stop there so as not to miss her aunt who must have been waiting impatiently. Her great-aunt Régina's impatience is celebrated throughout the family and her grandmother warned her to be obedient, discreet and polite during the few hours, overnight, that Rhéauna will spend with her. If she'd only known ... But Grandma Joséphine had also warned her never to drink from a water fountain because you don't know who's been there before you and what deadly unknown disease they've left behind ...

She opens the purse hanging around her neck. She could take out one of the nickels and buy herself an orangeade and a snack. The lemonade vendor is nearby on her left and he seems bored, maybe because he doesn't have many customers. He smiled at her two or three times, no doubt to encourage her to come over. She's well aware that she mustn't talk to strangers but you have to talk to a lemonade vendor even if he's a stranger, don't you? Otherwise how would he know what she wanted to buy?

She is about to make up her mind to dip into her little nest egg when she senses a presence nearby. A shadow in fact has just set down on her knees. She looks up. Her great-aunt Régina, red-faced and out of breath, has both hands on her chest.

"I'm sorry. I wanted to walk so I could save a little money and the station's farther than I thought!"

She's a tiny dried-out little woman with a yellow complexion – her brother Méo calls her Jaundice to tease her and it's the thing that she hates most of all in the world – she talks quickly and moves abruptly, driven by a perpetual motion that she can't hold back and that exhausts everyone else. She is squeezed into a threadbare coat despite the August heat and a silly-looking straw hat, vestige of the end of the last century, sits askew on her hair which is pulled into a salt-and-pepper pile, a complicated structure perfectly held in place that reminds Rhéauna of the illustrations she often used to see in the newspaper her grandfather reads.

Rhéauna gets off her metal bench and picks up her suitcase.

"If your place is far from here, *ma tante*, I don't think I can carry my suitcase all the way."

After a quick peck on the cheek – she smells too strongly of some flower Rhéauna doesn't know – Régina grabs the suitcase and sets out without waiting for her.

"I didn't say you'd have to walk, I said *I* came on foot ... We're going to take a taxi."

A taxi? What's that? She doesn't dare to ask, she'd also been told not to ask pointless questions.

The street they emerged onto when they left the station doesn't look like anything Rhéauna has ever known. It's lively, it's noisy, it's swarming with people, you might think that cars and people have been thrown down any which way, in big handfuls, and that no one, anywhere, knows where it is heading or why. An anthill of activity. No, not an anthill; ants know what they're doing ... A gigantic monster on rails – her aunt tells her that it's called a streetcar – drives past them, making an ugly clang-clang-clang that causes her to jump; sparks escape from the electrical wire hanging above that it follows with the help of a long metal pole fastened onto its roof, which connects them. Receiving too much information at a time, Rhéauna feels dazed. As if she knew, her aunt turns toward her.

"Big city's impressive, isn't it? Stay next to me, you could get lost in the crowd."

She holds up her hand to hail a car parked nearby. Rhéauna has never been in a car and excitement at the thought of travelling full speed through such lively streets makes her heart beat faster.

At first, the taxi ride through Regina thrills her. Everywhere, the streets are packed, people seem to run, not walk, cars mingle with horses in all kinds of harnesses, sedans, carriages, the horses neigh when the cars go too fast – men have actually been hired to follow behind them and pick up their droppings, there are so many! – on some streets the houses are three or four storeys tall. At one point the taxi goes past a kind of general store where she counts up to eight and she can't help letting out an exclamation of surprise.

Her aunt frowns, turns to the window to see what's going on.

"What is it? What did you see?"

"That store. It's eight storeys high!"

Disappointed not to have witnessed one of the urban dramas she's so fond of – a woman run over by a car or a frightened horse galloping off, or at least a traffic jam at a busy intersection because there are more and more of them as cars become more numerous, complicating traffic by terrifying the horses – Régina heaves an exasperated sigh.

"This isn't a little village, Rhéauna, it's a big city! You'll see plenty more eight-storey buildings!"

Rhéauna would like to call her idiotic, to tell her that she knows she's in a big city but that actually she's never seen a big city before and that it's normal for her to be surprised at everything she sees. She restrains herself, knowing that it would be pointless because she can sense that her grandfather's sister, as a city dweller, will look down on her and keep treating her like a perfectly ignorant country mouse. It's true that she hasn't seen anything, she's come from deep in the prairies, but is that any reason to make her feel uncomfortable? Her pride somewhat damaged she presses her nose against the car window again after shooting at her great-aunt a look into which she has tried to put all the contempt she can muster.

It seems as if everybody in Regina is dressed in their Sunday best. Nobody seems to be wearing everyday clothes, overalls for instance, which her grandmother calls dungarees – or old checked shirts or battered straw hats as they do in Maria on weekdays. No, they're all dressed to the nines. It looks as if they won't step outside without changing their clothes. Yet they bump into one another without even noticing! Why change to go out if they don't trade compliments? Especially when the men dressed like cowboys are so handsome under their enormous hats. She realizes then that they don't all know one another – there are so many more people here than back home – and she wonders how a person can live in a city full of strangers. Then she realizes that Montreal will be worse, as it's even bigger than Regina. That thought is enough to spoil her pleasure. She loses interest in what is going on outside the taxi and she lowers her head. Then pulls it up almost immediately because something has just happened around her, an abrupt change when the car was turning left, after blowing its horn: less noise, less coming and going, more trees, surprising peace and quiet all at once, after the downtown din. They have just turned onto a small street that could look like a corner of the countryside if the houses were less impressive and if there were fields of corn all around them.

Régina opens her big handbag, takes out a leather billfold and stuffs her hand into it.

"It won't be long, we're nearly there."

The car stops in front of a tiny house. Another disappointment for Rhéauna, who would have liked to stay in one of those eight-storey homes that must have an impressive view from so high up. She would even have been content with three. But Régina lives in a ground-floor apartment so small and so clean that Rhéauna, who has never smelled commercial disinfectant hanging over everything, immediately feels out of place. The house in Maria has always been well-kept, of course, Joséphine spends all day long working and cleaning, but after one quick glance inside her great-aunt Régina's suite – a living room, kitchen, a real bathroom, one bedroom – Rhéauna imagines her aunt is obsessed with cleanliness and that makes her uncomfortable. Everything is too-carefully positioned, calculated, the sofa cushions as well as the toiletries on the vanity, the new soap in the soap dish as well as the shining kitchen sink, and the little girl feels as if she is a big oil stain, indelible and all too visible on fabric that is too clean. Actually, it's funny, but her great-aunt's apartment reminds Rhéauna of her excessively elaborate and slightly ridiculous hairdo. Lacquered. The apartment is lacquered.

Régina asked her to wipe her shoes before coming inside, which she does, but she soon regrets not having removed them, even though they are new. They have been hurting her feet since this morning. She catches herself watching for traces of her passage on the rug. No, nothing visible. Oh, oh, her suitcase, which she set down in the entrance, may not be clean.

While she gathers up her things to put in the kitchen where they're less likely to be in the way or to get things dirty, the rumbling of her stomach reminds her that she's famished. Going up to her great-aunt who has put the kettle on for tea she says in a shy little voice:

"Could I have a snack? ... I haven't eaten anything since the lunch Grandma made me for the train ... I'm really thirsty, too."

As if she had just been waiting for that to get on her high horse, an excuse for expressing her frustration, Régina turns to her great-niece and starts yelling at her. It's so sudden that Rhéauna jumps and takes refuge in a corner of the kitchen, just in front of the bathroom door.

"Now that's going too far! Supper's in less than an hour. Can't you wait that long? You're a nice little girl, you're my brother's granddaughter and I've got a duty to look after you till tomorrow morning but I'm not your servant and I'm not here to cater to your whims! Joséphine should have warned me you'd be hungry before supper, you're a growing girl. I can give you some green tea and crackers because it's tea time but don't expect anything else, you won't get it! You'll eat when it's time to eat and that's that!"

Aunt Régina's stinginess is well-known – in fact, Méo blushes a little with shame when he talks about it because as he puts it so well, Jaundice will do anything to save a penny, even make a fool of herself – but Rhéauna had forgotten about it in the excitement of arriving in Regina and she remembers too late that her grandmother had told her not to ask her great-aunt for anything to eat, to wait until she offered. No matter how hungry she is. Because Régina isn't rich; in fact, she's rather destitute. Above all, she doesn't want it to show.

First mistake.

Rhéauna listens to her aunt's griping as she bustles around the wood stove. She wishes she were miles away, on the train to Winnipeg, why not? – she could have continued on her way, just changed trains and gone directly to her aunt Bebette whom she loves so much, couldn't she? – or in her own house, with her sisters and grandparents. She feels as if she's in a novel by the Comtesse de Ségur, *Sophie's Misfortunes* or *The Inn of the Guardian Angel*, where children are always bullied and unhappy and she'd rather be reading their stories than living them. A phenomenon like aunt Régina doesn't really exist in real life; it's too ridiculous. You might come across one in a novel, you laugh a little because it's absurd and you feel sorry for the character who's in the kind of situation that she herself is living through, but no one, ever, has lost her temper with Rhéauna just because she asked for something to eat. It doesn't make sense! Then she thinks about a book she tried to read last year but gave up because it was too scary. It was called *Oliver Twist* and it was written by a Monsieur Dickens and it started with a little orphan in an orphanage who dared to ask for a second bowl of thin gruel for breakfast because he was hungry ... She brings her hand to her mouth as she thinks about what happens to little Oliver after that.

All at once Régina seems to realize what she's doing, and she jumps as if someone has just called her back to reality by telling her off. She looks at Rhéauna, wipes her hands on the apron she's just put on and speaks in a contrite tone she never uses and that makes her seem even stranger. She stammers, she stutters, Rhéauna has trouble understanding what exactly she's trying to say, so confused are her words.

"Sorry ... You see ... So-so-so sorry ... I'm not used ... Usually ... See, I'm always alone here and ... Well ... See, I'm not used to ... I'm not used to having people ... Especially children ... I don't know anything about ... I don't know what to do ... I've got a nice dish of eggs goldenrod ... In a little while we'll have some nice eggs goldenrod ..."

She runs to the icebox, opens it, points to the egg sauce that in fact Rhéauna can't see.

"I made it last night ... I'll warm it up ..."

Grandma Joséphine says, though, that you should never reheat eggs goldenrod because it can go bad, that you have to eat it in one meal if you don't want to get sick ... Anyway it's so good that there's never any left. A tremendous gloom falls on Rhéauna's shoulders: she has a choice between eating some dangerous eggs goldenrod that's liable to poison her or to be left hungry until the next morning. She doesn't dare imagine what kind of bread her aunt Régina uses to make her toast in the morning ... Or butter to spread on it ... Or strawberry jam, if there is any ...

Régina goes back to the stove with quick little steps, burns her finger when she accidentally touches the kettle, lets out a little yelp more from exasperation than from pain, rushes to the sink to run cold water over it. Vigorously she works the pump, holding her injured finger under the metal spout.

"I don't know what I ... I never burn myself ... I don't know what ... Can you go sit in the living room? Wait there for me ... I'll bring your tea and crackers, I won't be long ... But don't watch, you can see how it upsets me ..."

Back in the living room, Rhéauna settles into a corner of the sofa, making herself as small as she can. Everything around her is distressing, the curtains drawn in the middle of the day; the ecru-lace headrests that very likely no head has ever rested on; the threadbare carpet, its designs long since faded, that barely hides the pitiful state of the hardwood floor; the furniture too big for the room, especially the upright piano that takes up nearly one whole wall. Why on earth does her grandfather's sister have a piano in her living room?

The absence of food smells worries her, too. In the house in Maria there is always an aroma of something simmering, a soup made from yesterday's delicious leftovers or the evening meal that has been cooking since morning. Or a cake that is rising in the oven. When you climb the stairs to the veranda, you are already glad to be there and the appetizing aromas make your mouth water. Here, no sooner have you arrived than you want to leave. Because it smells of nothing. Except for commercial disinfectant.

She has an urge to leave, taking her suitcase with her. Anywhere. Running. Even if it means losing her way or rushing at the first policeman she sees to ask for help. There must be hundreds of them here in Regina, whereas Maria has only one, a Monsieur Nadeau, who is jovial and always drunk. She is on the point of doing it, she's about to set her foot on the ground while looking in the direction of the door, her heart pounding, when Régina appears, carrying a tray with an old white china teapot flanked by two mismatched cups and a tiny plate of crackers. Rhéauna will never know then if she would have found the courage to leave her great-aunt's house without asking for her due, like a thief caught red-handed.

She sinks into the sofa cushions, takes a cracker, just one, and brings it to her mouth without haste when she would like to stuff it into her mouth and swallow it whole before grabbing the others with both hands. While she waits for the warmed-up eggs golden-rod. Which may be deadly.

Never in her life has she tasted anything so insipid.

Or seen food so pale.

Everything on her plate is white. And mushy. And runny. When her grandmother makes eggs goldenrod, it's usually to go along with a salmon pie in which you can always see a big piece of delicious pink flesh under the rich yellow sauce; but what her aunt has just set down in front of her is a plate covered with a kind of nearly transparent soup with a few pieces of hardboiled eggs floating in it that can't even colour the dish because the yellow is so washed-out. And chalky. No salmon pie, of course; that would be too good. Just a thin slice of bread, which by the way is fresh and delicious. If she weren't so hungry she could claim fatigue from her trip to save herself from this meal that promises to be disgusting, and go to bed right away, taking along the slice of bread without butter, but to her great displeasure her stomach started making its noises again as soon as Régina came in with the soup tureen, even if it had no aroma and, despite her disgust, she quickly grabs her soup spoon because the sauce is too liquid to eat with a fork. As she expected it has absolutely no taste. She is a little relieved; at least what she puts in her mouth and swallows as quickly as she can doesn't upset her stomach and will most likely check her hunger. Before it kills her.

The meal takes place in awkward silence. Earlier Régina let Rhéauna know that she doesn't know how to behave with children and the girl has nothing to say to this great-aunt who seems to be the one who takes the blame for everyone else's deeds, on the pretext that she is an old maid in a society where an unmarried woman is abnormal, and whom she has hardly ever talked to because she stays in her own corner, even during the lively meals at Christmastime. She doesn't say that what she is eating is good because she doesn't want to lie and her aunt, who knows that it isn't, doesn't ask her either. That is, Rhéauna cannot even claim that what's on her plate isn't good, it's only colourless, odourless and tasteless.

All of a sudden she thinks about school, about the last days of May, just before the final exams, when Mademoiselle Primeau taught them those three words that she thought were so beautiful – *colourless, odourless, insipid* – that she repeated them hundreds of times to her grandmother, who laughed as she told her that she couldn't use them to talk about the food at home. But here, tonight, she can use them and she wants to cry. Her first real meal away from home is a disaster. She wonders what they're eating now in Maria. She knows that they're sad, that her two sisters may be crying, but what they are eating is no doubt delicious, her grandmother would never dare serve them a horror like what's sitting in front of her, not even on a sad day like today.

When Rhéauna lowers her nose into her plate, her aunt thinks that she's being overcome by fatigue, but it's actually unspeakable dejection that is making her head droop. Her aunt taps her hand before she grabs her empty plate without asking if she wants another helping. Is she going to eat it again tomorrow? Warmed up a *second* time?

"You can go to bed whenever your want, you know, the train leaves early tomorrow morning. But Auntie has to warn you that she's going to play the piano for a while … I hope it won't bother you too much … your auntie can't do without it."

Because the eggs goldenrod were sitting on her stomach like lead, Rhéauna decided not to go to bed right after supper. In any case, it was no later than half past six when the dishes were done, the table cleared, the floor swept. They went back to the living room, went back to their places in silence and still had nothing to say to each other. Régina asked again how everybody was in Maria, especially the brother she adores despite the way he treats her. Rhéauna replied politely. Adding a few variations to her answers to make them more interesting. She nearly told the story about the peanuts in shells, but suspecting that her aunt wouldn't laugh, she restrained herself.

It has been going on for a good half-hour. Now and then, Régina smoothes her dress over her knees, as if to shake off non-existent dust, clears her throat as if she's about to speak but doesn't say a thing. She picks up an old magazine from the little table, leafs through it, puts it back, glancing toward the piano. Why doesn't she just sit down and play if she wants to so badly, what is she waiting for? A signal? From whom? As for Rhéauna, she drinks glass after glass of water, trying to get her meal down. But nothing works, the lump that weighs on her stomach seems to be getting bigger rather than being absorbed and she's afraid of suffocating to death in the middle of the night, in the bed that she'll share with her great-aunt. That's what worries her most: how will the two of them be able to sleep in the narrow bed that she spotted in one corner of the bedroom when she was looking around the house? After all, she's not going to press herself against the ancient body of her grandfather's old-maid sister the way she does with Béa and Alice to console them if they're sad or to warm them if the house is too cold. No, she'll ask her great-aunt for permission to sleep here, on the sofa, claiming that she doesn't want to disturb her. So much that she wishes she weren't there – a presence imposed on a person who obviously would rather be alone. The night before she wanted the night never to end; tonight she wants it to pass as quickly as possible.

Around a quarter past seven, Régina gets up and heads for the apartment door that opens on to the front balcony. Relieved, Rhéauna thinks that they are going for a walk in the neighbourhood and gets up from the sofa to follow her. But her aunt comes right back and seems surprised to see her standing in the middle of the living room.

"Where are you going?"

"Nowhere, I thought …"

Régina cuts her off as she turns toward the piano.

"I just wanted a bit of a breeze. It's too hot in here."

Resigned, Rhéauna goes back to her seat.

Then something unusual happens. As soon as Régina sits on the piano bench and even before she raises the lid that protects the keyboard, a remarkable change occurs in her, something subtle and radical that can be felt even though Rhéauna only sees her from behind. Her movements become more flowing, her hand strokes the varnished wood, her body, stiff as it had been, is now strangely soft, and it is with very palpable excitement that she opens the music book in front of her. She smoothes it, too, with the flat of her hand but her movement is much gentler than it was when she was brushing non-existent crumbs off her long skirt a little earlier.

She turns to her great-niece.

"This is Schubert. Do you know Schubert?"

She pronounces the name English-style, making the *t* ring out as if the Monsieur Schubert in question – whom Rhéauna has never heard of – were an American composer. Or a friend of hers in Regina who devotes his spare time to music.

The old lady's face is transformed. So is this Monsieur Schubert some kind of god that she reveres unconditionally? Rhéauna has seen that face on some of the sanctimonious women devoted to the Virgin Mary – Joséphine calls them holy cows – who are transformed at the moment of Holy Communion or before a particularly virulent sermon by the fat curé. Is her aunt Régina going to play some religious church music? On the piano rather than the organ? Rhéauna settles into her sofa. After all, better church music, even on the piano, than the unbearable silence that has been weighing on them until now.

The minutes that follow are so unbelievably beautiful that Rhéauna doesn't budge from her seat. She has never heard a piano in her life, she knows nothing about music – aside from the small church organ, there is Monsieur Fredette in Maria, the local fiddler who performs on all the birthdays and marriages but whose instrument shrieks too much to be called real music and Monsieur Fredette himself smells too strongly for anyone to hang around too long and listen to him – but what aunt Régina's fingers are coaxing from the white and black keys, the nearly unbearable happiness that she never suspected could be possible, the irresistible force that stirs and caresses her, transports her with ecstasy – though a few minutes earlier she had been thinking about running away from this damn house, she was so disheartened. Who would have imagined that so much beauty was hiding here with aunt Régina, the bundle of nerves the whole family fears, the quick-tempered woman who tolerates no annoyance, this slight and obviously fragile person who knows nothing about children: who would have imagined that she possesses one of the greatest secrets of the universe? And that she keeps it hidden here, inside these four walls, when she ought to be sharing it with everyone because everyone needs it to survive?

So that's what music is! It can be something other than Sister Marie-Marthe's wrong notes on Sunday mornings and the insupportable squealing of Monsieur Fredette's instrument? So it's true that it can be beautiful?

It begins softly, gentle as a lullaby murmured by an adored grandmother. Even more, that it's a melody known forever – it sounds familiar the first time you hear it – but as soon as the music is imprinted on the brain and you're convinced that you could never shake it off – just as you are beginning to hope that it will stay that way, with no variations, because it's perfect – all at once the rhythm changes, develops, it rises and falls like laughter, it growls, too, it's threatening and it brings tears to your eyes because something terrible is hidden there along with an immense joy and, just as suddenly, it becomes melancholy again and the oh-so-beautiful melody from the beginning returns, powerfully, more glorious than ever because of its tremendous restraint. That's what you want to preserve; in fact, you want to carry it around for the rest of your life – that simple little melody from the beginning and the end which will have the power to soothe you during the difficult moments of life and to ornament the happy moments with one more rapture. It doesn't end either, it seems to fade away, it blurs until you can no longer hear it. It goes on, it must go on, it cannot stop, but it can no longer be heard, that's all. The hands are no longer wandering over the keyboard, no vibration surges from the instrument, yet it perpetuates itself in the silence that comes after.

It lasted how long, five minutes? Twenty? Rhéauna couldn't say, all she knows is that she would like it never to stop. That is the meaning of eternity. The music of this Monsieur Schubert. When aunt Régina's hands leave the keyboard and move onto her knees, Rhéauna would like to hurl herself at the keys to replace them in order to get back the happiness that was too short, that doesn't have the right to disappear.

A second or two of silence fall over the living room at the end of the piece, then you can hear timid applause that seems to be coming from outside. Rhéauna looks out the open door. When she looks back at her aunt as if to ask her for an explanation, she realizes that Régina is smiling. You can't say that it's a beautiful smile, Régina's face isn't beautiful, but it's a smile that illuminates, irresistibly sincere. And in the end, she can allow herself to think that it is in a sense beautiful.

Rhéauna gets up, crosses the living room, steps out onto the balcony. Dozens of neighbours have gathered outside great-aunt Régina's house. Some have brought chairs, as if they knew that there would be more than one piece on the program that night. Others are stretched out on blankets spread over the meagre grass that's beginning to go yellow because there hasn't been enough rain. Couples hold hands, whole families are peaceful and quiet, an old gentleman in a wheelchair seems to be consulting a music book. As soon as they see Rhéauna emerge from the house they applaud. Surely they don't think that she is the one who's just produced those phenomenal sounds. No doubt they know Régina-Coeli Desrosiers, they know that she is the great musician, not a poor little girl who's just arrived from the far-off prairies and who had no idea that Monsieur Schubert existed! Turning a bit, she realizes that her great-aunt has followed her and that she is the one being applauded. Rhéauna steps aside to give her room. Régina, red-faced, makes a quick little bow and goes back inside after asking Rhéauna:

"Do you want some more?"

Does she want some more! She wants some until tomorrow morning, until her train leaves for Winnipeg, until her death, she wants some until her death. She will ask her mother for a piano when she arrives in Montreal, she'll throw herself at it as if her life depended on it – and her life does depend on it now, she's certain; starting now she will console herself for everything with the music of her great-aunt's friend, that Monsieur Schubert who invented it all, all that unbelievable music!

Before she sits at the piano her aunt turns to face her. She's no longer the same person and Rhéauna hopes that she will never see the other one again.

"They do that every evening."

"Is that why you opened the door?"

"Yes."

"What do they do in the winter? You can't open the door then. Do you play during the winter?"

"I play all the time. Every evening. All year round. Winter ... in the winter they can't hear me and they wait for summer. But maybe it's good for them to take a break ..."

She sits down at the piano. Opens another music book.

"Did the same man compose that?"

"No, another one. Long before him. But you'll see, it's just as beautiful."

"Why don't you say so?"

The question has come out by itself and Rhéauna blushes. Her aunt looks at her.

"Why don't I say what? What are you talking about?"

Rhéauna coughs into her fist, takes her courage in both hands, dives in.

"How come you never said you can play the piano? I didn't know and I bet my little sisters don't know either."

"Life's like that, some things we want to keep to ourselves, Nana."

"But everybody'd be so happy to know how good you are. And ... maybe Grandpa would stop saying mean things about you all the time."

Another smile appears on Régina's lips, this one sad, a smile not of joy but of resignation that brings back to the surface the aunt Régina that Rhéauna never wants to see again.

"Nothing could stop your grandfather from saying mean things about me, Nana. And I think it's a good thing he doesn't know I've got some talent. It suits him."

"Why does it suit him?"

"Grown-ups are more complicated than you think, Nana. You mustn't ask questions like that, the answers might disappoint you."

"Grandpa could never disappoint me. I love him too much."

"That's what I'm saying; go on loving him. Meanwhile, listen to this ..."

Night has fallen without her being aware of it. The pieces of music, each more beautiful than the rest, succeeded one another all evening, now bubbling mischievously, now slow and sombre enough to break your heart. Finally, Rhéauna joins in the applause

that rose up between the pieces, clapping her hands enthusiastic-
ally. Louder than anyone. She looks at her great-aunt in profile,
follows the movement of her hands on the keyboard, the swaying
of her head during the slow movements. She guesses at the movements of her feet on the pedals under her long skirt. No longer is
she the same person and it's this one, the woman in raptures at the
piano, that she wants to remember, not the bad cook or the sour
shrew who doesn't know how to behave with children. It doesn't
matter that the eggs goldenrod was so bad and that Régina was
impatient with her if it all hides such a gift. This is the first time
in her life that she has met someone who has a genuine talent, in
any case, aside from being able to cook marvellous dishes or, in
her grandfather's case, to tell stories that go on and on and are
never boring, and she is overflowing with admiration. She doesn't
understand how it happens, how her aunt is able to read music
as if the notes were words on a page, then transfer them to her
fingers, give them so much meaning, so much emotion – and never
lose her way! The force of habit? The repetition day after day of
the same pieces? Again, it hardly matters. What *does* matter is the
indescribable happiness it offers her, the rose-coloured night that
is falling with no one noticing, the prolonged applause coming
from the sidewalk in front of the house, her aunt plunged into the
music to the point of forgetting everything else, the warmth that
she feels deep inside herself, that she couldn't name but that she
wants to feel forever, like a votive light, because it is consolation
for everything. No, that's not true, it's no consolation at all. If she
let herself think about what awaits her tomorrow, on the train, or
in a few days when she arrives in Montreal, she knows very well
that her heart would swell with bitterness, that tears would come
to her eyes, that she would be as unhappy as before her great-
aunt's concert, but in fact the music of Monsieur Schubert and the
other composers helps her to not think about it, and she is grateful
to him for this moment of respite before the inevitable avalanche
of events descends.

With the concert over, Régina rises slowly, tucking away a lock of hair that had moved during her excitement.

"Did you like that?"

Rhéauna can't speak. Her aunt understands, goes and shuts the door to the apartment after waving at the neighbours who are sending a heartfelt *Merci*.

"Time for bed now. You've got a long train ride tomorrow."

Rhéauna manages to extricate herself from the sofa. She has to come back to reality, get into her nightgown, brush her teeth in the bathroom, pee as she's been desperate to do for some time. And sleep. But she's positive she won't be able to. For reasons different from the night before. Will she be able to carry all that music with her, to remember the melodies, so beautiful, so captivating, to hum them at difficult moments? No, probably not. Already they're getting away from her. She would like to grab hold of her aunt's music books, wishes she could read them like the books by the Comtesse de Ségur or by Monsieur Dickens. But no. That requires knowledge, information that she doesn't have. It can be learned, of course, but she may not have her great-aunt's talent. Finally, she is condemned to be one of those who have to be content to listen.

The bed is narrow but Rhéauna no longer feels uncomfortable at the thought of lying next to her aunt. She could ask to sleep on the living-room sofa as she had intended, presumably so as not to disturb her, decides no, that might be impolite or tactless.

Régina switches off the bedside light.

Rhéauna thinks that she ought to say something, to congratulate her grandfather's sister, thank her. But how? Her words will never be as striking as what she has just heard.

"I never heard that, a piano, *ma tante*."

She senses the old woman turning to her, feels the warmth of her body next to her own. Her great-aunt Régina isn't cold after a concert.

"Pretty, isn't it?"

"It's more than pretty ... It's ... it's ... magnificent."

Régina wraps her arm around her great-niece's shoulders and they fall asleep almost immediately.

This is the first time since the beginning of her adulthood that Régina has slept with someone. But that, no one will ever know.

Régina-Coeli Desrosiers has never married.

Everyone knew that the unattractive young girl, shy and awkward, would be an old maid. The youngest child of Rhéau and Simone Desrosiers, she had been brought up to help her mother and serve her brother and sisters. A late arrival in her parents' life, most likely unexpected, unlike her siblings she hadn't been able to enjoy their affection, discreet but palpable. On the contrary. Her mother had always made it clear, without showing any regret or guilt, that she had not been desired and she treated her like a servant, with no signs of affection or words of encouragement.

She had never had a companion and she didn't seem to care. She had seen her brother, Méo, marry that idiotic Joséphine Lépine and then her sisters: first Bebette with some obese individual who was even more insufferable than she herself, if that was possible, the indispensable Rosaire Roy, king of the Canadian Pacific Railway; then Gertrude, who quickly left for Ottawa to tie the knot with a young lawyer named Wilson, then die of sorrow in strange circumstances and leave behind the appalling Ti-Lou of whom it was said that the life she led was far from respectable and who was known as the she-wolf of Ottawa. As the house was being emptied, however, Régina-Coeli's personality changed. Or maybe, released from her obligations, free at last to be herself, she let herself go, showing her parents her real personality. Or the one that they'd fashioned for her with their constant frustrations and reproaches. She had not been born sour-tempered, she'd become it. Because of the rest of the family. She had grumbled while serving her brother and sisters, complained about their whims and demands, but to date she had never dared to behave with anyone else as she allowed herself to do from then on with her parents; she sent them packing despite the respect that she owed them for the simple reason that they were her parents, neglecting her duties as cook – she hated cooking and now managed to ruin meal after meal with a kind of dogged will to displease that was very effective – and doing the most rudimentary household tasks.

She hadn't looked at men; they weren't yet aware of her existence. On her twenty-fifth birthday, she had officially declared herself an old maid and her parents had given up for good any thought of one day getting rid of her. They had made her without wanting her, now they had to put up with her. Till the end. Of their lives or hers. Her mother, as a good practising and narrow-minded Catholic, saw her as a punishment for sins that she hadn't committed; her father, a good defeatist and submissive farmer, as one more necessary evil in an already difficult life.

And all that time the existence of Régina-Coeli Desrosiers – her double-barrelled name came from her mother's somewhat excessive devotion to the Blessed Virgin – would have been terribly pathetic had she not had music to console her. For everything.

Music had come into her life by chance. One of the nuns who taught at her school in Saint-Boniface – the family had not yet left Manitoba, the Desrosiers's native land – one Sister Marguerite-Bourgeoys, who played the parish organ on Sunday and spent her free time at the piano the rest of the week, had noticed little Régina-Coeli's obvious fascination with the instrument. She'd started by hanging around the nun and her piano after the catechism lesson on Sunday, which always ended with Mozart's *Turkish Rondo*; then she quickly moved on to questions, precise and often relevant, until one fine day she asked permission to touch the keyboard, just to see how it would sound under her fingers … Sister Marguerite-Bourgeoys had asked her if she wanted to learn to play and Régina-Coeli had answered yes. She was the only one in the family who showed a little talent or even the slightest interest in any art, no matter what.

And so the nun started to teach her secretly the rudiments of that difficult instrument, most of the time at dawn before classes began. Régina-Coeli had to leave as soon as classes were over to prepare the meals – at noon and in the evening for her family who – it was obvious from how her brother and sisters behaved with her – mistreated her. She learned to play piano then unbeknownst to the others; no one at home or at school was aware of the ordinary little girl's new interest in classical music.

Régina-Coeli was not an exceptional student and she often displayed a difficult nature, irascible when things didn't go her way – a fingering technique particularly hard to master, a piece that was complicated to decipher, the cold that numbed her hands in winter, the dampness of summer that made the ivory of the keyboard slippery; she would throw a tantrum, hit the piano as if it were a human being, even say bad words she'd heard who knows where that made Sister Marguerite-Bourgeoys blush. Perhaps Régina-Coeli was taking revenge on the piano for what her family made her put up with. The nun was severe as seldom as possible, however, because of the tremendous, sincere passion for music that she sensed was growing in her student who'd learned to read scores in record time and whose tremendous determination to master the instrument, to subject it to her will, was wonderful. But when everything was going well – if Régina-Coeli managed to play one whole piece without a mistake, for instance – she was transformed, radically changed, one could see the beginnings of the pianist she could become, it was obvious from the fluidity of her movements and the intelligence of her performances. Then Sister Marguerite-Bourgeoys would flush with pride. And when, after a year of lessons undertaken with such great seriousness, the little girl began to understand that music could be *interpreted*, that you weren't limited to transferring to the keyboard precisely what you read on the score, that on the contrary you were free to play as much what the piece of music made you feel as the printed notes, she had thrown herself into the piano the way others might do into drink, sin or religion. It had become the centre of her life, her panacea, her reward, her consolation. And all, oh joy, with no one else's knowledge. Because during all those years, she hadn't said a word to her family circle. She'd asked Sister

Marguerite-Bourgeoys to keep the secret but the nun, so proud of her pupil, had let out word to some of her colleagues and then Régina-Coeli Desrosiers's lessons, though early in the morning, drew something of a crowd. Even the school principal, one Sister Jésus-de-la-Croix, a strict and rather chilly woman, was not averse to the occasional visit to the small room where, it was said in the religious community, divine melodies rose up for the greater glory of God. Her first audience then was a group of black-and-white wimples who thought they had before them a revelation of God on earth, though what was happening before their eyes was on the contrary the raw, pagan passion of a woman, neglected by her family, for an art that was saving her life. Most likely, they would have thought that passion guilty and reprehensible if they had imagined it for what it was. But they chose to remain in ecstasy without thinking.

No one in Régina-Coeli's family ever knew that she devoted herself to the piano. With remarkable talent.

And when she left school at fourteen, she found herself deprived of all music. For ten years. It was out of the question to ask her parents for a piano. Music had never been heard in the house and, in any case, they would have told her that the living room was too small for such a massive instrument. Or that they were too old to put up with that pounding away all day long. Or too poor to pay for something so useless. Now and then she would slip into the school music room and her former teacher would let her satisfy her passion for an hour or two, but rumours began to fly about the nature of their relationship – it's fine to be a teacher's pet when you're at school, but when you leave, you must never go back – and Régina-Coeli had to give up the piano with no hope of remission. She said her goodbyes to the old, much-loved instrument with a Chopin nocturne, but she couldn't do justice to all the subtleties and reproached herself for years, mentally correcting her final performance, a failure, correcting it, polishing it, but too late.

That was how, little by little, she became the sour-tempered Régina-Coeli Desrosiers everybody learned to hate. She only had to give in to her natural inclination toward the impatience, anger, rage that the existence of the piano in her everyday life could lull for a while, and to which she could devote herself. As Chopin, Schubert and Mozart were no longer there to give meaning to her life, she had concentrated bitterly on the role that fate seemed to have in store for her, that she seemed unable to escape – the role of servant to everyone else. Her parents were old, her older siblings were far away, raising their own families, so the work was lighter, but Régina-Coeli went at it as if the house were full of people all year long and the Desrosiers home became the cleanest one in Saint-Boniface, the one that was always held up as an example when anyone talked about a well-run household, where no one would have wanted to live, however, because of that shrew who ruled over everything there or, so it was said, who poisoned the existence of anyone who dared to approach her.

One fine day she told her parents, just like that, point blank, that she was leaving Saint-Boniface for Regina. She needed a change; she'd been thinking about going away for a while and she'd got a job at a library in Saskatchewan that was looking for a bilingual archivist. At first her parents seemed not to understand, then after she'd explained that, once she turned twenty-five, she wanted to be on her own. They'd asked why, adding of course the usual criticisms: she didn't have a heart; she was abandoning them in their old age when they'd been so good to her; she would destroy her soul in that city where hardly anyone spoke French; she would become a loose woman to be pointed at by others: to which she responded that people already pointed at her and that she wanted to go far away, cut off from everyone she'd known until now. To start a new life. Then, in a moment of weakness, she promised to tell them before she left the real reason for her decision.

On the morning of her twenty-fifth birthday, Régina-Coeli, whose parents, no doubt in retaliation for her imminent departure, hadn't asked what she wanted for this birthday when she would "don Saint Catherine's bonnet" and join the ranks of official old maids, put on her prettiest dress – she had two, a pale yellow one for weekdays that she'd worn to do so much scrubbing and cooking, and a sky-blue one for Sunday which confirmed that her mother had devoted her to the Blessed Virgin, Queen of Heaven – and the hat that she usually kept for Sunday Mass and asked her parents to follow her. Rather, in a voice that brooked no retort, and they had no choice but to do as she asked, wondering what on earth she wanted from them. On the morning of her birthday, no less. The three of them inched their way across the parish of Saint-Boniface under the surprised looks of their neighbours who'd never seen them all on the street at the same time: her, small, dried-up and plainly nervous; them, hesitant, dragging their feet a little because they didn't know where she was taking them.

She helped them climb the big stone staircase of her old school, greeted the few nuns they ran into on the long corridor and took them to a small, bare room in which a big, decrepit upright piano had pride of place. She pointed to chairs and they sat, frowning. She sat on the piano bench, facing them.

"You asked me why I wanted to go away?"

She turned around, opened a music book, raised her hands above the keyboard.

And what swept over her parents kept them in their seats. It was more than music; it was an ocean of mixed sensations, a deluge of sound so powerful that it twisted their hearts and knotted their stomachs, a whirlwind of feelings, too numerous and too intense to be experienced all together, that made them want to run away and at the same time drown themselves in it forever. Not only had Rhéau and Simone Desrosiers never heard anything like it but the storm of sound set off by their own daughter, whom they'd always thought was too ordinary to take care of herself or to wonder who she was or if she had needs, desires, fancies. Placid themselves, never knowing anything close to an uncontrollable passion, they couldn't have imagined such a flame in one of their children, and for a moment they thought that their senses were deceiving them, that the piano player was not Régina-Coeli, their so-nondescript daughter who had never distinguished herself in anything at all except cooking and housework, but someone, a music student or nun, who was hiding in the next room. They had to face facts, though, and they listened to the piece all the way to the end. They saw their daughter for the first time in their lives and stayed glued to their chairs, wide-eyed, arms crossed on their chests. Were they moved or upset? Were they experiencing this moment as a revelation after years of intentional blindness? Régina never knew.

The piece over, she let a few seconds pass before turning to face them. Would they shower her with insults or stiffen as usual in an oppressive and empty silence? As if what had just happened hadn't?

At last, she turned in their direction.

"That's why I want to go away."

They were already standing in front of their chairs: he, with his hat on; she, clutching her purse against her stomach.

Ready to be on their way.

✕

When she awoke the next morning, Rhéauna rediscovered the unpleasant great-aunt she'd met at the station the day before. Cold, stiff, pinch-lipped and frowning. Gone was the passionate woman pinned to her piano, vanished the rapturous performer of Monsieur Schubert and Monsieur Chopin. It was as if she wanted to make what she'd exposed of her real personality disappear in front of her great-niece, a vice that she had to keep hidden, a shameful flaw, and concentrate on fixing breakfast, grumbling.

She wakened Rhéauna quite unceremoniously, shouting at her from the bedroom doorstep:

"I'm going to think you're dead! You've barely got time for breakfast before you leave."

She has already forgotten that she'd just shared the warmth of her bed with a little girl she'd charmed and overwhelmed with great swaths of unsettling music. She is herself again after her everyday fit of madness, her nourishment, her reason for being, and now is acting as if she doesn't know that the day at the Regina Public Library lying before her will be nothing but a long, tedious prelude to the ecstasy awaiting her tonight. She has traded her inspired performer's costume for that of a grumpy archivist everyone's afraid of. As if the one didn't know the other. Or the more interesting of the two didn't exist in the daytime.

Rhéauna is discouraged. The porridge, too runny to be porridge, is the same colour and pretty well the same consistency as yesterday's eggs goldenrod. The toast is made from a hard, stale loaf, as if the delicious bread from the night before had dried on the counter all night, and the milk has a funny smell. Not sour, but nearly. She knows, though, that she'll have a long journey from Regina to Winnipeg and she tries hard not to show her disgust for what she is forcing herself to eat, which like last night's food is rolling around in her mouth. She makes a few stabs at conversation, comes up against a wall of silence, finally resigns herself, with her nose in her glass of milk.

Her great-aunt drinks black coffee without swallowing anything else. Maybe she doesn't like her food either and prefers to eat out ... In Maria it would be unthinkable. Everyone eats at home and never, ever, would they even think of eating elsewhere, except when they're invited by relatives and always for supper; here in Regina, though, in such a big city, there may be what her grandparents call restaurants, magical places that Béa dreams of, where for a sum of money and in no time at all they cook whatever you want, like the lemonade man in the station but more elaborate.

She tries not to think about Montreal.

With her suitcase packed again and her coat on, she waits for her great-aunt on the balcony. Another taxi will come and Régina lets her niece know that she's beginning to cost her a lot. Rhéauna nearly offered to pay for the taxi but she was afraid that would break her budget, which is fairly slim. As on the day before, she doesn't have a lunch and will have to buy something before she boards the train. But just before she starts down the steps to the sidewalk, Régina slips her a brown paper bag.

"Something to eat on the train ... Winnipeg's a long way away."

Rhéauna shudders inwardly at the thought of what might be in the bag. Should she get rid of it without even opening it for fear it might take away her appetite?

She looks out at the store windows that file past. She will have crossed this city twice without stopping, without meeting anyone but this strange great-aunt who changes depending on the time of day, one half of her not seeming to know about the other one's existence. A walking lie.

She knows that all the people she has seen on the streets of Regina since yesterday just speak English and that, anyway, even though her English is fairly good, a real conversation would have been difficult. In Maria, she could stop and continue a conversation with anyone where she'd left it the last time she'd met that person and … No, she has to stop thinking about Maria so much, it doesn't help to compare everything to her little village. That's all over, all in the past. The tremendous scale of the adventure she's embarked on with no one asking her opinion comes back to her all at once and, as she gets out of the vehicle, her anxiety has her bent in two. Régina thinks that she's tripped over something and tells her to watch where she puts her feet. She feels like replying in the same tone of voice. But what good would it do? She keeps quiet, takes her suitcase, climbs the steps of the enormous stone staircase.

Régina has no trouble finding the gentleman who is supposed to look after Rhéauna on the train. He's from Montreal, a student who earns money for his studies by crossing Canada from coast to coast as a baggage handler, shoeshine boy or occasional childminder. He has a funny accent, he rolls his *r*'s and Rhéauna wonders if everyone in Montreal talks like that. She is reassured to realize that she's not the one with an accent, he is.

Now it's time for farewells. She would like to jump into her great-aunt's arms, perhaps tell her that she suspects the older woman has some great sorrow that's impossible to share; she'd like to tell her, too, that the secret is safe with her, that she'll never talk about it, to anyone. Of course Régina's chilliness makes it impossible. Rhéauna must be satisfied with a dry kiss on her cheek. The train is about to take off, the Montreal fellow has picked her up to put her in the coach, as if she weren't big enough to do it by herself. She'll have to say something. Nothing comes to her. Her great-aunt tries to make something that could pass for a smile. It's a pitiful sight.

"Say hello to your great-aunt Bebette. It's been a long time since I've seen her …"

Then, just as the door is about to close on the little woman she'll probably never see again, a sentence emerges from Rhéauna's mouth that she hasn't felt coming. She looks Régina in the eyes and tells her, with a sad smile:

"I know you're unhappy, *ma tante* Régina from Regina."

DREAM ON THE TRAIN TO WINNIPEG

Heaven is full of archangels.

She knows that they're archangels because of their immense wings; if they were ordinary angels their wings would be smaller, their faces less radiant, their songs more fluty. They have low-pitched voices, archangel's voices, and they chant in unison a kind of litany made up of a single note, an o stretched out to infinity, that actually reminds her of the howling of the train when it has left the station or when they want to warn a village of the danger represented by its imminent passage. Clear the track, get your children out of the way.

Archangels are stunningly beautiful, as all angels are supposed to be beautiful, especially archangels, but their song is frightening because it gives the impression that a train is approaching and that it will come too close to not be dangerous.

Heaven is so full of them they have trouble getting around. Some, who refuse to make way for the others, jostle and, if they weren't busy producing their long, drawn-out o, they would probably be shrieking insults at each other. She realizes that they are city archangels.

She is all alone in the midst of the traffic of archangels, so beautiful but so disturbing, and she doesn't know what direction to take. She could ask of course, but do they know how to do anything besides pronouncing the endless o, the incessant drone that gets on her nerves because she knows that it's fastened down up there in Heaven, eternal as the stars, and she must learn to live with it. Do they themselves know where they're going?

They suddenly seem to become aware of her presence and they turn in her direction, all together, like a herd of cattle when a train actually does pass. Maybe they will talk to her, help her, tell her where to go and how to get there. Instead they stop their insistent chanting and a great silence takes over Heaven. As unsettling as the din that came before. She raises her hand in the same way she saw her great-aunt do to hail a taxi and she's about to ask them where she is and what she's doing there, when one of the archangels, the tallest, the finest looking, the most imposing, starts to beat its wings, quickly copied by others – hundreds, thousands of others. The beating of wings replaces the litany heard a while ago, a beautiful sound of birds taking flight rises into the sky. She even expects to hear the cooing of pigeons or the cries of nighthawks. But they remain silent while the beating of their wings speeds up, amplified, until they form a kind of whirlwind that shakes her, takes hold of her and lifts her off the earth. Instead of falling into a hole like Alice in Wonderland, she rises up toward the sky like a rocket on the feast day of Saint John. The whirl of wings lulls her, makes her soar, turns her in every direction, faster and faster. She sees them, the archangels, who are waving at her in a farewell that she does not understand because she hasn't even had time to be introduced.

When she slips through them – a tiny hole in a sea of archangels – she feels as if she's an arrow that is piercing a target, or a bullet penetrating an animal's skin. She turns toward them. They are now lower than she is. She's afraid that she has killed them. No, the beating of wings has stopped, the o stretching to infinity has started again and they've begun jostling one another again, paying no attention to her.

Now she is all alone in the middle of the sky. It's cold – the sun is a pale winter sun – the whirlwind is nauseating her and she has lost her suitcase. She will start falling again at any moment. Will the archangels down below form a carpet to receive her or will she crash to the ground? The ground? No, the seat in the train. She is on a train. A moving train. And it's shaking her up.

Then, on the horizon, a flight of wild geese makes its appearance. A mother wild goose, cackling and joyous, followed by seven goslings exhausted by their mother's speed because she doesn't want to miss the arrival of the train.

The young man who is supposed to look after her until Winnipeg – his name is Jacques and she quickly realized that he is supposed to make her journey as pleasant as possible – is sitting on the seat facing hers. He is holding a tray with all kinds of good things to eat. They look delicious. Her mouth waters.

"How much does it cost for all that? I may not be able to pay for everything."

He smiles, sets the tray on her lap.

"Don't think about that. Eat. I threw out the lunch you had with you … It didn't smell good."

The train bellows, cows turn their heads in the direction of the passing train, a flight of wild geese crosses the sky.

✖

It's the third time he has come to sit beside her on the worn leather seat. After the snack, during his second visit, he gave her material for drawing, but as everyone has always told her, she's no good at drawing, so she contents herself with lining up in her finest handwriting – hard to do with coloured crayons – some of her favourite words in the French language: *mélancolie, silhouette, mandibule, onomatopée* … Others, too, which she finds gentle to the ear – *aérien, foisonnant, litière* – or whose sound she finds evocative – *carabine,* for example, which sounds, in her opinion, like the object that it names. (When she says the word good and loud – *carabine!* – she hears the sound the rifle makes when her grandfather goes hunting for hares, in the cornfield in front of the house.)

She doesn't understand them all, of course. She remembers looking up each one in her grandmother's old dictionary when she came across them in a novel; in fact, it is one of her greatest joys. But if some are engraved in her memory, others slip away from her. A little earlier she was frozen for several minutes over *circonlocution* – one of the longest words she knows, along with *onomatopée,* and the most beautiful – but couldn't remember the meaning. That was the question she prepared for Jacques if he should turn up for a third time.

When he arrives then, with a blanket because it's a little chilly in the car, she gets up from her seat, shows him the word written in good round letters, all even, the way Mademoiselle Primeau had taught her.

"What does that mean, *cir-con-lo-cu-tion,* Jacques? I used to know but I can't remember …"

He seems somewhat surprised by her question.

"You're young to know a word like that … Where'd you get it?"

"In my head. I mean in the books I've read. But I've held on to it. I started reading when I was little, you know. I like words. I think they're beautiful. And I like to remember them. Look, instead of drawing I wrote a whole page."

"Listen, I don't know if I remember exactly what it means but I'll try ..."

He talks to her about roundabout means of expressing yourself without saying exactly what you want to say, of a number of words with just one meaning. She knits her brow, slightly lost.

"I don't really understand. Mademoiselle Primeau always told me that you have to be clear when you talk ... Give me an example."

He thought it over, scratching his head, knitting his brow in turn.

"It's hard just like that, point-blank ..."

"What's a pointed blank?"

"Look, one question at a time ... We're going to start with *circonlocution* ... For instance, if I'm looking at your page of writing and I tell you that your handwriting isn't bad, that's a circumlocution because I took a detour, used several words to say something that I could have said more directly. I could have just said that your handwriting is beautiful ... That's also called a periphrasis, or a euphemism, or ..."

He smiles at Rhéauna's wide-eyed astonishment.

"I've come up with some words you don't know, eh? It's complicated, for sure. The French language is always complicated ..."

"Well, the words you say are really complicated, even more than the ones in books by the Comtesse de Ségur ..."

"Looks like you're going to stay in school even if you're old enough to work ..."

She doesn't know why he is laughing, she didn't intend to be funny. But laughter feels good so she decides to join in. Then he sits down beside her to explain the meaning of the term *point-blank*.

"Do you understand?"

"Yes, I guess so."

She wasn't really listening to him, though. She's just watching his beautiful lips move without taking in what emerges from them.

Because she thinks he's very handsome. Very. Despite his advanced age. If he is nearly twice as old as she is – he confessed that he would turn twenty in a few months – he doesn't come across as arrogant like the boys in Maria who, once they're old enough to get married, become arrogant, they puff out their chests and make jokes they claim are dirty, slapping their thighs, that she understands only rarely. No, there's nothing crafty in his eyes. When they light on her, it's at her that they are looking, as she is now, a little girl, and not what she'll become in five or six years. She doesn't feel as if she's being judged or assessed as future goods. The boys in Maria like to make obscure remarks that always have to do with what the boys and girls they will become can do together. For them it's terribly funny but the girls tend to think they're silly with their pimply faces and hypocritical eyes. She suspects that they're forbidden things that have something to do with the prohibition against playing with the boys in the cornfields, but what things? And why?

The train is chugging across the prairie. Jacques is explaining words she has never heard, but she's not listening. She is looking at his mouth.

Usually the excitement she feels in the presence of something that interests her or someone she likes comes from a part of her body near her heart; it's warm, it's pleasant, often she has experienced a kind of dizziness when her grandmother, kissing her, said that she loves her, or over a huge ice cream cone on a summer afternoon, or when she received for her sixth birthday the doll who closes its eyes that she'd coveted for so long. That warmth, it seems, that floating sensation is what we call love. At least that's how it has always been explained. With a warning, though, to watch out if it gets to be too strong. But what she feels in front of this tall, handsome, grey-eyed young man – she's never seen eyes that colour, she didn't even know it existed – doesn't seem to be located in her chest. Yes, her heart is pounding, faster even, but the warmth, instead of rising up to her head, is going down toward her lower body, and it curls up a little higher, around her solar plexus. She wonders if she has to go to the bathroom. No, it's not that. It's something else. It's new, mysterious and, strangely, it makes her feel uncomfortable. As if she were guilty when she hasn't done anything.

If she got up now, right away, if she went up to him and kissed him on the mouth, what would it mean? And why does she want to do it all of a sudden? What's got into her? She'd firmly pushed away Fabien Thibodeau, a boy at school, when he wanted to lure her behind a barn to play doctor and now she wants to kiss an adult on the mouth! What can it mean? That she would like to play doctor with him? But he's way too old!

"Have you got a stomach ache?"

She is startled.

"What?"

"Have you got a stomach ache? You've been rubbing your stomach … Are you sick to your stomach? Maybe it's what you ate, or the motion of the train …"

"No, no, I'm fine. My stomach doesn't hurt. I don't feel sick, well, maybe a little … A drink of water would help I think. Or some orange juice."

He gets up, obviously worried, and nearly runs to the dining car.

She leans her head against the window. Outside, cows chewing hay watch her go by. Placid. Happy. Do cows ask themselves questions? No, cows don't ask themselves questions. Lucky them. She raises the window, takes a deep breath.

She feels as if she has brushed against a danger. If he hadn't interrupted the thread of her thoughts to ask about her stomach, would she have done it, would she have got up and kissed him? On the mouth? Would she have had the courage? The nerve? And afterward, what would have happened afterward? The sensation of warmth around her solar plexus has subsided but her heart is still beating too hard. The coolness of the glass does some good. She takes more deep breaths. What is she going to do when he comes back? Drink the orange juice and send him away with a thank-you? But that's not what she wants! She wants him to stay, to look after her, talk to her, to …

What exactly is it that she wants? After the kiss … What would have happened after the kiss, what comes after the kiss? Caresses. After the caresses? Others, more precise? But how? How precise?

Jacques comes back with a cold glass of orange juice. It's good. She didn't realize how thirsty she is and drinks it in two long gulps that tickle her throat in a nice way.

"Thank you. That felt good."

"I hope you don't have a fever."

He leans across, touches her forehead. It feels soft, it feels warm, she wants to cry. Oh, please, leave your hand there, don't take it away … It will cure me if I have a fever.

"No … Your forehead is cool … You're just tired from the trip."

Will he sit down again, take up their conversation that was so interesting, where they'd left it? Likely not, he has work to do. Earlier, he talked about shoes to shine, meals to serve and other people – adults who, like her, need help – whom he must look after. He's right, she's not all alone on the train and she has to let him tend to his business if he wants to pay for his courses at the university to become a doctor. A young doctor. The only doctor she has ever known is old and he doesn't always smell good, so she finds it a little hard to imagine Jacques with a stethoscope around his neck. Say, that's another beautiful word – *stethoscope* …

She wishes he would stay. A little longer. The shoes to be shined can wait. And it's not yet time for the evening meal … Adults are supposed to be able to manage on their own whereas she …

But how can she hold on to him?

"I know you aren't married, you don't have a wedding ring, but have you got a fiancée?"

It came out without her realizing. She said it to gain time, to keep him from leaving. She has the impression, though, that she has asked the wrong question because he straightened up all at once as if she had insulted him. She was indiscreet, that's not polite, and she wishes she hadn't said it. Her grandmother would insist that she apologize. But she doesn't have time, he speaks first.

"No, I don't have a fiancée."

It seems as if he wants to run away, but why is he so uncomfortable, the question she asked was perfectly ordinary!

"Why do you ask?"

She has to be careful about how she replies. She senses that he would be easily hurt. She chooses her words carefully:

"At your age some of the boys in Maria are already married with children …"

He tilts his head a little, sits on the edge of the seat. He looks as if he's going to slide off onto the dirty floor. As if all at once he's the one who needs help from her.

"In town, Rhéauna, we don't marry so young."

"Everybody calls me Nana. Rhéauna is too serious. It's a name that nobody knows and no one ever remembers …"

"I remembered …"

"You're different, you go to university …"

"Okay. I'll call you Nana if you stop saying *vous* to me. You don't say *vous* to your friends, Nana, you say *tu*."

His friend! He sees her as his friend! If she could not get off at Winnipeg to meet her great-aunt Bebette but stay on with him all the way to Ottawa, to Montreal, she would. And she would gladly go all the way to Vancouver with him … Why not spend the rest of her life always moving like that – Montreal to Vancouver, Vancouver to Montreal – with someone who thinks of her as a friend, who would always be nice to her, whom she could admire without his realizing it, love secretly, instead of being subjected to the life that awaits her in Montreal, full of the surprises, with people she doesn't know and dreads to meet? To grow up on a train beside a perpetual medical student? She knows it's ridiculous to think that but it fills her with a wild hope and, for a while now, that strange sensation in her lower body has come back. She's going to do it, she is going to get up and kiss him …

She looks up. And suddenly stops.

Something about him has changed. He is as handsome as ever, his impossibly grey eyes still set off that same mysterious dizziness, but a sadness that she hadn't been aware of has appeared on his face, which has turned pale. She guesses that what he is going to say is important. Like at confession. She doesn't know why but she senses that he is going to confess to her, that it will be hard for him, that she has to listen carefully. That a secret he has never shared with anyone will be revealed here, in a train on the way to Winnipeg, to a little girl who may not understand what it means and will be annoyed with herself.

All the same she assumes a look of concentration to listen to him. And tilts her head, like him. Or like the priest in the confessional when what you have to confess to him is very ugly and you hesitate. Is that why he is hesitating? Because it's going to be ugly? She pricks up her ears, waits patiently.

It takes a while. He doesn't speak right away. He seems to be searching for words, changing his mind, she could swear at a certain point that he's about to leave the car, then all at once he takes a long breath and says in a very gentle voice:

"I don't like them. Women."

That's all.

It's true that she doesn't understand.

So she decides to smile.

"Does that mean you're going to stay an old bachelor?"

He raises his head.

"Probably."

"My grandfather always laughs when he says he should have stayed an old bachelor, that women are just a pack of trouble. Is that what you think, too?"

"No ..."

"Can you play the piano?"

The change of subject seems to astonish him.

"Why do you ask me that?"

"I've got an old auntie who's an old maid. She's my grandfather's sister. You met her at the station in Regina; she brought me. She plays the piano. It's so beautiful to listen to ... It seems to be the most important thing in her life. If she's an old maid does it mean that she doesn't like men, that she thinks they're a pack of trouble?"

"No. Maybe it just means that she hasn't met the right one."

"Same with you ... Maybe you'll meet the right girl someday ... Maybe even on the train, you never know ..."

"No, when I say I don't like women that's not what it means ... You'll understand later on ... Meanwhile, forget all that ... I don't know why I told you ..."

A kind of fog creeps into the region around her heart. This time though it doesn't go lower; it stays there, like a weight. It's cold and it makes her want to cry. She would like to tell him that she understands, to console him because it seems to upset him terribly, but she does not yet know the meaning of what has just been revealed to her and she stays there, dumbfounded, helpless to come up with anything at all that might help this handsome, grey-eyed young man she would willingly follow to the ends of the earth, who has just confided a mystery that for her is impenetrable.

Her smile is so sad that he mustn't smile.

"Forget that. I shouldn't have ..."

He is on his feet, he's going to leave.

She has to think of something. Just one sentence. A little nothing for consolation, like her grandmother's remarks when everything is going badly, when she has one of those fits whose source she doesn't know, that scare everyone because they are so unlikely coming from her.

"Maybe if you learned the piano ..."

He practically ran out of the coach, one hand over his mouth.

Silly child! That's not what she should have said! She's made him run away, she won't see him again, he probably won't say goodbye when they get to Winnipeg. She has destroyed the dream of travelling across Canada with him for the rest of her life.

Outside, the same never-ending fields of grain pass by again and again. The sky is too blue, the clouds too white. She would like a good dark storm with lightning and thunder, what her grandmother calls a condensed end of the world. Hail, too, to behead the corn, destroy the harvest, overturn the train, bring to an end this whole damn journey, the unexpected end of the road, lifeless life in a world that she doesn't want to know, that's going to be imposed on her though no one has asked for her opinion. And to stifle the tragedy that she has just suspected in Jacques, that she doesn't understand because she is too young, but that she knows is serious, irrevocable, irreparable.

When she left Maria, she cried; this time, she feels like wrecking everything.

She unfolds the blanket, lies down on the seat.

She knows that she won't sleep.

She only wants to die.

✕

Before going to bed the night before, Jacques had left the carefully polished shoes outside Compartment 14. Shining boots and shoes is the job he hates the most, so he was somewhat relieved the previous evening to find the corridors of the sleeping car nearly empty. Just a few pairs, including this one, had been left in front of the closed doors. He had been able to go back to studying earlier than usual. But in the morning a Canadian army major named Templeton had brought his shoes back, telling him they weren't polished properly, that the army would never accept such a slap-dash job and that he'd have to do it all over if he didn't want a new, official complaint to the conductor. He hadn't argued – the customer is always right, especially when he's wrong – and Jacques had brought the shoes to his small cell. In the beginning he'd thought of giving them back as is to see if major Templeton would notice, then decided not to take a chance. He needs this job to continue his studies and he doesn't want to lose it.

He is now bent over the left shoe, he's just spat on the toe which in his opinion was perfectly clean and rubs it like a maniac with his chamois square. No doubt a waste of energy because these shoes are perfect! He has put off starting the job in the hope that Major Templeton would have to walk around the train barefoot, but he just saw him in the dining car, shod in gleaming boots and more arrogant than ever. The officer eyes him scornfully before pointing to his footwear.

"These are clean boots, my boy! You ought to spend some time in the army, that'd make a man of you!"

He didn't have the nerve to ask if shining shoes properly was the prerogative of a real man, if it was the kind of idiotic thing they put into soldiers' heads, and he turned his back after saying that his shoes would be ready in less than half an hour.

All this pointless rubbing allows him, however, to think back to the conversation he's just had with young Rhéauna, to the confession that had escaped him when he couldn't hold it back from a little girl who didn't know what it was all about. Never before had he talked about it to anyone. It was a secret he'd kept buried since early adolescence when he thought that he was the only boy to have that kind of thought, which haunts him and has several times brought him to the edge of the abyss. He knows now that he's not the only one, that there are others who have the same tastes and the same desires as his, he has informed himself, read articles, was appalled by the story of Sodom and Gomorrah in the Bible, but those he'd encountered – a chance meeting, the look in someone's eyes in a crowd – put him off because they were never equal to his expectations. Because those expectations – and this is one of the things that disturb him most – are to a large degree aesthetic. It's beauty that he's looking for in men like himself but he has never yet located it. Not even once. They're never handsome enough, they're too fat or too thin, and it's their fear of discovery above all that can be read in a bitter crease of the mouth that makes them ugly. Is he like that, too? Can he be spotted in the crowd because of that lost look, that easily detected panic that smells of victim ready for sacrifice? Does he have the look of the damned that he sees in others? Does it make him ugly, too? And maybe he's not handsome enough either for the aesthetic criteria of the men on the prowl he sees now and then, even here on the Montreal-to-Vancouver train ...

Brought up Catholic like all Quebeckers by parents who were always talking about God and the Blessed Virgin and with only crass ignorance to guide their behaviour, he'd been so naive as to go to confession when he became aware of his condition in early adolescence. He suspected that what he felt was not altogether normal, but would never have imagined that it was so monstrous. The priest had frightened him so much that, for months, he could hardly sleep, considering himself both sick and dirty, convinced that he was a pariah no one would ever want, condemned to be alone on the fringes of society. He'd tried to change, to direct his dreams and fantasies toward women; he took cold baths – the priest's advice – he punished his body, he prayed to God, begging to be turned into a boy with healthy ideas, but nothing changed and what he saw when he was masturbating – also forbidden, considered dangerous for both mental and physical health by the priests – even if he made a nearly superhuman effort to disguise it, erase it, transform it, was still the body of a man.

At nearly twenty not only is he still a virgin, but he has never seen a man naked. His own body is the only one he knows and, if he mentally undresses someone, it's always himself, with his puny physique, hollow-chested and nearly hairless, that's so unappetizing. Only his eyes are attractive, his mother has always said so, but grey eyes, especially when they're your own, aren't enough to fulfill the dreams of caresses and kisses of a young man filled with odd urges.

He has even gone so far as to wonder cynically if he'd only decided to become a doctor in order to see naked men! Since he has been attending university he has studied in detail all the art books in the library, he has crammed himself with paintings from all eras – the sturdy physiques of the Renaissance, the lankier ones of the nineteenth century – he has been moved by the perfection of Greek and Roman sculptures, but there's not one image, no matter how beautiful, how inspiring, by which he wants to be intoxicated; it's a genuine flesh-and-blood man with sounds and smells, with amazing, unexpected reactions and an infinitely renewable capacity for sensual pleasure. But his religion and his society forbid it. He's actually convinced that he is afflicted with a serious, debilitating vice and he asks himself every day how he'll be able to live the rest of his life if he's not able to change his nature.

And he has just expressed all of that out loud for the first time in two short sentences in front of someone innocent who perhaps will never even know that it exists or, on the other hand, will, like the rest of society, see it as a dangerous mental illness that must be cured at all costs, or at least overcome.

Does he feel relieved? Did saying those words to someone else, even one who is unaware of the importance of what's going on, do him any good? He would like to answer yes. That the mere fact of, once and for all, having said aloud in an intelligible voice what has been tormenting him for so many years has rid him, even if only a little, of the anguish that is crushing his heart. But no. He is well aware that she was not the right person and that it wasn't the right time, that it came out in spite of himself, in vain, and nothing has changed, he is still alone with his pain over the Canadian army's pair of shoes and his shoeshine kit.

Before his confession he was filled with rage; now he feels drained of rage. Is that any better?

A gentleman in uniform and cap has just shouted something in English; it can't be far to the station in Winnipeg. Nana again presses her nose against the window, which she has just closed. The fields are smaller; big, rich people's houses speed by, often protected by enormous, leafy trees of unknown species, there are no more cows on the horizon. A paved road runs along the railway tracks; dozens of cars or more drive by, blowing their horns to greet the train. It slows down a little, blaring like a nervous animal and spitting smoke, then turns left. A city stands out at the end of the plain. Much bigger than Regina. A genuine big city, her grandfather had said, a *capital*. She had asked what a *capital* was, he told her that it was an important city, where the government of a country or a province was located. Regina was the *capital* of Saskatchewan; Winnipeg, much bigger, was Manitoba's. She immediately lost interest in the word. Not beautiful and too official.

She was not aware of anything when she left Saskatchewan for Manitoba. Except for the city at the far end of it, she knows this landscape; it's the same as back home, but she had hoped that, when she left her province, she would find a different panorama from the one she was used to – mountains, maybe, at least one big hill with forests (she's been dreaming for so long about seeing a forest). No, prairies still, even if there are more trees and smaller plots of land, with an omnipresent sky that eats up everything, even the silhouette of the city that's approaching – wheat, corn, oats, barley. She'll never get away from it!

She turns her head, cranes her neck a little. Jacques didn't come back to see her. She'd had a hunch that he wouldn't, while hoping she was wrong. She would like to say goodbye before she gets off the train, tell him that she hadn't understood what he'd told her but that, when she did understand later on as he'd told her she would, most likely when she was grown up, she would have a kind thought for him, even if it was ugly. Because, though his words had been unclear, it was because what he'd confessed was something not very nice.

So men exist who don't like women. What do they do? Are they alone for their whole lives, old bachelors buried deep inside their big, deserted houses? Without ever having children? The question she asked Jacques earlier comes back to her. Does it mean that her great-aunt Régina doesn't like men? And is that something serious or ugly? Will Jacques be unpleasant with sudden mood changes like her great-aunt? She wishes she could get answers now, right away, wishes she could leave the train knowing what will become of him, if he's going to succeed in life, come into his own as a good doctor. But the future – her own as well as the kind young man's who looked after her during the journey – is not a novel to be read at bedtime, and all that she can do, she knows it, is to decide that, as of now, the Prince Charmings from her books will have grey eyes and, in secret, they won't like women, whatever that means. She thinks it's *romantic* and she can't quite understand why.

Another whistle of the train, this one more prolonged. A few jolts, the wheels screech against the rails: they have arrived. A huge brick structure appears, the train enters it through a long tunnel, a wood-and-metal platform starts to unwind along the car. It seems as if the train is motionless, that the platform is moving, more and more slowly. One last little jolt, one last blast of the whistle, a final sputter of smoke and everything stops. A weary animal has just come back to the stable.

Loads of excited people are running in every direction, talking in loud voices, standing on tiptoe trying to see inside the cars. Hands wave, shouts rise up from the platform. Among all these people is her great-aunt Bebette, whom she's fond of but doesn't feel like seeing.

Another night in a strange house with too-old people who will ask her too many questions.

She gets up, heads for the exit. Her suitcase is there somewhere in the storage area. Good and heavy.

Jacques is standing at the top of the three steps, holding her suitcase and wearing a sad smile.

"You weren't going to get off the train without saying goodbye, Nana!"

She felt her heart leap in her chest. A solid punch that cut her legs out from under her and made her stagger. And the heat in her solar plexus has come back all at once. She is convinced that she won't be able to say a word, that everything will be stuck in her throat, that she's going to come across as a little idiot.

He crouches in front of her, puts his hands on her shoulders. She is taller than he is and has to bend down to answer him. Maybe that's what helps her speak. Because she does manage with no problem.

"I thought it was up to you to come and get me and take me to my aunt Bebette …"

"You're right, that's my job. But mainly I came to say goodbye, that I was glad to meet you, to talk with you, and to advise you not to be afraid of Montreal or of the life that's waiting for you there with your mother. It will all be fine, Nana, you'll be happy, your mother will be nice, you'll make friends … Sometimes a change is good, Nana. You think it's going to be horrible and in the end you realize it's better that way. I'm not expressing myself very well, but I just want to tell you that I hope you'll be happy."

Will she ever love someone as much as she loves Jacques at this moment? She doubts it.

And she kisses him on the mouth, right there in front of everybody.

And tells him:

"I don't believe you. But it doesn't matter."

135

3

BEBETTE

No sooner has she stepped onto the platform than she is drowned in a surge of arms, heads, clothes in many colours. Her name is shouted, people kiss her, children hop and skip around her, her feet get trampled, adults laugh, in the midst of the hubbub her suitcase disappears as if by magic. You might think that everyone in the station when the train pulled in was there to welcome her, and she doesn't know which way to turn, especially as she doesn't recognize a soul. Have they made a mistake? Do they think she's someone else? No, it's her own name that she hears and she thinks she can recognize in the curve of an eyebrow or the roundness of a cheek a reminder of great-aunt Bebette's looks. And so she starts to reply to the kisses and hugs, she laughs, too, and shakes hands and asks people she's certain she doesn't know what's new. A prisoner of the whirlwind of sounds, of smells and colours, she walks away from the train without realizing it – she has the impression that she is being taken away as children were in some of the novels she has read where they were sold to go and work in the mines – and all at once she realizes that she's in the waiting room, an area even bigger than the one in the Regina Station, more impressive and noisier, too. It could hold not the Sainte-Maria-de-Saskatchewan church but the whole village! She is dazed, tired. She wonders when someone will finally explain to her what exactly is going on when a loud *saperlipopette* rises up nearby, making everyone around her freeze. It's no longer her name being shouted, she's no longer being hugged. The group surrounding her is divided in two, like the Red Sea opening for Moses.

And her aunt Bebette appears.

She's a very capable woman, fat, with creamy skin, feared by her grandfather's family as much for her all-consuming good humour as for her authoritarian, manipulative and nearly despotic side. A born dictator, she controls her children with an iron hand and enveloping arms. She is an attentive mother with terrible fits of temper, sentimental but sometimes with a heart of stone. She is generosity personified combined with malevolence. Rhéauna has always heard that Bebette is two individuals at once: the nice and the not nice. Even more than her sister Régina-Coeli's moods, Bebette's are feared and she takes advantage of that always to do as she likes, making everyone take her advice, intervening where she has no business, overly curious, intrusive – but so charming when she wants, so understanding and magnanimous, that she is forgiven for everything. She is the centre of attention wherever she goes, the life of parties and the most distraught at funerals. She reigns and leads the people around her with a satisfaction that she doesn't hide and does everything in her power, which is great, to keep it that way.

Rhéauna, however, knows only the positive side of Bebette's personality. She has often heard about her famous outbursts, her severity, her aggressive side, but for her that's a kind of legend because never has Bebette, who has been fond of her since she came out west, shown her the dark side of her personality. She is always charming with her and then some. When they get together over Christmas, she gives her all kinds of presents and kisses, which smear her face with a thick coat of dark red, nearly blue, lipstick. Her gruff, good-natured lady's voice makes her laugh and encourages her to eat her fill whereas her grandmother tries to persuade her to watch her diet to stay healthy and not get fat.

"*Saperlipopette*, Rhéauna, you're a big girl! I nearly didn't recognize my sweet girl!"

Her *saperlipopette* is also famous in the family. Never in her life has Bebette sworn, she doesn't need to: she just has to open her mouth, deliver her booming *saperlipopette* and everything comes to a halt – people stop what they're doing and the world stops turning. She shouts it with such self-assurance, such an intense modulation in her voice, that no curse from Quebec – neither *tabarnac*, nor *câlice*, nor *sacrament*, nor even a *crisse de câlice de tabarnac de sacrament* – could equal it. It is a thunderclap that hits you in the middle of the forehead, leaving you paralyzed and helpless. And shaking with fear.

But the one she's just pronounced in front of Rhéauna is a caress, a whopper, maybe, but a caress all the same. You sense in it affection for a beloved great-niece and maybe a grain of pity for this child who must cross an entire continent to join her mother and begin a new life. It's a *saperlipopette* all right, and it rings out loud and clear under the vault of the waiting room, but it is also a rather rough expression of love from the bottom of her heart. Some of those present – though they'd never admit it – are even a little jealous of this little girl who's come from the depths of Saskatchewan to be imposed on them as if she were a queen and already is enjoying the leniency of the dreadful Bebette.

"How do you like this reception, little girl? Eh? I'll have you know there's nineteen of us! Nineteen people that came here to meet you! I'm not sure even Queen Victoria would have brought out such a crowd if she'd taken the time to visit us out in the Canadian West when she was alive!"

Rhéauna, who can't think of anything to say, merely smiles without looking at anyone in particular.

Her aunt bends over her. A mixture of spicy sweat, bar soap and cheap perfume. After the loud smacks on both cheeks, Rhéauna knows that she looks like a clown because Bebette's lipstick always leaves smears that are nearly indelible and need several washes to disappear, but she dares not wipe it in front of the older woman for fear of irritating her.

"You must be ready to drop, you're so tired. Climb in with me. My buggy's the biggest, my daughters' are smaller … And now, Rhéauna dear, welcome to Saint-Boniface!"

"Aren't we in Winnipeg?"

"Yes, but we're from Saint-Boniface and we've decided that the station belongs to us, too … We call it the Saint-Boniface Station even if it upsets the people in Winnipeg … *Saperlipopette,* let me wipe off that lipstick … Look at you – people will think I've slashed your face!"

She wets her thumb with the tip of her tongue and starts to wipe Rhéauna's cheeks. The little girl feels as if her face is being torn away. Or that her cheeks are being rubbed off.

"Okay, that'll do for now. We'll finish up back at the house … There's a nice hot bath waiting for you …"

The clan moves like one person, or a gaggle of geese: Bebette in the centre, taller than anyone else, bustling, prattling, regal, the others surrounding her like a queen bee whom they serve without debate. She gives orders, delivers a few slaps, shoots off a couple of well-placed *saperlipopette*s, not her loudest, though, and drags her great-niece behind her by the hand.

When the train pulled in, Rhéauna was the object of everyone's attention, probably because Bebette had given orders, but the little girl feels as if for a few minutes now she no longer exists because everyone is paying attention to her aunt, the natural focus of the group, and she knows that won't change. Bebette must not often, or for very long, agree to be on the fringe of her family's attention and she probably doesn't need to give orders for things to resume their normal course.

A dense group among a thinner crowd made up of aimless onlookers and hurried travellers cutting across the waiting room, a tight knot of cries, of laughter and smells, not all of them pleasant, Bebette's tribe cuts a path toward the exit of the Winnipeg Station.

Bebette turns to Rhéauna after pushing away one of her grand-daughters who was trying to get a little too much attention and wanted to grab her other hand.

"I didn't introduce you to everybody yet … We'll do that at the house, but there's so many people I know you won't be able to remember all the names … I brought all my daughters and their children – my boys are at work – all my daughters-in-law are here, too, with my boys' children and, I'm telling you, that makes a whole lot of people for me to manage … I've even got a couple of great-grandsons in the batch ... See, I didn't want you to arrive all by yourself, or to feel lost. I wanted lots of happiness when you got off the train, I wanted you to feel that everybody'd been waiting for you ..."

"Anyway, it's a change from Régina."

"I'm not surprised. Poor Régina – is she as boring as ever?"

"No, I wouldn't say that."

"Yes, you can, dear. My sister Régina-Coeli is the most boring person who's ever been created! She was put on earth to make us die of boredom and she's way too good at it in my opinion. A punishment! My sister Régina-Coeli is a punishment! And not even from God, but the devil!"

Everyone laughs. Too loudly. Some protest. As a matter of form.

"Oh, come on!"

"Don't say that, Grandma ..."

"She isn't that bad ..."

"After all, Mama, she's your sister ..."

"I like my aunt Régina."

Bebette puts an end to it with one sentence.

"I didn't say I don't like her. What I said was she's crazy, with her delusions of grandeur!"

Why bother arguing. Aunt Bebette probably doesn't even know that her sister plays the piano to survive her unbearable loneliness.

"Does she still play that crazy music of hers? Does she still think she's a great artist? Does she still put on those free concerts for her neighbours, the darn fool? She's crazy, all right! She thinks we don't know anything but it all comes out in the end!"

Rhéauna doesn't have time to answer. They've just gone through a metal door and emerged onto a large street, livelier than Regina, to the head of a line of splendid, spic-and-span buggies that look roomy and comfortable. They look as if they've come from the general store in Winnipeg for their first race across the city to celebrate her arrival.

Bebette is already lifting her long skirt.

"Mine's the first one up front. Pretty, isn't it? I just had it fixed up. I'd like to tell you it was in your honour but really, it needed it. Come on, the others will follow us."

They are alone in a huge contraption smelling of new leather, axle grease and horse manure. He's off like a shot when Bebette delivers a whistle that must act like a *saperlipopette* or a crack of the whip and Rhéauna, thrilled, is glued to the back of her seat.

If Regina's streets surprised her, Winnipeg's take her breath away. An open war seems to have been declared by three means of transport: automobiles, which are numerous and roaring, street-cars and horse-drawn carriages. The resulting pandemonium is indescribable. People everywhere, dust, noise, strange odours, very different from the horse manure she's used to smelling on Maria's one street, acrid stenches that catch at her throat and give her an urge to cough. When they're not simply congested, the avenues around the station are blocked, with everyone yelling because no one can move; the horses take fright, they neigh and kick, children are running all over, whining, and the police don't know at whom to whistle. Rhéauna tries to see everything at once and doesn't stop moving on her seat. Her great-aunt places a firm hand on her knee.

"Stop squirming, Nana, you look like you've got worms …"

Rhéauna tries to be still, to observe everything without turning her head too much. In vain.

"I've never seen a thing like that, *ma tante*! Not even yesterday in Regina."

Bebette smiles, puffs herself up as if she owns the city of Winnipeg.

"The big city's really something, isn't it?"

Her great-aunt Régina had said the same thing the day before, she'd used the same words, at nearly the same time of day, about a much smaller city and in a much smaller crowd. She wonders if she would be just as impressed by the streets of Regina now that she's in Winnipeg. If she went back to Regina right now, would she think the streets were peaceful compared to these, when they'd seemed so spectacular twenty-four hours earlier? Do we end up getting used to all that? To changes? To the unknown?

Her great-aunt leans over to her and talks to her very softly, as if to reassure her.

"You'll have to get used to it, they say it's even worse in Morial. Apparently, they've put lights at the corners of the streets there to help the traffic. I don't know how it works but apparently, they've already done it in the United States, in Salt Lake City I think ... I read that in the paper. A green light to go and a red light to stop. I don't understand how, but if it works ... You can't stop progress, can you?"

The buggy swerves violently and Rhéauna almost ends up on her knees on the floor, which is covered with a royal-blue carpet.

"You have to sit properly, Nana, or you could get knocked out ... *Saperlipopette*, you have buggies in Maria, don't you? You know how they work!"

The store windows are full of exotic things: strange household devices; electrical appliances that look nearly menacing, their use mysterious; big reproductions of pictures showing beautiful landscapes in blazing colours or people frozen in odd, stiff poses; fabulously rich clothes. She even sees a whole display of wedding gowns! It all rushes past her eyes and she only has time to note its existence but can't fully understand what she is seeing. Will she be able to hold it all in her memory and think about it later?

Her great-aunt takes off her enormous hat covered with birds and foaming tulle that made her look like a monarch, untouchable, and all of a sudden she seems more human. Less impressive at any rate. And smaller. She sticks a long pin into the fabric of the hat, then sets it down between them. Then she tidies the hair that has escaped from her hairdo – grey curls in a loose knot on the top of her head. That way, in profile and despite her portliness, she resembles closely her sister Régina-Coeli.

"It'll be quieter in Saint-Boniface! And *saperlipopette*, at least people will speak French."

✕

It's a country road in the middle of the city, like the one in Regina the day before. The frame houses resemble that of her grandparents, with verandas wrapped around three sides and everything, but instead of overlooking a cornfield, they face other houses, painted similar colours and equally worn down by bad weather. They could be a row of houses sitting in front of a gigantic mirror. And multiplied to infinity because Rhéauna saw several other streets like this one when the buggy turned off what seemed to be the main artery in Saint-Boniface, an avenue nearly as busy as the streets around the station, but whose name she hasn't been able to read yet.

After travelling through downtown Winnipeg, the buggy went across a metal bridge, the Provencher Bridge, then crossed a square where stood a very beautiful cathedral, and great-aunt Bebette said in a tone that contained a certain amount of relief:

"We're home now, *saperlipopette.*"

On the veranda of the last house on the right, painted sky blue with white shutters, a pachyderm is waiting for them, slumped in a dilapidated rocking chair, his head back, apparently asleep. Rhéauna had found the word *pachyderm* in a book about animals. It seems to mean the same thing as elephant. This is the first time she can use it for a human being. She knows people who are big, of course, Madame Houle and Monsieur Cantin, for instance, and even Bebette are all fairly corpulent, but this one is even bigger and she finds it hard to believe that he's going to extricate himself from the chair in a little while, stand on his feet, say something, go inside the house with them. She imagines him rather as an unmoving guard, like a huge hound attached to a chain so he can't run away, or as a gigantic garden gnome. A presence that is reassuring despite his immobility. As she climbs the few steps that lead to the front door, she realizes that he is a very old gentleman with pure white hair and incredibly short legs. Maybe because his torso is so huge, his limbs seem truncated – two little arms, two little legs – and Rhéauna wonders if he waddles when he walks, like a gnome in a fairy tale. A giant gnome. Who rolls along instead of walking.

Rhéauna smiles despite her fatigue.

Bebette walks past her, lays a hand on the man's forearm without waking him.

"This is my husband. He's big."

The buggies that were following them have stopped behind Bebette's and the other eighteen people who greeted Rhéauna when she got off the train have already swept into the garden in front of the house, up the steps, through the front door. They're of all ages, there are even some children, but in her opinion most are rather old to be stirring up this whirlwind of excitement around her on their own initiative: she doesn't really understand why they're fussing around her so much, she doesn't know them, all she knows is that they are part of Bebette's family. They seem to know her, though, they call her by name, they ruffle her hair, welcome her again to Saint-Boniface, and wish her good luck on the rest of her journey. They talk loudly, they laugh, a skipping rope appears out of nowhere and some little girls – the only ones who are ignoring her – sing a counting song she's never heard that says something about a cow that's lost in a cornfield and counts the cobs … She senses that this evening will be very different from yesterday's and that no doubt she won't have the peace and quiet she needs if she's to rest from her long trip. Will they keep following her till she leaves tomorrow morning? They must have their own houses, surely they don't all live with Bebette! Anyway, the house wouldn't be big enough, which reassures her a little.

Her suitcase has just appeared beside her but she doesn't see who brought it. A very elegant lady in a dress of wine-red satin with greenish glimmers takes her hand, squeezes it a little too hard.

"Poor little girl … I knew your mother very well. We played

together when we were little. We were the same age. She wasn't easy …"

Why is she talking about her mother in the past like that? She still exists, even if she's at the other end of the country!

Bebette claps her hands, all heads turn toward her.

"Thanks for coming out like this, everybody, it was nice of you! I'm sure our little Rhéauna is glad to have you all here … But now I think you can go home, she must be tired, and you've got supper to make … If you want some lemonade or coffee, there's gallons."

No introductions. She won't know their names though Bebette has promised to introduce them one by one.

Conversations stop dead, this is probably the signal they've been waiting for to leave. Rhéauna understands that she's guessed right: no one in this noisy group has chosen to come and meet her at the station, they probably didn't want to, it was all laid out by Bebette. They had no choice but to accept the orders of this energetic woman to whom it seemed very hard to say no about anything, so strong was her personality, she was the undisputed leader of the family whom they feel obliged to obey without argument.

The house is cleared out in no time, no coffee is requested, no one comes back to welcome her or to wish her good luck for the rest of her journey. You could say that she ceases to exist for the second time.

Now Rhéauna is all alone with her great-aunt Bebette. And the mammoth with the too-short limbs goes on sleeping despite the racket all around him.

At first, she refused to climb into the steaming bathtub that takes up the whole back wall of the bathroom just under the open window through which any curious passerby could no doubt see her playing in the water. Back home she washes herself while standing in a basin on the back veranda in summer and, in winter, in front of the wood stove where her grandmother places three kettles full of warm water; it takes five minutes and there is no question of lingering, unlike her two sisters, who always take their bath together to save water, and love to shout and spray one another with dirty water in imitation of battles at sea. All they know about battles at sea they've gleaned from picture books – Saskatchewan has very few large expanses of water and boats are rather rare – and they picture themselves as Caribbean pirates, especially as Captain Hook, the most-hated character in children's literature because he wants to destroy Peter Pan and kidnap lovely Wendy, or as Long John Silver, the most ferocious pirate of all time. Grandma Joséphine had read *Treasure Island* to them the year before and they still haven't got over the vastness and the cruelty of the sea; the twenty-foot-high waves that can swallow a boat in seconds; the food full of worms that sailors sometimes have to make do with; boats that pitch and roll; flags that sport the skull and crossbones; cannons that produce as much smoke as noise. All that is what they try to illustrate in the half-full basin of water, but they have to stand up during their improvised wars because they can't even kneel in their too-narrow ocean.

When great-aunt Bebette told her that she should take a bath before supper, Rhéauna saw herself standing in a basin, scrubbing herself with a big square cake of soap, the same kind that everyone in Maria uses because Monsieur Connells doesn't sell any others even if certain village ladies often complain because of its poor quality. Instead, she found a massive, all-white bathtub, an enormous rectangular monster with lion's paws that resembled a coffin already filled with steaming, scented water. She told Bebette that she preferred to wash herself one parish at a time, the way she did at home, and her great-aunt burst into laughter that Rhéauna is convinced made the house shake.

"*Saperlipopette*, Nana, this isn't the country, we're in the city, we've got running water! And don't tell me you're afraid of my bathtub, too! It's one of the finest in Winnipeg! The biggest one in Saint-Boniface!"

"I didn't say that it wasn't beautiful, *ma tante* ..."

"No, but it scares you, doesn't it?"

"No, I didn't mean that ..."

"Nana, you aren't the first person who didn't want to! I'm used to it! When I had it put in for your uncle Rosaire a few years ago, nobody but him even wanted to get close to it. I practically had to carry my children in my arms one by one to convince them to try it! Even the ones over forty! Their excuse was they didn't live here to get undressed but I made them all try. The whole gang! The oldest and the youngest! It took pretty well a whole month. And they all loved it! Some are even going to put one in at their place, that's how much they liked it! It's wonderful, you'll see, it's like swimming in a lake. Heated!"

Rhéauna had to let herself be talked into it because she knew that she wouldn't win with this great-aunt who might very well behave with her as she'd done with her children and force her to try the darn tub, no matter what. (She imagined the beautiful lady in the wine-red dress she'd seen a while ago, who was so dignified, taking off all her clothes in front of her mother – or her mother-in-law, if she's the wife of one of Bebette's boys – just to make her happy, slip into the bathtub while covering the lower part of her body ...) Great-aunt Bebette is really very strange.

Finally she edged her way to the steaming creature. It was mainly the odour that made her decide to dip a finger in the water. Bebette told her it was called *rosemary*. That rosemary, apparently, wasn't used just for cooking. She also explained to her that it was an exotic oil from far away. That it would soften her skin. Take a bath in water full of oil? A kind of salad dressing? But apparently this was no ordinary oil:

"On the label they say it has therapeutic powers! And I know something about that – Rosaire claims that means medical, but Rosaire sees medication all over – but I say when you use a five-dollar word like that it must be important! I bathe in it every day, *saperlipopette*, and besides always being clean and soft, I smell as good as a flower garden! Although I can't say I'm any healthier."

Rhéauna has finally bent over the bathtub, already more tempting now with its unknown fragrance, put one finger into it, then her hand. It is softer than ordinary water and it makes her realize how tired she is. She feels a weight between her shoulder blades. She hunches her back.

Bebette seems to be reading her mind:

"Ten hours on the train, my pet, wears you out. Take your clothes off, get in the tub, soak yourself for a good half-hour, then tell me what you think."

She has been soaking in that divine aroma for a good half-hour now and she'd like to stay in it forever, it's so relaxing after the shuddering of the train and her anxiety in the face of the unknown. Her head feels as rested as her body. The soap she used to scrub her entire body also smells of rosemary and she wonders if that aroma will follow her long after she gets out of the tub. Monsieur Connells's soap doesn't have much smell at all and if you know that you're clean when you step out of the basin at her grandmother's, you also know that you still smell the same.

When the water cools down, she just has to turn on the tap on the left – there are two! – Bebette told her that the hot water tank was full, whatever that means. And if the bath is too hot, the tap on the right dispenses cold water. She switches blissfully from lukewarm water to water that's nearly boiling, her body takes on a beautiful red colour, she feels weak, gradually glides toward sleep. Maybe she actually goes to sleep without realizing it.

Then all at once, just as Jacques is making his appearance with his big grey eyes and his sad smile, her Prince Charming who doesn't like women – she should have kissed him longer instead of being satisfied with a quick little peck, she didn't even have time to taste his mouth, to enjoy the coolness of his lips – the bathroom door opens and there stands Bebette holding a big white bath towel in front of her.

"*Saperlipopette*, Nana, I've been telling you to get out of the tub for ten minutes! Were you asleep? That thing is to take a bath in, not to drown! I told you half an hour, not the rest of the night! You'll be so limp when you get out you won't be able to eat all the good things I've cooked. It's suppertime and your great-uncle Rosaire doesn't wait. Now get out, dry yourself with this towel, get into your clean clothes and come to the table with us!"

As she gets dressed, she dreams of finding a bathtub like that in her mother's house in Montreal. At least she'd have that consolation.

Two white china plates laden with steaming corn sit proudly in the middle of the dining-room table. It's the first of the season – it was late this year and everyone who lives in western Canada is unhappy. For them it represents summer's end, harvest time, back to school – Rhéauna is happy she can finally eat some, but she's a little surprised to see that there's nothing else on the beautiful hand-embroidered tablecloth. Two dozen ears of corn, three places set, two pounds of butter and that's all. And why two pounds of butter anyway? Unless they're expecting company ... Or corn is Bebette's equivalent to Régina-Coeli's eggs goldenrod. And is only one dish served per meal in her grandfather's family? But when they come to visit at Christmas or Easter, the many members of Rosaire and Bebette Roy's family always bring lots of good things prepared with care and enthusiasm by the women in the clan.

But it's pretty to look at, this tableau in yellow and white. In any case it gives you an appetite, she can hear her stomach growl.

Then great-uncle Rosaire makes his entrance on the arm of his wife who supports him under the armpits. He takes tiny steps, bent over, legs apart. Sweat stands out on his forehead and his shirt is wet in front and under the arms. He must only move for a meal or a bath, at least that's what crosses Rhéauna's mind. She doesn't know how to behave around him. Say hello as if everything's normal? Or ignore him and make small talk with Bebette while he stuffs himself because that's probably what he will do? There's a reason he's so big ... He leans against the end of the table before he manages to sit down on a big wooden chair, the only one that can support him and which creaks under his weight. All at once Rhéauna remembers that she has often asked her grandparents why aunt Bebette's husband never came to Maria. She had the answer before her eyes and it's not a pretty sight.

How much could he weigh? She thought about the word *pachyderm* a while ago, now what comes to her mind is a whale. He's as white as a whale and he seems equally uncomfortable out of water ... And his weight must be close to that of a little cachalot ...

The silence is becoming heavy. Bebette ends it by speaking to her husband.

"Say hello to Rhéauna, Rosaire. She's my brother Méo's granddaughter. Maria's daughter. You remember Maria Desrosiers, the one who left at the beginning of the century to live it up in the east, in the United States, in Providence, Rhode Island? Well this is her daughter! She's on her way to Montreal where her mother's just moved for some reason or other ..."

A very small voice emerges from the mass of flabby flesh, surprisingly sweet and with a natural affability breaking through. A good little boy who speaks politely.

"I know who she is, Bebette, you've been talking about her visit for a week now ... I saw you arrive a while ago with the rest of the gang, but I was going to sleep ... Hello, Nana, how are you?"

He looks at her for the first time. His tiny eyes are an amazing blue that is somewhat reminiscent of the gown on the statue of the Blessed Virgin, but with red veins as if he suffers from a permanent head cold. Piggy eyes. She can't stop herself from sketching a faint smile. An elephant, a whale, a pig – the entire animal kingdom will be represented if this keeps up! What will she think about when he starts to eat his corn? A cow? Will he start ruminating like Valentine, her grandfather's cow?

"Welcome, Rhéauna ... But your name isn't Desrosiers, is it?"

"No, Uncle Rosaire, it's Rathier ..."

"That's right, your mother married a Frenchman from France ... Wasn't long till she was on her own again. That'll teach her ... Anyway, welcome, Rhéauna Rathier. You're a real pretty little girl ... And tempting like all the girls in your family ..."

Rhéauna sees Bebette stiffen a little and suspects that Rosaire's compliments are usually reserved for her and that she doesn't take it kindly when they're meant for someone else.

Bebette wipes her hands on her apron, forces a smile that's supposed to be gracious but looks more like a cruel, sardonic grin.

"Okay, time to eat. It's good to gab but the corn's getting cold, *saperlipopette!*"

This time the *saperlipopette* is very serious; Rhéauna pulls out her chair.

"There's a dozen for your uncle Rosaire. See, he likes his corn and he eats a lot during the two weeks when we can get it fresh … What we don't eat tonight I'll roast on the wood stove tomorrow morning, Rosaire likes that as much as toast … Do you eat corn out there? You can eat all you want but be careful, there's something else afterward … I cooked chicken, potatoes, new peas. And a raspberry pie 'cause they're nearly over …"

Rhéauna wonders if there will be a whole chicken for her uncle and another for her and her aunt. She immediately regrets such a rude thought, hangs her head. It's very different from last night's supper.

Since she was a small child she's been taught to spread a thin coat of butter on four rows of her corn at a time so that nothing drops onto her hands or her plate. And to chew for a good long time because corn is hard to digest. And that indigestion from corn can be fatal. Great-uncle Rosaire doesn't seem concerned about these trivial matters. He places the blazing hot corn on the pound of butter, turns it around so the whole ear is thickly coated, salts it and throws himself on it, grunting. The little girl has never seen such a thing. He devours a cob of corn in less than a minute, it's all over his cheeks, butter is dripping onto the table, he hiccups, he labours, he belches, his breathing is hoarse and jerky, there is sweat standing out on his forehead. As soon as one ear is finished he drops the empty cob onto his plate and takes another. All under a kindly look from Bebette who picks at hers because she claims that she doesn't like corn very much. She seems, though, to feel a need to apologize for him: she wipes her lips with her napkin and looks at Rhéauna, smiling.

"He's only like that when he's eating corn. You'll see, he'll calm down in a while …"

Rhéauna is appalled at the mere thought that he is going to eat something else after his dozen ears of corn but she doesn't dare say a word and bends over her plate.

Looking up, she suddenly catches a strange look on her great-uncle's face. Right in the middle of a grunt, while he is chewing at an incredible speed, he gives her a kind of pleading look, as if he is asking her for help … She realizes then that he can't stop, that it's a kind of sickness, that he could die of it, like a horse that's left behind in a field of oats. Here's another animal to add to the list … Not a cow, though. Rosaire doesn't ruminate, he devours!

She looks at Bebette. Does she know? Has she, a ten-year-old little girl, come here to guess something that's as plain as the nose on your face, that her great-aunt, an intelligent woman, doesn't see? Or prefers not to? And why? Bebette had said earlier that he would calm down when the chicken arrived but is that true? Does he eat everything like that? And most of all, does he always have that pleading expression when he swallows his food as if he were eating for the last time? Would he like to be stopped by force? Does Bebette let her husband eat because she feels sorry for him? But excuses him to keep up appearances?

"*Saperlipopette*, Nana, you aren't eating! Aren't you hungry?"

No, she isn't hungry. She puts her ear of corn on her plate.

"You don't like corn?"

"Maybe I'm too tired to eat …"

"Oh, come on, a child your age has to eat! You're still growing! Pretty soon you'll be a big girl!"

She tries to pick up her corn, nibbles a couple of mouthfuls. Will she be able to eat it again someday and not think about uncle Rosaire? About his pleading expression? But why doesn't he say so? Why doesn't he get up from the table, throw his plate on the floor, saying that he doesn't want any more, that he's sick and tired of being fat, of eating like a pig? Who knows, maybe he likes it. Eating too much. And being a pitiful sight.

But Rhéauna has misunderstood her great-uncle Rosaire. In part, anyway.

Rosaire Roy had built a fairly respectable fortune as foreman during construction of the western branch – the last and most difficult one – of the railway that henceforth would cross Canada almost from coast to coast, east to west. He was present at the opening of the final section that runs through the Rockies into British Columbia when he was about to retire and saw it as the crowning achievement of a long and fruitful career. He witnessed the creation of the famous *pâté chinois*, the British shepherd's pie with added corn, a commodity that was local, abundant, filling and invented by Asian cooks to nourish the men working on the railway. He ate more pork-and-beans than any human could tolerate. For years he slept in disgusting barracks that smelled of grime, sweat, pork-and-beans farts, in a tent or under the stars but never in a hotel because he would have felt as if he were looking down on his men. He grew ecstatic over the beauty of Lake Louise during the full moon and he fed the elk that wander freely on the streets of the glorious village of Banff. Most of his life he followed the railroad when the Canadian Pacific Railway was being built, far from his hometown, Saint-Boniface, now and then for several months at a time, often suffering from loneliness but always thrilled by this unprecedented and unique project that would link the Atlantic Ocean and the Pacific – a revolutionary metal road on which he was an enthusiastic worker. Essential, too. Which didn't keep him from making seven children with Élisabeth Roy, née Desrosiers, the one love of his life.

There exist some old yellowed photos showing him bare-chested with his arms crossed, in front of the first locomotive to have crossed the border between Manitoba and Saskatchewan, others scarcely more recent that show him on board the train which inaugurated the section that winds its way through the Rockies. A last one, the one of which he's the most proud, shows him in front of the incredible panorama of Vancouver's English Bay in the summer. He is already big but the virile strength that now emanates from him commands respect. One can sense that he's a foreman who doesn't just show up on easy days.

His trips home to Winnipeg were always a source of joy for his family because, as a father, he was considerate, amusing and generous. There'd been whores, of course, who followed the workers across Manitoba, Saskatchewan, Alberta, and toward the end, British Columbia in covered wagons, lavishing on them some human warmth – it's necessary for the body to exult, especially when you're young and vigorous – but that was a simple call of nature, a bodily function that served only to relax and that he didn't condemn despite the Catholic religion which was uncompromising on the matter of an absolute prohibition against knowing other women than one's own. His affection he reserved for his Bebette, and for his retirement – to be taken as late as possible, when he was close to seventy, a unique situation at the Canadian Pacific Railway – the children grown up, married, parents themselves, he planned with her an end of the line made up of sweet things and little treats. He had money in the bank, his house had been paid off for ages, they were going to travel, but this time *inside* the train. They would visit his wife's family who were scattered from one end of the continent to the other – uncles in Vancouver, nephews and nieces in Calgary, Ti-Lou in Ottawa, the loathsome Régina-Coeli in Regina and maybe even Maria in the United States. And in particular, Joséphine and Méo outside Saskatoon, whom they both adored. His own family was quite sedentary and he'd never had to travel very far to run into them. But never mind, they would put on giant celebrations and invite everyone they knew on his side. Bebette could be in charge of it all with her ringing *saperlipopette*, run to her liking, parade beneath her unbelievable hats with nothing to worry about except seeing to it that the great celebration at the end of their lives turned out to be a success. It was one exciting plan that alas never materialized.

Rosaire Roy had always been a corpulent man, what his wife liked to call a force of nature as she gazed at him with adoring eyes. He loved to eat, a lot, for a long time, greasy things drowned in thick sauces and rich desserts that gave him delicious sugar thrills. The doctors at the job sites told him to control himself if he didn't want his heart to burst in his chest, but he laughed, patted them on the shoulders and left, telling them that he'd bury them all because he loved life so much.

Until that cursèd day in 1908 when he'd learned, just as he was about to retire, that he had cancer of the prostate. When the doctor had told him that at his age the disease would progress slowly, that he could look forward to more fine years, he refused any surgery. Then he told Bebette, sparing her as much as possible. She had burst into protests, oaths – for once in her life she had cursed, using an extensive and impressive vocabulary, a combination of blasphemy from Quebec and oaths of a sexual nature imported from the United States – she had cursed heaven and life that was playing such a lousy trick on them just as they were getting ready to make their dream come true, now, after so many years of separation imposed by his insane job. For the first and only time in her life, her *saperlipopette* hadn't been able to express all the horror she was feeling and she'd been forced to draw on the vulgar vocabulary that she'd always condemned.

When she had calmed down a little, Rosaire had told her that after carefully thinking it over, he had something important to ask her.

This happened in the kitchen, over a cup of what Bebette's family called Indian tea, a strong, dark herbal tea that kept you awake even more than coffee.

They were sitting face to face on either side of the table, where an apple pie that Bebette had just taken out of the oven was cooling. It was a beautiful day in spring, they should have left Winnipeg for Vancouver a few days later. Their bags were packed, the letters announcing their visit had no doubt already reached their destination. The relatives on the other side of the Rockies must be delighted about the visit from their Manitoba cousins they hadn't seen for so long, Bebette and her famous *saperlipopette*, Rosaire with his vast repertoire of dirty jokes picked up along the Canadian Pacific Railway track.

Rosaire had reached out and gently squeezed his wife's hand.

"It's another sacrifice I have to ask of you, Bebette."

She had held out the other hand and he kissed it over the embroidered cloth.

"I don't have to tell you that I don't feel like going on a trip …"

"I understand, Rosaire, it's all right, it's not a sacrifice …"

"That's not the sacrifice … You see, I say sacrifice but I don't know if it's the right word. It's more like I want to ask you for a favour. But favour may not be the right word either … I don't know what to call it … Maybe you won't want it, maybe it'll even shock you …"

Anxious, she pulled away her hands, which she'd brought to her heart.

"You can't want us to separate because you're sick! You can't want to go to the hospital! I can live it with you, take care of you, *saperlipopette*, I'm not heartless!"

"No, it's not that. It's not that at all! I don't know how to … Look … You know how much I love to eat … how much I love your cooking … I've had to do without it for a good long part of my life and now … Don't think badly of me, Bebette, but I'd like to die while I'm eating. Eating your cooking. I'd like to eat everything I like, without thinking about my heart, without thinking about my prostate, eat your roast pork, your pork *cretons*, your *tourtière*, your eggs goldenrod, your roast veal, your desserts that are the best in the world. I'd like to pass away with a full belly, Bebette, in a year, in five years, it doesn't matter, but I'd like to die when I'm full, drunk on fatty sauces and your homemade fudge! Don't say no, Bebette, don't tell me it's suicide, that our religion forbids it, that we'll be punished, especially me, I know all that. No, help me! Help me to die happy and fattened up instead of wasting away and getting thin."

This time it was she who took his hand.

"It's true that it's suicide, Rosaire, and the Catholic religion forbids it, and we'll both be punished, me as much as you, but *saperlipopette*, if the good Lord is mean enough to pull that trick on us, we'll pay for our sins when the time comes. I'm not taking any time to think it over, Rosaire, because if I did I'd end up afraid of the fires of hell and tell you no, so I'm telling you yes right now. You're going to eat so well, Rosaire, the whole city of Saint-Boniface will be jealous of you! Everybody's going to want to die like you, fed by Bebette Roy, the greatest cook in all the Canadian West!"

They never talked about it again. Starting on the day after their conversation, Rosaire had sat down in front of an endless meal that would go on until he died. Five years later he had gained a hundred pounds, he had trouble moving around, he sometimes suffered brief diabetic comas, but he didn't lose his nerve: three times a day, sometimes more, he settles in over the delicious food that his Bebette has prepared for him, he grunts, he breathes heavily, he belches, most of the time alone with his wife because he doesn't want to impose all that on anyone else, especially not his children and grandchildren and, if someone asked him, he would most likely declare that he was happy.

His heart doesn't burst in his chest, he has no digestive problems, life has given him an iron constitution despite the cancer that is gnawing away at him but without torturing him, and that is all he wants.

It's all delicious but the presence of the fat man who does not respect any of the table manners that her grandparents had instilled in her – no elbows on the table, no noisy chewing, never talking with your mouth full – takes away her appetite a little and Rhéauna eats less than she should. She'd been very hungry when she went to the table. And it smelled so good! But why does her great-aunt Bebette let her husband behave like that? Rhéauna suspects there is some mysterious reason, a secret only they know and she struggles all through the meal not to look too much in her great-uncle's direction so as not to embarrass him.

Meanwhile, her great-aunt tries to keep the conversation going with anecdotes, each one less interesting than the others, about her family, illness, children's words, her sons' success, her daughters' good marriages. She also talks about the struggle of Saint-Boniface to remain francophone in the English sea of western Canada. Like Maria in Saskatchewan but bigger and more influential, with the hope of a genuine right to speak in Parliament and in French! They'll win. Oh, yes! One fine day they'll win. But she quickly realizes that her great-niece isn't listening and finally she stops. She eats in silence, something not seen often, whereas Rhéauna is content to nibble at Bebette's chicken with celery, one of her famous specialties, for which she usually gets only compliments but that this night, for the first time, is met with indifference. It's not normal for this child to eat so little. Could she be tired from her trip? She looks at her husband. Or disgust. She wanted to warn Rosaire to mind his manners a little around the little girl but she forgot. After all, it should be up to him to think of it, right? She's angry with him all at once and angry with herself for being angry with him. Poor man. The latest news about his health isn't good, she has to go easy on him ...

At dessert she remembers all at once that Rhéauna was born somewhere around the end of summer. Good, finally a subject that will interest the little girl.

"It's your birthday soon, isn't it?"

Rhéauna looks up from her plate where she has just stuck her fork into the still-warm raspberry pie, even if she has no intention of tasting it. Her grandmother has always told her not to play with her food, that it's rude. And this is the first time she hasn't wanted to throw herself at her dessert ...

"That's right, I forgot. It's on September 2."

"September 2! That's next week!"

"Yes, it's always when we go back to school.

Bebette gets out of her chair, arms akimbo as if she were angry and Rhéauna wonders why.

"Will you be all by yourself with your mother in Morial?"

"I guess so ..."

She hadn't thought about that either. It's true, she will be all alone with her mother on her birthday. No presents from her two sisters, wrapped up behind her back and flourished like trophies, no upside-down cake with canned pineapple and maraschino cherries from a jar, no fancy sandwiches cut into triangles without crusts. She's going to cry, she can feel that she is going to cry, but she mustn't because she doesn't want her great-aunt to know how much she doesn't want to go to Montreal. Not tomorrow, not ever.

"But that's terrible! How old are you going to be?"

"Eleven."

"Eleven years old and all alone with your mother who probably doesn't even know how to make a cake because she's spent her whole life in a cotton mill! That's terrible ... Did you hear that, Rosaire? The child turns eleven next Tuesday and she'll be in Morial all alone with Maria Desrosiers who probably can't even boil water!"

It's obvious that Rosaire isn't listening and he barely looks up from his plate.

"We're going to have a party for you, Nana! Would you like that, a nice birthday party?"

Rhéauna would like to protest, she definitely doesn't want to see people tonight, she wants to go to bed, forget the fat uncle and the mountain of food he's just gobbled, not think about her long train ride the next day and sleep. If she can ...

Bebette has already picked up the wall phone.

"Do you know your mother's phone number in Morial? I'm going to call her, we're going to postpone your trip, we're going to have a party for you tomorrow night, it doesn't make sense ..."

She has to do something to keep Bebette from calling her mother, from delaying her departure, from having a party! She doesn't want a party. There's nothing to celebrate! Never again will there be anything to celebrate!

Bebette rummages in a notebook hanging on the wall under the telephone.

"I thought I'd written it in my book ... Ah, here it is!"

Rhéauna gets up from the table, goes to her great-aunt who is already maniacally cranking the phone that will put her in touch with the local telephone operator.

"Don't bother, *ma tante*, please don't bother! I have to leave tomorrow ... Maybe my mother will take me to a restaurant for my birthday ... I heard there's lots of restaurants in Montreal ..."

Bebette gestures to her to be quiet.

"Hello, Madame Gendron? This is Bebette Roy. How are you? Me, too, thanks. Listen, if I want to call long distance to Morial would it take long? Is that so? My goodness, the telephone is modern! Look, I want you to call Amherst 2361 in Morial for me ... That's a big phone number, isn't it, not like here! Do you know how it works? Do you have to write out the whole word *Amherst*? Ah, just the first two letters ... Go ahead then, do it, I'll wait for your call ..."

She hangs up, all excited.

"Just think, apparently it only takes a couple of minutes ... And I read somewhere it won't be long till we can put in those numbers ourselves! It's unbelievable to think that you can talk to somebody at the other end of the world whenever you want!"

Rhéauna has gone back to her seat at the table. She can't stop Bebette from talking to her mother, but she has to find some way to stop her from carrying out her crazy plan.

"I'd really rather leave for Ottawa tomorrow, *ma tante* ... Otherwise the trip will be too long, I'll be too tired when I get there ..."

Bebette laughs as she pinches her cheeks. It hurts.

"You're talking like a grown-up, Nana. Stop being so reasonable and let's celebrate! You'll have fun. Don't you like parties? Most children adore them! When I was little, there was nothing I liked better than a birthday party!"

The phone rings. Bebette jumps, spins in a pirouette that's amazing for a person of her age and corpulence and throws herself at the phone.

"Hello, Madame Gendron? Ah, it's you, Maria!"

Her mother is there at the end of the line! A wave of emotion breaks in Rhéauna's chest, shaking her, she feels tears come to her eyes, has trouble breathing.

"It's your aunt Bebette! How are you, little girl? I hope I'm not disturbing your supper. What? What do you mean, you finished long ago? Eh? How come you're an hour later there? What do you mean, a time difference? It's already dark where you are? That's impossible!"

Her mother is there at the end of the line! She can even hear her voice but can't make out what she's saying. She could talk to her! She could take the receiver, press it against her ear, bring her mouth up to the microphone and talk to her mother!

"Yes, sure, she's here! You've got a lovely little girl, lucky you! I don't know how you could get along without her for so long! Sure, you'll talk to her afterward ..."

Her mother wants to talk to her! All her fatigue flies away, the disgust that had overwhelmed her when they were eating disappears, her mother whom she hasn't seen for so long wants to talk to her! Bebette gestures to her to come up while she goes on chattering.

"Listen, I'm not going to stay on the phone, this is long distance and it costs a fortune, but I wanted to let you know that Nana's going to spend another day with us, if it's okay with you. I just realized, her birthday is next week and she'd be all alone with you in Morial, so I decided to put on a big birthday party for her here tomorrow night. There'll be a bunch of us to celebrate, *saperlipopette!* I'm going to invite the whole family. I'll change her train ticket, too, the one to Ottawa and the one to Morial ... Don't worry, we'll take care of her! And I hope everything's all right in Morial ... Bye!"

She holds out the receiver to Rhéauna who is standing paralyzed in the middle of the dining room.

"Here, but make it quick, it's long distance ..."

Rhéauna can't move. Her feet are glued to the floor, her heart is pounding, she feels as if she's about to faint.

"*Saperlipopette*, Nana, make up your mind! If you don't want to talk to her I'll hang up, time's flying!"

She finds the courage to take a few steps, to hold out her hand.

"Tell her there's likely a train to Ottawa that comes in every day at the same time ..."

Rhéauna holds the receiver to her ear. Her mother is there, at the end of the line, in person, as if she were standing beside her.

"Hello, Mama?"

"How are you, sweetheart?"

It's her voice. It hasn't changed. It's just the way Rhéauna remembers it, warm and with a joyful note that makes it quaver. It's the voice she's heard so often in her dreams. That she's missed so much.

"I'm fine ..."

She can't think of anything else to say. She looks at the phone numbers that her great-aunt Bebette has jotted on the wall below the telephone and can't think of anything else to say.

Bebette heaves an exasperated sigh.

"Hurry up, talk, say something, *saperlipopette*, anything at all, at least ask her how she is … It's been years since you've seen her, you must have something to say!"

Rhéauna manages to open her mouth.

"How about you?"

That's all. She hears breathing at the other end. Her mother is waiting for her to add something – but what? There's too much to say in not enough time … She rests her head against the wall.

"I can't wait to see you …"

That wasn't true five minutes ago but now, all of a sudden, it is. She wishes she were in Montreal already, to snuggle up to her mother, smell her fragrance, cry against her neck, blow her nose on her dress, tell her she loves her and say how much she has missed her. Reproach her, too, for abandoning her sisters and her, to hit her even, claw her. Claw her and kiss her!

"Me, too, darling, I can't wait to see you. But it looks like we'll have to wait another day … Your aunt Bebette didn't even ask for my opinion … But I think it's a good idea to have your birthday there, in Saint-Boniface, because I work nights and it would've been hard … Listen, there's a beautiful room waiting for you, just for you, you're going to love it here … But hang up now, or it will cost Bebette too much. Bye, sweetheart … I can't wait to see you."

A click. Rhéauna removes the receiver from her ear, looks at it. She feels a hand on her shoulder, then on the back of her neck.

"She couldn't talk to you any longer …"

Bebette takes the receiver, puts it back in place.

"Maybe you're too young to understand but you have to pay for long distance by the minute and …"

Rhéauna cuts her off, raising her head.

"If I give you the rest of the money for my trip to Montreal will you call her back? I didn't have time to tell her that I love her …"

Her pillow is soaking wet, her handkerchief unusable for a while now and she's exhausted from crying so much. She is at the same time at the halfway point of her journey and torn between two poles: she already misses Saskatchewan so badly but, for several hours now, she's been wanting to be in Montreal with her mother. She can't have both, she knows that; in fact, she's sure that Saskatchewan has disappeared from her life forever and she hates the tugging that is making her for the first time want two conflicting things at once. She has tried to console herself with the thought that probably she will soon see her sisters; the prospect of the definitive loss of her grandparents, though, has made her sob as if she had just learned that they'd died. She knew, of course, that this separation was definitive but she feels as if only now has she *understood* that it's no longer an idea but an irrevocable fait accompli. She is mourning her grandparents even though they are still alive.

And the party that's being planned for tomorrow infuriates her. Bebette could at least have asked for her opinion, find out whether she wanted a party or not, if it was important to her to be turning eleven! And most of all that they are marking it with balloons and multicoloured confetti and everybody singing "Happy Birthday." She has no desire to see again the eighteen hysterical individuals who met her at the station, or to pretend she was thrilled that they were taking an interest in her, the poor child people feel so sorry for, who would be spending her birthday all alone unless they took charge! She doesn't want to be taken charge of. She'd rather spend her birthday in silence, have them forget about her visit to Saint-Boniface or keep a vague memory of a polite little second cousin who passed through their lives discreetly, without bothering them, and then disappeared without a trace.

But no.

She heard the dreadful Bebette howl on the telephone for a good part of the evening, issuing commands; ordering a pink-and-green cake – that's right, even the colours! – from her daughter Gaétane and party sandwiches from someone she called Lolotte who might have been Colette or Charlotte; protest when someone told her that they might not be able to attend the party; threaten with plenty of deafening *saperlipopettes*; promise with veiled words abuse that would be remembered for a long time if they weren't present and proud to be; laugh excitedly when she got a new idea. In fact, Rhéauna is beginning to wonder if her great-aunt Bebette is planning this party for herself, to pass some time, to fill an evening, to busy herself because she has nothing to do in life but feed her obese husband. Besides, it isn't normal for a woman her age to need so badly to plan a birthday party for an eleven-year-old child! After all, she is only the sister of the child's grandfather, not her grandmother!

Rhéauna punches her pillow a few times, tries to find a bit that's not wet with tears. She won't sleep tonight, she can feel it, and the party tomorrow night will be a nightmare even worse than she can imagine. Actually, she didn't see many children this afternoon. Does that mean it's going to be an adult party, a party for old people, a children's party with no children, something boring and endless with everybody pretending they're enjoying themselves when they're actually bored to death? Will the guests eat the fancy sandwiches reluctantly in the hope that the goddamn party will be over as soon as possible and the goddamn child will finally disappear?

All that's missing from Bebette's plans, which are doomed to be disastrous, is for her to dress her Rosaire as a clown, though it is rather amusing to imagine Rosaire dressed like a buffoon! Rhéauna smiles in spite of herself, is annoyed with herself to have thought of something so mean, pulls her knees up to her stomach and starts to hum as she used to do in Maria whenever she was sad. It relieves her a little but not enough to put her to sleep.

Something that her mother told her comes back suddenly. Something that hadn't struck her at first but that suddenly seems very important. She unfolds herself, turns onto her back, looks at the ceiling where the light from the streetlamp in front of the house, and the night wind, are drawing ghosts on the curtains.

Her mother said that she works nights. When will they see each other if she goes to school in the daytime and her mother works at night? Why make her come to Montreal if they have different timetables? A strange suspicion, a vague concern creeps into her head. She can't say what it is but she knows that it's disturbing, maybe even threatening.

Her mother hasn't brought her to Montreal because she missed her; there's some other reason that she doesn't want to own up to. A secret. She needs her but she can't say why. Like in a novel.

In her circle, they thought at first that Bebette Desrosiers had been put on earth to make them happy. Vivacious, amusing, generous, she assumed the role of the eldest of the Desrosiers girls and very early was giving orders in place of their mother – a woman of delicate health who had nearly died giving birth to her last child, Régina-Coeli – who trusted her because she was structured and responsible. But she'd been quick to take her role a little too seriously. Although still the funny Bebette that they knew – in fact, she used her sense of humour to get out of the difficult situations in which she often found herself – she had started to rule over everything in the house, each person's tasks and timetables as well as organizing meals and the family budget. She still made everybody laugh, while showing her own astonishing self-confidence. And appearing curt when she felt that she should be, which was pretty well all the time.

And so she had transformed herself without too much trouble into the tormentor of the little sister that she saw, as did other members of the family, more as a servant of the household than as the youngest daughter of the Desrosiers family. Bebette gave the orders, Régina obeyed. It wasn't written down anywhere, it was just something they accepted without argument. And it had gone on for years.

The two sisters had never been close. An open animosity had in fact been established because both had a short fuse and the slightest thing would send them into fits of rage that were often exacerbated by the frustration of one or the touchiness of the other: Régina-Coeli was regularly fed up with being picked on by everyone in general and Bebette in particular, even though that was the role she'd taken on long before, and her older sister accepted no resistance to her often peremptory orders or to her cruel and at times unjust criticisms. Next came endless, monster, screaming matches that went on and on, always crowned with slamming doors or dreadful meals. Although Régina complained to their father, an alcoholic farmer who, since his wife had taken sick, preferred his animals' company to his children's, nothing changed: Bebette was still the undisputed boss of the Desrosiers tribe, Régina the servant.

Her sister's comical side also got on the nerves of the cold, skinny Régina who lacked any sense of humour and she let her know. And so the two sisters grew up, each on her own side, without trying to understand one another, Régina devoted in spite of herself to the well-being of the others, Bebette snowed under by responsibilities too great for a girl her age.

Bebette, though, had had a radiant childhood made up of discreet searches and surprising discoveries because she was interested in everything: what animals do to reproduce; what makes nature so angry that she creates blizzards and electrical storms; what makes birds fly and snakes slither. And human beings laugh. She liked to laugh herself and to make others laugh since her early childhood, she had played clown to stimulate family get-togethers, consulted her books of jokes that had belonged to her father and of which she'd learned long extracts by heart – she liked people to be cheerful and she wanted it to show. She had the nuns at school laughing and even – it had happened several times – the priests at confession. She was an invigorating ray of sunshine and everyone adored her.

Until the arrival of Régina-Coeli anyway, when overnight she found herself head of the family with adult responsibilities and problems she didn't always understand. For some years she tried to settle everything with her gift for repartee, she managed to shut them all up all the time, no one dared talk back to her and everyone submitted to her. She always got what she wanted with the help of a well-placed joke, a clever pun, her reputation for shouting her head off. She ruled, she was feared, but she was very unhappy when she realized one day that she wasn't sure she was respected.

That was when she became a dragon. To get some respect.

Her sense of humour disappeared all at once as if she'd wakened one morning miraculously transformed and had forgotten who she'd been the day before. No more joking or punning or clown's faces, Élisabeth Desrosiers was henceforth the serious head of a household and, if anyone didn't like it, they'd better watch out.

As soon as her new character was found – at first her brothers and sisters had thought it was a joke but quickly realized that it was serious, definitive and that they'd better get used to it – she'd begun to search for something that would belong only to her, some personal detail, some expression to be associated only with her, that made you say when you saw it or heard it that you couldn't help thinking about Bebette Desrosiers. Like Queen Victoria's lace bonnets. Or the Blessed Virgin's blue robe. She had tried all sorts of things: extravagant hats you could spot two blocks away or clothes so severe you might think that she'd joined a religious community; also, the stentorian voice that she'd had to develop as head of the family and that she made even more threatening or – something totally unlike her – a soft voice in which you could, however, sense a chilliness that sent a chill up your spine and even curses that weren't oaths but did make an impression. *Tabarnouche*, for example, derived from the Québécois *tabarnac*, which itself sprang from the liturgical *tabernacle*: it was quickly discarded as too vulgar; or *lime green*, which she thought was pointless even if it had the merit of originality; or a *flute* uttered at the right time, in the right place, which she thought was too short to be effective. When she finally found what would make her a celebrity and even a legend all over Saint-Boniface – her famous *saperlipopette* – she still held on to her extravagant hats and her stentorian voice. The latter reinforced the devastating effect of the well-timed interjection whereas the hats gave her a queenly bearing.

And so she unearthed her *saperlipopette* in an old French novel, published in the mid-nineteenth century as a serial that for some unknown reason had turned up in Saint-Boniface. The word was used by a ridiculous *gendarme*, the comic relief in the story, who brought it out on many and varied occasions. She had immediately thought the word interesting because it had *five* syllables you could emphasize in turn according to need: *sa*per-li-po-pette!, sa-*per*-li-po-pette!, sa-per-*li*-po-pette!, etc. and she'd tried it out rather timidly on her family and friends. With no real results. They had looked at her, frowning, some had burst out laughing – Régina-Coeli, for example, ultimate insult to her authority – Méo had even asked her where she'd got that word they'd never heard before, that took off in every direction. She hadn't been discouraged and had polished it in front of her mirror that evening – for some time she'd been entitled, as the eldest of the daughters, to her very own bedroom – copying querulous expressions and trying to make the word snap like a whip, her forefinger pointed and brows tightly knit. She'd realized that by separating the first two syllables and speeding up the other three – *sa-per-lipopette!* – while using a hollow, disturbing voice, she achieved a fairly satisfying result that actually impressed her.

She had used it first with the young grocery delivery boy – "Sa-per-lipopette, Tancrède, can't you do something about those muddy boots!" – who had left the house white with terror. Well, that was something, at least it scared the children. After that she had hurled it at the woman in the post office on Boulevard Provencher who had jumped as if she'd been hit and tried to excuse the faltering Canadian postal service for an inexplicable delay – the package she asked for had never existed, Bebette just wanted to try out her oath on someone she didn't know to test its effectiveness – then at the butcher whom she'd accused, leaning heavily on theoretically scandalized *saperlipopettes*, of pressing his thumb on the scale when he weighed the meat. He'd apologized – so it was true! – and had shown her out himself after making her a gift of three enormous pork kidneys that no one wanted except the Desrosiers family who oddly enough was fond of them. As for the mailman, he had reacted to her *saperlipopette* as if he were grappling with a rabid dog that was about to tear off part of his pants along with a good long strip of bleeding flesh.

She had waited, though, before bringing it out to her family. Convinced that she finally had the right way to terrorize them, she particularly didn't want to relive the flop of her first attempt. She waited for the auspicious moment, the winning conditions.

The key event, the moment when you could say that she'd finally found the devastating character she was looking for, had occurred at one of those meals, a Sunday supper, when everything seems to be working toward creating a disaster. It started with the soup, which, besides not tasting of anything much, had been served lukewarm, which the father had always hated. Bebette had used the opportunity to show how sarcastic she could be with her sister. Her father had given her a smile of complicity; that had been her reward, for he very rarely smiled. Most likely because he was usually loaded. And fuming. Régina-Coeli had apologized, claiming that the oldest ones – Méo and Bebette herself – had delayed coming to the table, that she'd had to shout several times that the soup was served and getting cold. Bebette had swallowed the reproach, telling herself that Régina-Coeli had it coming to her. Then the roast veal was overcooked – charred according to Bebette – the potatoes lumpy, the gravy too thin and the dessert, a blueberry pie, a specialty of Régina's, too dry and not sweet enough. More and more depressed, she served, cleared the table with her head down and back bent; she tripped on the rug and couldn't stop apologizing.

During the whole meal you could feel the tension growing between Bebette and Régina-Coeli. Régina gave in to her sister's criticisms; Bebette overstated her exasperation a little to set the scene for her final explosion, the official entrance of the ringing and lethal *saperlipopette* she'd been preparing for so long and that would finally confirm her, so she hoped, in her role of head of the family, because her father was too weak to assume it and her mother too sick to take over.

The opportunity presented itself when the coffee was served, pure slops according to Bebette, insipid dishwater you wouldn't dare serve to the beggar who came to the door at Christmas, a disastrous end to an atrocious meal.

Until then, Régina-Coeli had put up with everything, hardly saying a word, content to shake her head at her sister's rude remarks or taking refuge in the kitchen to hide her rancour. But she reacted very badly to the criticism of her coffee. Because she had tasted that coffee and thought it excellent. In any case as good as that morning's which hadn't elicited any rude remark. Maybe even a little better. And so Bebette hadn't finished her remark that denigrated her supposed dishwater when Régina, who once again was going to leave the dining room without asking her due, had gone back to the doorstep, returned to the room and rested both hands on the table as she leaned toward her older sister.

"I put up with a lot tonight, Bebette, during the whole meal, but you aren't going to criticize my coffee! It's good, my coffee! And I forbid you to claim that it isn't!"

Overjoyed at the opportunity being offered her on a silver platter as they say, Bebette stood up, regal, gave the table a slap, just one but resounding, and fired off her first *sa-per-lipopette*, delivered the way she'd rehearsed it in front of her mirror so often, like a great actress sure of the impression she would make; the first two syllables carefully separated, *sa-per*, then the last three in one burst, *lipopette*. It fell like a blade on the history of the Desrosiers family: from now on there would be the time before the *saperlipopette* and the time after, that of Bebette and her terrifying oath that frightened everyone, putting an end to any discussion and settling everything to her advantage.

Everyone in the room had frozen. A talented caricaturist would have had time to sketch each member of the family, wide-eyed and open-mouthed, so long were they motionless. Lightning had just struck the house. Bebette stared at them all one by one to make sure they'd got the point, even her parents who lowered their heads, too. Ending with Régina-Coeli, who was the first to move and run off to the kitchen, where shortly after she could be heard slamming the dirty dishes around in the sink. The meal ended in nearly religious silence and Bebette got up from the table without saying good night to anyone. In her room, planted in front of her mirror, she allowed herself a victorious grin. Thank you, Régina.

And so the legend of Bebette Desrosiers's *saperlipopette* was born, then spread at dizzying speed through the parish, then over all Saint-Boniface. Bebette became the person you didn't want to hear saying *saperlipopette* – it made the children howl, the old folks cry, teenagers tremble – to the point that in the end people were willing to do whatever she wanted to avoid it. When she was walking on the street in one of her incredible hats, head high, gaze provocative, people crossed the street to avoid her. The butcher never pressed his thumb on the scale, the woman at the post office shook when she appeared at her metal wicket, Tancrède invented fits to get out of delivering grocery orders for the Desrosiers family.

It was not respect that Bebette inspired all her life, it was fear. But she never made the distinction.

Only one man resisted it, though, that *saperlipopette* of hers, a foreman on the Canadian Pacific Railway, a giant who would never be impressed by the Desrosiers dragon, who would even love her as seldom had a dragon been loved. And she wouldn't bother him, would never fling an offensive *saperlipopette* at him because she knew that it would be pointless, that it would never have an effect on him. Without letting herself be totally dominated by him, something she could never do – she will allow her beloved Rosaire to resist her, to discuss the soundness of her decisions, to hold her back sometimes when she has a tendency to go too far with manipulation and emotional blackmail. Out of love. Out of devotion. Out of admiration. But that's another story ...

That *saperlipopette* is still striking today, in 1913, years and years later. It's famous now across the entire city, it is discussed, feared, it's the subject of zany or terrible legends, Bebette having long ago replaced the werewolf and the bogeyman in the inhabitants' nightmares.

Anyway, Rhéauna, who's not too bothered by it, maybe because she isn't from Saint-Boniface and doesn't feel obliged to play along, keeps hearing it all evening, sometimes murmured to be convincing, sometimes shouted to terrify. Always on the phone. And it seems to work because that blasted birthday party the next day is gradually taking shape as the hours pass. Along with the pink-and-green birthday cake – Gaétane; and the crustless sandwiches – Lolotte; apparently there will be huge platters of raw vegetables (celery, carrots, radishes) adorned with yellowish-orange pimento cheese – Olivine; stuffed olives, as much tomato juice and orange juice as anyone wants; salted peanuts – Camille; and even party hats and bags of confetti – Bebette herself.

Rhéauna is in despair.

All the next day she feels as if she's invisible. No one has time to look after her, they're too involved with getting ready for her birthday party! Bebette is hysterical, loads of people come and go, carrying enormous packages that they set down everywhere but mainly in the kitchen. Bebette exclaims happily like a child or shouts acid criticisms – when Gaétane bursts into sobs, Rhéauna guesses that her pink-and-green cake is not a great success – women of every age run and shout, children cling to their skirts without even glancing in the direction of the birthday girl. Rhéauna, who can't help thinking about Christmas, more or less expects the arrival of a Christmas tree cut by hand that morning – are there forests around Saint-Boniface? – or to see a man dressed up as a ho-ho-hoing Santa Claus. She is quick to realize, though, that she is just a pretext: Bebette likes to gather her family and friends together, have a party for any reason at all, that's plain to see. She's only happy when there is life around her and she leaps at any pretext for organizing a family party. And if there's no reason she makes one up, as she's doing today, with rather ridiculous energy that is very close to despair. No one but her needs this party, no one wants it, so why is she working so hard? To pass the time? To shift her attention away from her huge husband? Rhéauna wishes she could beg her to call it off. Knowing that it would be pointless, that Bebette wouldn't listen to her, she simply dreads what lies in wait for her that night: an excellent meal most likely but one she'd happily do without; surprises prepared too quickly to be of any real interest; a pointless hustle and bustle around a sad little girl who had not been expecting so much.

Around one o'clock that afternoon, Bebette pushes in front of Rhéauna a tall, pale young girl who seems to have trouble staying upright, she's so thin, and who stubbornly keeps looking at the threadbare motifs in the living-room carpet.

"Nana, this is your third cousin Ozéa. She'll look after you till tonight ... She's awfully nice, you'll see ..."

Most of all she's so boring, maybe because of her pathological shyness that keeps her from asserting herself and makes her express everything in the form of a stupid question:

"Want to do something? Like what? Have you got lots of dolls back home in Maria? Have you got one that opens and closes its eyes? Can you talk English? Is it true you aren't a real orphan and you're going to be with your mother and help her work in the house of some rich people in Morial?"

Accustomed to the energetic suggestions of her sisters, to their healthy aggression, to their curiosity about everything in nature – animals, plants, insects, even the most repulsive – Rhéauna is taken aback in the presence of this city girl who's dressed like a doll in the middle of the week, who's too clean, too quiet and has just one thing in her mind: to stay clean.

"No, I can't play marbles, my mother won't let me play in the dirt, she says it's all right for little girls in the country ..."

Rhéauna feels more like slapping her than playing with her. She'd been told that city children are sassy, unruly, that they know more, too, because they often go to school longer but instead she finds herself with this mildly retarded scaredy-cat little girl – she was born in Saint-Boniface, a big city, she's thirteen years old and she's never heard of the Comtesse de Ségur, the ignoramus! – who's only interested in her own little self.

The day turns out to be long, then. And challenging.

Rhéauna wanders from room to room with the anaemic Ozéa while everyone is bustling about in the house. She tries to read – a novel taken from her suitcase which she has read several times and never tires of – but her third cousin looks at her as if she'd come from another planet.

"Don't you like to read, Ozéa?"

"I like it when I'm all by myself."

She gets the message, puts the book down.

"Okay, so we have to find something to play … What do you play in the city in the afternoon?"

Another uncomprehending look.

"Let's walk. That's something I like, walking …"

"Okay, sure, let's walk."

"Grandma Bebette doesn't want us to leave the house … This isn't my neighbourhood. We might get lost."

"We won't go far … Go ask her, tell her we won't go far, we'll stay on this street … Tell her I've got a good sense of direction …"

"She'll say no."

There is something final about this statement. Rhéauna realizes that no negotiation is possible: if Bebette has decreed that they won't step outside the house because Ozéa is too dumb to avoid getting lost in Saint-Boniface, they won't leave the house and that's that.

A red crepe-paper streamer with "Happy Birthday" printed on it in gold shows up in the dining room around the middle of the afternoon. Some great-uncle or first cousin or second cousin or third cousin hangs it up, bellowing too loud for it to be sincere, a song that's reminiscent of *Partons, la mer est belle* but barely sounds like it, it's botched so badly. He even sends some winks her way that he hopes will suggest they're in league with each other but that she refuses to answer. After all, she isn't going to show enthusiasm she doesn't feel for a streamer in English!

Gradually she does regret her stubbornness at refusing to be the centre of attention amid the frenzy created by Bebette's friends. Something new, like guilt, is making her feel sick. She decides then to ride it out. She tells herself that all those preparations, the excitement, is happening because of her, for her, to celebrate her birthday, that it all springs from a very laudable intention on the part of these generous people who insist on underlining the passage in their lives of a little girl who'll be all alone on the night of her birthday in the company of the mother she barely knows, and that they're doing everything possible to make her forget it.

She spends long minutes sitting in the parlour next to Ozéa, who does nothing to break the silence. She no longer dares to read so she won't hurt her cousin's feelings. She's bored to tears, convinced that the day will never end. She looks out the window. Rosaire is sitting in his chair. He is snoring, an empty plate beside him.

At one point Ozéa gets up without warning her and tries out some rather clumsy dance steps. Probably she wants to show her country cousin that she takes ballet lessons which cost a fortune and will make her into a genuine young lady, but she only makes herself more ridiculous because she has no talent for dancing. Rhéauna hides her giggles with her hand. She doesn't know a thing about dancing but she does know that what she sees now is grotesque. She tells herself that at least something is happening! Ozéa, soon exhausted, stops her demonstration as quickly as she started and sits back down in her chair, giving Rhéauna a triumphant smile, as if to say, Just you try it, you'll never learn that in Saskatchewan out in the back of beyond! Rhéauna would like to tell her about her adventure in the cornfield to terrify her a little.

Then nothing interesting happens and the afternoon is torpid once again. Rhéauna finally falls asleep – the flight into sleep – and wakes up with a stiff neck because her head had been at an uncomfortable angle.

A small miracle happens: it's nearly six o'clock, the afternoon finally passes. Ozéa presses her ear against the gramophone from which emerges the voice of a woman being flayed alive. It seems as if everyone has forgotten that she exists. But the real test will soon take place.

It begins with Bebette who sweeps into the parlour, a vast apron around her waist, her hair a mess, face red from excitement. "It's nearly ready! No one from Rosaire's side answered the invitation but it doesn't matter, we don't need them! Besides, they don't even know you, Nana. They're nobodies. Dull. Especially at parties! Us, though, we know how to have fun. Not like them. Funeral faces with pointed hats on their heads, that's not our way. There's just little Gabrielle I'd have liked you to meet. Her and her mother. They've got their heads screwed on right. She's just four years old, the little monkey, and she can already write her name. Believe me, that child will go far ... But you don't even know which one she is ..."

She is talking too much and too quickly because she's nervous, that's plain to see. Rhéauna wants to tell her to calm down, take a deep breath, everything's going to be fine even though she's not so sure herself.

"Did you have fun with your cousin Ozéa? She's nice, isn't she, like I told you!"

Ozéa, terrified, hunches her shoulders. She's afraid that Rhéauna will denounce her, tell her grandmother how boring she turned out to be. She's so pale that Rhéauna is afraid she'll faint in the middle of one of Bebette's sentences. Who goes on with her monologue.

"Have you got a pretty dress, something to wear tonight? Go and change now, and hurry, people will soon start coming. I told them to be here early because it's a children's party. We usually do them in the afternoon, but this is a weekday and people are at work ..."

All at once Rhéauna realizes that Ozéa has taken an afternoon off school to be with her. She shouldn't have bothered.

"Hurry up! Come on now, *saperlipopette*, go and change. And you, Ozéa, go and help your mother set the table! Is that your dress for tonight? Haven't you got something dressy, something, you know, something like a party outfit?"

She disappears before Ozéa can say anything.

Rhéauna feels a little sorry for her over having to deal with that woman all the time. She goes to her room to change.

As soon as the first guests arrive, hysteria takes over the house. There are a good dozen people, Rhéauna doesn't know if they're one family or several because they're of various ages – two old adults not much younger than Bebette and Rosaire, it seems to her; others in their thirties who could be as old as her parents; then teenagers, children, a baby. They talk non-stop, they laugh at anything, each one wishes her "Happy Birthday" several times. They move around so much that the house seems already full when the party has barely begun. Others arrive hot on their heels, even noisier if that's possible, then still others. An endless parade of rustling long dresses and hats covered with tulle and birds of every colour take over the house, staccato remarks addressed to no one in particular are delivered with no hope of a response, inarticulate shouts and laughter come from who knows where – all that amid dizzying comings and goings that intensify minute to minute. They have impossible names – Althéode, Olivine, Euphrémise, Télesphore, Frida, Euclide – which they cry out with slaps on the back or between hugs and kisses. The women race in every direction to set the table, the children howl because they're hungry, a call-and-response song – already! – bursts out in the living room but doesn't have an echo, which is odd: the refrain, rhythmical and full of double entendres of course, is shouted at the top of his lungs by a fat, red-faced man, then nothing, no responses, the girl in the duck pond behind the house in the middle of the woods, digga-doo, digga-dun-day gets no response and the somebody's uncle who sang it, in the middle of the living room, waving his arms, looks like a damn fool. He's told as much by a tiny woman, curt and idiotic, probably his wife or his sister maybe, who doesn't weigh her words as she points her finger at him. He swallows, hunches his back and goes back to the ranks of the men who'll be bored on the doorstep all evening because really, a party for the eleventh birthday of a little girl they don't know is not by a long shot their idea of fun. They'll take refuge in strong drink, as usual – "frisky" alcohol – according to Bebette – before they start to fondle any grand-nieces who are old enough. And to set off the evening's first drama. They gather around Rosaire, the older men will talk about the Canadian Pacific Railway, about the good old days on the work site with no women to pester them; the younger ones will once again envy them that life of freedom surrounded by untamed nature. Bebette is everywhere and nowhere at once: everywhere she's not expected – she surprises some little girls who are laughing about one of their cousins who's been wearing eyeglasses for a while now and she yells at them so many insults and *saperlipopettes* that they all burst out sobbing – and nowhere when she is needed: "Where's Aunt Bebette? We can't find the candles for the cake! Aunt Bebette! Aunt Bebette!" Barely half an hour since the last guests' arrival the lady of the house calls out: "Come and get it while it's hot! Eat up before it freezes!" They all race into the dining room where a huge U-shaped table is set up. There are also two tables for the children in the kitchen but soon it's obvious that they don't provide enough space. Then in no time, the mountains of food brought by everyone and hastily prepared that same day by the women, who didn't scrimp on sugar or fat, is being devoured pretty well all over the house. It's like Christmas: tourtières, apple pie, roast turkey, pigs'-feet stew; and Easter: an enormous ham, already sliced and spread over two vast white china plates surrounded by potatoes prepared four ways (mashed, boiled, baked, roasted); a fresh ham that Lolotte's husband had smoked a few months earlier and was keeping for a special occasion; maple syrup pie; the little fried pastries called nuns' farts. Not to mention platters of raw vegetables and the inevitable corn on the cob. It is all delicious, of course, and needless to say, abundant. Everyone eats a lot and quickly. At first, it seems like too much food, but there are nearly forty of them passing plates between mouthfuls and, in the end, the women are afraid they'll run out.

But there is enough for everyone, even the greediest. The one who is overlooked in all the commotion was the birthday girl herself, whom they abandoned to her fate after they embraced her because there were more important things to do – as if the reception itself were more important than she is – who spends a good part of the evening alone at the end of the adults' table, watching them eat, laugh, shout. As soon as they'd cleared their plates the children left the kitchen, racing and shrieking all over the house. Some went upstairs to play hide-and-seek and who knows, maybe doctor as well. After the main dishes, delicious and filling, when an incalculable number of salads appeared as if by magic, the men who'd held back since the beginning of the meal, simply devouring everything in sight, warmed up and began to hum and tap their feet. Call-and-response songs finally got a response, the women turned red and hid behind their hands when the allusions became too risqué – "She says whoops, does Farlantine, she says spuds and your poutine, put your mmm, put your mmm, right next to mine!" Then, after a particularly dirty couplet, Bebette stands up and shouts to everyone: "The singing and the dancing are for Christmas! This party's for children so hold back! Meanwhile we've got something more important to do if you get my meaning ..." All eyes are on Rhéauna who realizes right away that the birthday cake ceremony is about to begin. She wishes she could go on being forgotten while observing them, they're so funny, she'd have liked to hear the rest of the call-and-response song, too, but this is a birthday party and that means birthday cake, you can't avoid it ... She forces a smile that is meant to be innocent, as if she doesn't know what is going on and sighs, resigned. She'll have to act surprised, listen to the song, blow out the candles. A breath of complicity descends onto the wreck of the table. Nudges are exchanged, excited hilarity hidden behind hands. Suddenly the children appear as if by magic. Someone must have told them or maybe their instincts inform them that the cake is on its way. The lights go out in the dining room. Two women enter the room, carrying the pink-and-green cake on which eleven candles flicker. The inevitable "Happy

Birthday to You" rises up in the dark, sung off-key but sincerely, vibrantly, happily. The last part is stretched out in the traditional way: "Happy biiiirrrrththday, dear Rhéééeaaaaunaaaa!" Then come cries, endless applause, everyone tells her to make a wish before she blows out the candles. She complies gracefully, telling herself that it's nearly over. When the candles are out, the other children want to know what she wished for while the adults tell them she has to keep it secret or it won't come true. A moment of calm settles in around the table while everyone samples the cake. It's true that it's not much to look at, it's rather shapeless and the icing has already started to ooze; it turns out, though, to be delicious. And as Gaétane puts it so well, probably to apologize: "It may be ugly but it tastes like cake!" The ingestion of fat and sugar is gradually taking effect, it shows in the tone of the conversation. While they serve the coffee, the women, hands on their hearts, talk about the *Titanic,* which sank in the North Atlantic last year, an event that traumatized them all the more because they're so far from an ocean – a natural phenomenon they have trouble imagining from deep in their vast prairies where salt water doesn't exist – and they've never seen a big ship. Since they're talking about serious matters now, Bebette slips in the oft-repeated story of her far-off uncle, pride of the Desrosiers family, who fought alongside Louis Riel and was hanged with his leader in Regina in 1885. She wipes her eyes as if she'd known the martyr well or witnessed his hanging, and her children laugh at her a little. "Honestly, Mama, you never laid eyes on him and you talk as if he was your best friend!" She gives them a little *saperlipopette* of protest, blows her nose, then glances in Rhéauna's direction. "That child has a long trip tomorrow … All the way to Ottawa, by way of Toronto. It's going to take all day." They look at her and nod. "As far as that's concerned …" "She needs her sleep." "Poor child." "We'd better be going." "Well, I guess we'll be on our way …"

And there, while they all look on in commiseration, after such an amazing demonstration of kindness and generosity toward someone they hardly know, whose eleventh birthday they wanted to celebrate, a little late now but with such intensity it makes her shiver – not for long, a few quick seconds, it's gone as soon as it starts – Rhéauna all at once, not knowing where it comes from – feels happy. It's as violent as it is brief. It's complete, round, warm. She would like to hug them all one after another and ask them to forgive her for not being able to appreciate this wonderful party that was put on just for her as if she deserved it. She would kiss them all on both cheeks, even Uncle Rosaire who nodded off as soon as he'd downed his three pieces of cake. She would tell them she'll never forget them, that later on, when she's grown, when she has children, she will describe with tears in her eyes this extraordinary evening, she would tell Bebette that the festivities will always be some of the most beautiful in her life, but she knows that's impossible because of her shyness and only whispers a little, "Thanks so much for everything," before she gets up from the table.

Only Bebette is aware that she's upset.

✖

Late that night, her great-aunt Bebette sat on the edge of Nana's bed and took her hand. She talked to her looking down, as if she had reason to reproach herself.

"I hope you understand that there wasn't time to get presents. If we'd known I'd've covered you in gifts, you'd have had all kinds of lovely surprises, but as it was last-minute ..."

Tell her it doesn't matter, that the party was enough, that anyway she didn't ask for so much; make her understand that their generosity touched her, that it will be a bright spot in her memory ... But nothing comes, she sits there motionless, her hand imprisoned in Bebette's, unable to express her gratitude. She can't understand why. If her grandmother were beside her she would throw her arms around her, embrace her. She would describe the party in detail as if she hadn't been there, make comments on each of the guests ... But she doesn't actually know them, for her they are a kind of multiple assembly of individual elements that don't have a personality of their own. She has made the acquaintance, in a perfunctory way, of just three: aunt Bebette, uncle Rosaire and cousin Ozéa, the others are costumed characters burdened with unbelievable names who've passed in her field of vision without leaving a trace: they sang, they ate, they laughed, they bellowed "Happy Birthday" in unison, and then they went home. That's all. She knows, though, that the women worked all day for her, that they baked, grilled, roasted, decorated, but not one came over and talked with her. They gravitated around Bebette, their mother or grandmother or mother-in-law without paying much attention to the person being feted, and all Rhéauna could say was that they'd been very generous. Even that, she couldn't express.

Her aunt pulls the covers up to her chin. She could have been about to kiss her. No, she, too, holds herself back.

"Try to sleep now, you've got a long day tomorrow ... *Saperlipopette*, practically eighteen hours on the train! All by yourself! You leave early tomorrow morning and you get to Ottawa late tomorrow night ... I talked to Ti-Lou, she said she'll arrange to meet you at the train station ... And she'd better or she'll have to deal with me! But she's never been all that dependable, she's somebody that could send a taxi for you ... Now I know she's my sister's daughter, but I tell you she's something else ... Be careful around her, Nana, don't believe everything she tells you, she'll often talk nonsense. She's what they call a loose woman, your grandmother must've told you, and those women are dangerous ... If we'd been able to avoid having you stop there we'd've done it, but going directly from Winnipeg to Montreal would've been too long, we didn't want you to spend a night on the train ... And we don't know any-body in Toronto, we haven't got any family there, so who would have looked after you if we'd decided to have you spend the night there? Nobody in our family likes Toronto, so we avoid it as much as we can ... But here I am talking away, I'm keeping you awake ... I'll fix up some leftovers from tonight for the train ... You'll be having two meals and their food probably isn't very good ... Now go to sleep, sweetheart."

A hand brushes her forehead, then the light goes out and the bedroom door closes. It's very dark, she's not quite sure now which way is up and which way is down, she feels as if she's floating. Her grandmother would say that she's too tired to sleep. She has to, though, she needs a good night's sleep, but bits of the evening come back to her, images that are blurred because there is so much movement, strong odours of stodgy food and overheated bodies, a whirlwind of powerful sensations that make her feel as if she's flying above her bed.

Eventually she falls asleep, thinking about the archangels that inhabited her dream between Regina and Winnipeg.

✖

The sun has barely risen when they arrive at the station.

This time they're alone – no nervous relatives, no mad race across the waiting room. Rhéauna even has to drag her suitcase while her aunt struggles with the big bag of food she has brought. Bebette tugs Rhéauna with her other hand as if she fears losing her in the crowd that's as dense and hysterical as the one the day before, despite the early hour. They are shoved with no apology, criticized repeatedly for being in the way or not moving fast enough. Bebette lets out two or three well-placed *saperlipopettes* and, each time, a path opens before them as if by magic.

"Your grandmother told me there's someone who's supposed to look after you on the train ..."

"Yes, on the train from Regina his name was Jacques and he was really nice ..."

"Maybe he'll be on this train, too ..."

"I don't think so ... He was just going to Montreal, then he was leaving again for Vancouver ... He does that twice a week during his summer holidays. And I guess that will be his last trip this year ... If we meet him he'll be heading the other direction ... In the train that's going west."

The locomotive is already sending off its plume of smoke, the motor growls, some white vapour escapes from between the wheels of the cars with their doors open.

"Look, there it is, your car ... You're lucky, it's a new one ... Where are you supposed to be meeting that man?"

"I don't know, it must be in the car ... Jacques was waiting for me right at the door, at the top of the steps ..."

"If you ask me it isn't normal to trust your children to strangers like that ... Anyway, I hope he's different from the fellows my husband worked with on the job sites all his life ... I'm telling you,

I wouldn't have trusted my daughter to those men ... Actually I never trusted my daughters to anyone, I wouldn't let them travel, they had enough of their father always being away and I'm glad!"

"It's their job to look after children who are travelling alone, *ma tante* ... or, well, it's part of their job ..."

"I'm sure it is, but I hope they investigate those men before they hire them! With all the raging lunatics on the loose ..."

"He was a student, he's going to be a doctor ... Don't worry, *ma tante.*"

"Students can be crazy, too, you know! If I never worried in my life, little girl, I wouldn't have got where I am today!"

Suddenly she spots someone she knows farther along the platform, sets her bag of food next to her great-niece and runs over.

"Stay there, I won't be long ..."

Rhéauna, worn out, sits on her suitcase and takes a look in the bag. It smells good – roast pork and ham. And mustard. When she got up an hour earlier, she wasn't hungry; but now she would like to plunge her hand into the heap of food and take out a sandwich without crusts, the soft part all moist. Pork or ham, it doesn't matter, she loves them both. She has to wait till noon, though, or be all alone in the car without her dragon-aunt to make her stop eating.

Bebette has just approached a very tall and very slender lady dressed in black who seems to be about to board the train, too. She is standing straight and looks severe, hands folded on her stomach. From a distance, she doesn't look relaxed. Something like a Régina from Manitoba, but much taller. All that Rhéauna hopes is that she won't have to take this long journey in the company of so sad a person ... The hat of the lady in question, battling crows above a foaming nest of tulle, bears some resemblance to Bebette's; they must go to the same hatter. Rhéauna knows they're talking about her because both are looking in her direction. Gesticulating. She has the feeling that she's going to have not one but two guardians during her trip between Winnipeg and Toronto, then Toronto and Ottawa.

The two women approach. Bebette looks relieved; Rhéauna

tells herself that she has guessed correctly. Her aunt dusts her off almost from head to toe, then introduces her as if she were the dirtiest little girl in town even though everything she has on is brand new. "Rhéauna, this is Madame Robillard. Madame Isola Robillard. She's a friend of mine. And she's agreed to look after you during the trip ..."

"But, *ma tante*, there's somebody who is supposed to do that!"

"Two are better than one, *saperlipopette* ... Especially when you know one of them ..."

Madame Isola Robillard smiles at her. It's a lovely smile, a little cold maybe but not without kindness. Still, Rhéauna hopes that the woman won't monopolize her during the journey ... She wants to read, to eat at her own rhythm, to sleep if she feels like it; she has no intention of rhyming off her pedigree to a stranger she'll never see again, just to pass the time.

"Are you going to Ottawa, too?"

The woman leans over to her – in fact, she bends double – though Rhéauna isn't all that small. And she talks as if she were dealing with a four-year-old. Rhéauna thinks to herself, "It's going to be a long trip!"

"No, just to Toronto. I'm going to meet my son. He's a doctor."

"Are you sick?"

"No, no, not at all! Aren't you funny! I'm going for a visit because I haven't seen him for a long time. Since he can't travel because of the operations he does every day, I'm the one who goes to see him."

She straightens up, looks at Bebette.

"I'm not wild about Toronto but what can I do? It's the price I have to pay to see my boy!"

Bebette grabs her niece's suitcase and the bag of food.

"All right, time to board the train, it's about to start. You can tell each other everything during the trip. Now don't ask so many questions, Nana! Madame Robillard is kind enough to look after you but you mustn't bother her! Understand? The journey will take all day and maybe she wants to rest ..."

Isola Robillard lays her hand on Bebette's arm.

"I've just got up, Madame Roy, I definitely don't need any more rest."

Rhéauna thinks that Madame Isola Robillard must like nothing so much as to be asked about her son and all his works, and decides to avoid the subject as much as she can.

Bebette pushes Rhéauna onto the small metal staircase, climbs up behind her.

"I'm going to get you settled ... We'll try to find a quiet spot ..."

A corpulent, red-faced young man appears and Rhéauna realizes that he is her new Jacques. But he doesn't speak a word of French and her English, while passable, won't let her keep up a real conversation. So she'll have to fall back on Madame Isola Robillard if she needs anything. And no doubt put up until the bitter end with her praise of her doctor son in Toronto.

As for Bebette, even though she speaks with an accent you could cut with a knife, she'll be able to make herself understood by Devon, another weird name, and the directions she gives him about Rhéauna are precise, long and detailed.

He tries to protest – is he telling her that he knows his job and to mind her own business? – she won't let herself be impressed and talks non-stop for a good five minutes. She even found a way to pronounce *saperlipopette* as if it were an English word, which sounds perfectly ludicrous; nevertheless, she scatters it through her advice and warnings.

Just as the doors are about to close, Bebette makes a move that amazes Rhéauna. The train whistle has already been sounded two or three times, the ritual *All aboard!* has already rung out several times, too, Devon pushes Bebette toward the door, telling her she'll break her neck if she waits too long before jumping off the train when with no warning, the old lady throws herself at her great-niece, takes her in her arms, hugs her tight and kisses the top of her head.

"Bye, bye, sweetheart! Take care of yourself! Pay attention to your cousin Ti-Lou and don't let your mother push you around!

Fat tears run down her cheeks while she plasters two huge, noisy, fat kisses on Rhéauna.

"The Roys have done their best for you, *saperlipopette*, now it's time for you to look after your own self ... You can do it ... Yes, you can ..."

The car begins to move, Bebette hurries down the steps, turns around and waves, looking grim.

Isola Robillard rubs her earlobe after taking off a mock-diamond rhinestone pendant earring.

"That woman is very high-strung."

Rhéauna replies:

"She's my grandfather's sister! And yesterday she gave me a birthday party even though my birthday isn't for a week!"

"That's what I said! She's high-strung!"

The exchange ends there.

Which doesn't mean that Madame Robillard is silent. One-way conversations don't seem to bother her and, if Rhéauna had been stunned by her great-aunt's monologue during supper, Madame Robillard's has her rooted to the spot. It's an unending stream of pointless words, an inexhaustible and incredibly stupid logorrhea of hackneyed clichés repeated to infinity. She talks as she takes off her hat and gloves, as she positions her sharp backside on the straw seat, as she smoothes the pleats in her long black skirt, as she opens a small suitcase that holds her cosmetics and her medicines – she claims to be sick, rolling her large, protruding eyes – and when she blows her nose. Even that doesn't stop her from talking.

Bebette should have warned her that she'd be coping with a blabbermouth!

She carries on of course about her devotion to her only son, about the sacrifices she has accepted to bring him where he is today – one of the biggest hospitals in Toronto. She also talks about her boy's wife who's not worthy of him and doesn't know how to manage him – Isola's own words – about the children she hasn't given him, depriving her of grandchildren and great-grandchildren. What use is old age, will you tell me, without grandchildren! Then she tackles the subject of the many charitable causes on whose behalf she has exerted herself for years now and that are very lucky to have her because without her ... She talks about people Rhéauna has never met as if they were acquaintances she'd seen the day before or about whom she was dying to have some news. In the first half-hour of the journey, while the train is slowly leaving Winnipeg and its suburbs, Madame Robillard refers to dozens of people by their first names, never explaining who they are, no doubt taking it for granted that everyone knows the same people she does and that Rhéauna will be able to sort them out.

Not once does she ask the little girl how she feels, if she wants anything to drink or eat, if she needs to go to the bathroom, what she thinks of being required to join her mother in Montreal, an unknown and dangerous city. The only time she refers to it in fact is for a long-winded anecdote several decades old about a visit she and her son Denis had paid to that dreadful place in mid–heat wave that ends with an unusually violent diatribe, a sentence without appeal:

"You think it's hot out west in the summer? If you want to know what a real heat wave is, little girl, just try Montreal in July. True, you'll be there next July ... Anyway, you'll see for yourself that I'm right! It's worse than hot, it's sticky! Myself, I wouldn't live there for all the gold in the world. Especially not in summer! We're lucky here in Saint-Boniface and we don't even know it. That's what I tell them all the time but I don't think anybody listens to me. Though I'm not stingy with my advice! But no, they behave as if they don't hear me. Everyone! Even my own son!"

Rhéauna stopped listening to her a while ago. She is resting her head on the window and looking outside, trying to mix Madame Robillard's voice with the sound – clackety-clack, clackety-clack, clackety-clack – produced when the wheels of the train rub against the metal rails. Another repetitious motif.

The landscape that unfurls before her eyes is as repetitious as

Madame Robillard's soliloquy or the sound of the train. Rhéauna wonders when she will leave behind these tunnels with no exit. She won't get to Toronto until suppertime and to Ottawa very late at night. Is Madame Robillard going to talk like that all the way to Toronto? And never stop?

Fields, more fields, fields with no end. Is Canada nothing but an enormous field of grain? With no horizon? She has been promised a mountain in Montreal, but Montreal will turn out to be nothing but a field of wheat like the others, a super-size Sainte-Maria-de-Saskatchewan church with a mountain in the middle to make it a little different? Lost in the plains? Can you hear the corn grow in Montreal?

Devon has come to see her several times but she doesn't understand a thing he says and merely nods. Like an idiot. Isola Robillard has offered to translate; Rhéauna turned her down, claiming to understand perfectly well everything Devon says to her.

Her first meal on the train – wolfed down in third gear when they were crossing a fairly large town whose name she couldn't see – is accompanied by disjointed comments from the old biddy who skips from one subject to another without even seeming to notice. To fill the time, thinks Rhéauna, or because she can't stand silence. Rhéauna could plug her ears but she won't; she knows that would be impolite. And so she lets Madame Isola Robillard gab away all she wants while she tries to focus her attention on what's going on outside. Which turns out to be harder than she'd have thought. After all, some of the stories are very sad, some fates frankly tragic, that's all very interesting, she can't deny – diseases horrible and violent, incredible accidents, zany separations – and above all, she doesn't believe that one person on her own could know so many unfortunate destinies. In the end, her accumulation of insoluble calamities and irreversible catastrophes bores her to tears.

She is about to fall asleep, she feels numb, her eyes close by themselves – the delicious but so heavy pork sandwich (with fat from the roast) that she just ate probably has something to do with it – when some twinkling in the distance, a nearly imperceptible movement behind the trees that line the railway tracks, a shimmering across what seems to be an enormous flat surface attracts her attention. She presses her forehead against the window.

Water! It's water! As far as the eye can see! There! Very close, just behind the edge of the trees! She's never seen so much water in her whole life! At least not since she left Rhode Island, but that was too long ago, she's forgotten everything about Rhode Island. It shimmers, it gleams, it shatters into broken lines of waves that crash onto the shore, and sunbeams broken into a thousand pieces that wash onto the riverbank seem to be floating over it all for the sheer pleasure.

She stands up on the seat – who cares about good manners? – and presses her hands on the glass.

"There's the ocean, Madame Robillard, look at the ocean!"

"The ocean! Honestly, Rhéauna! We're in the middle of the country! There's no ocean in the middle of Canada! What's in the middle of Canada, Rhéauna?"

She leans across the space between their seats.

"I asked you something, Rhéauna, what's in the middle of Canada? You must know, they must have taught you in that god-forsaken hole in Saskatchewan!"

"The Great Lakes. The Great Lakes are in the middle of Canada."

"So why did you say it's the ocean?"

"There's so much water, Madame Robillard! It can't be just a lake! It has to be an ocean! A lake is small, you can swim in it, it dries up in the summer and turns into a duck pond! But that … That … It can't dry up, there's too much water, it's too big, it's too beautiful!"

"There's a reason it's called the Great Lakes, little girl … We've just passed Fort William so it must be Lake Superior you can see and it's not salt water. It's not a sea. Seas are way farther away, ahead of the train and in back of it. Far away. I've never seen them because I don't want to go that far, not to the east or to the west.

We're going to turn south in a little while and head for Toronto. Where we are now I can say that I'm halfway there ..."

And resumes her monologue where she'd left off: her sister-in-law Aline came over for a cup of tea the other night to tell her some incredible tale about an eccentric travelling salesman, one Michel Blondin, who ...

On the pretext of an urgent need to pee, Rhéauna gets off the seat and rushes toward the toilet. She meets Devon, who asks where she's going. She tries to explain in English but he doesn't understand and finally she indicates the bathroom door. He blushes to the roots of his hair and lets her go.

But she doesn't go into the smallest room, which probably stinks to high heaven. (Her grandmother warned her never to use the toilets in public places, not even when she gets to Montreal, because you never know who's just come out and what they might have left behind that's dirty and dangerous. Bugs, diseases, nameless and deadly ... Not to mention the smells. It's fine to put up with your own family's smells, it's nature, but not strangers', I mean, really!)

There is a door just ahead of the little room that she wants to avoid. Rhéauna leans on it, puts her forehead close to the rectangular glass.

It's so beautiful!

The train is now closer to the water, there's an opening in the curtain of trees, the railway track now follows the vastness of Lake Superior.

She has dreamed since early childhood about the oceans described in the books she's read, she has spent hours over the black-and-white illustrations of raging waves or slack seas, stocked with boats or not. It was all magnificent and made you want to take off, to see salt water rise up, agitated, at the slightest wind; the skies pouring out in colossal, destructive torrents; ships trying to clear a way and end up they never know where, but nothing had prepared her for what she sees before her. For the movement. Especially the movement. The water's undulation, the gigantic mobility, the monumental breathing she'd have been unable to imagine when she was splashing around in the calm little ponds outside Maria.

The train follows the shore and the waves, unimpressive as they actually are, that seem to her like mountains in motion, for she has only seen very small spurs of water lap at shores that weren't even beaches.

She has pressed both her hands on the glass, stuck her face there. She wishes she could shed her clothes, shed her skin even. She doesn't know what that means but all at once she feels an irresistible urge to take off her well-behaved, obedient-little-girl's outfit – the coat that's too big, the ridiculous hat, the brand-new, Nile-green dress, though she thinks it's so pretty, the socks, the shoes, the white cotton underpants – to be stark naked on the shore of Lake Superior. Then she would remove her skin, which is also a costume, a kind of disguise that hides something more important, *herself,* that hides herself, she's sure of it. She would fold her bones, pack them in her suitcase and leave behind what was left of her ... What? Her soul? ... At least that's what the fat priest in Sainte-Maria-de-Saskatchewan would maintain, yes, she would allow her soul to dive into the sea. Because it is a sea, an inland sea, not salt water maybe but still a sea. Her soul would sink straight to the bottom, among the reeds, the cattails, pebbles, fish, and she would go and live with them, planted in the silt at the exact centre of her journey between Maria and Montreal. A place that *she* would have chosen. From the bottom of the water she would watch once a day as the train went by heading east and tell herself that she'd nearly – oh, it was so long ago – gone to the end of the railway line, to a mythic city in the province of Quebec, an island with a real, big mountain, where everyone spoke French and her mother was waiting for her.

She wishes that the train would come to a halt, that the panorama before her eyes would freeze, that time would stop. To let a lost little girl be found. At the bottom of the water.

Then the train negotiates a slight turn toward the south en route to Toronto and the sunset sweeps over everything. The sky turns from calm to fire.

She has seen sunsets before, though. Sitting on Grandpa Méo's knees, she was often thrilled by the yellows and the oranges floating over the fields of grain behind the house, their two heads strained toward the west where Méo claimed that the day would end in the swirls of the Pacific after it had hooked its feet into the Rocky Mountains. Méo also said that it was the most beautiful moment of the day, of every day, the blessed hour when you had to be silent before such grandeur and look at it and thank providence – he didn't like the word *God* – for having invented it simply for the pleasure of our eyes. So that the farmer who worked like an animal all day long can tell himself that his day hasn't been wasted.

But a *double* sunset, what a gift! First the sunset itself, magic and sublime, then as well its reflection blurred by the movement of the waves, its colours transformed by the water, the red becoming gold streaked with green, the gold becoming green streaked with red, the clouds looking at each other's belly, comparing themselves and sizing one another up self-importantly, vying for the light, all mixed together, stirred, overturned, inverted, the top half solemn, impressive, the lower half furious and wild. A silent end of the world, a symphony without music.

She wants to stay! Here! Now! Wants this moment never to end. Wants the train to not advance. Wants the sun to not move. Wants the little girl gazing at it all to exist only plunged into the mad colours. A painting. That couldn't be hung anywhere because it would be too beautiful.

A hand on her shoulder. The perfume of old lady unique to Isola Robillard, her exasperating voice.

"I was getting worried, I thought you'd been taking a long time. I was afraid you couldn't find the toilet."

Then she in turn glances out the window, bringing her hand to her heart.

"It's true, it really is beautiful, eh?"

And goes on without even catching her breath.

"It's exactly what I was saying to your aunt Bebette the other day when she came to bring back my big kettle that I cook my beans in ... Madame Roy, I say to her, in your opinion, now tell me honestly, there's no one around ... is there anything in the world more beautiful than ..."

✗

Isola Robillard is well aware that she talks too much. She's been called a chatterbox, a blabbermouth, she's been threatened count-less times with being shut up by force, eventually she isolated herself – her son and daughter-in-law in Toronto are terrified at the prospect of her arrival – but she talks and talks, over and over with no end, to herself or to everybody, not because she's afraid of silence, that would be too easy, she'd just have to leave the house, throw herself into the crowd and listen to the unremitting din of the city; no, the reason lies elsewhere.

Actually, she is afraid of being boring. And every day of her life, since her husband's death, she turns nasty to avoid being invisible. If only she were unaware of it, if others went into hiding to talk about her neurosis, if they laughed at her behind her back, but no, she knows it, it's repeated to her non-stop. "Will you keep quiet, Madame Robillard?" (Her butcher who starts to curse every time he sees her come into his shop.) "Will you shut your trap once and for all or I'll tear your guts out!" (Her brothers and sisters who do everything they can to avoid her, but she always manages to discover where they're hiding.) She simply can't help talking. She is convinced that she'll disappear into the scenery unless she talks, that people will forget she exists, look right through her, go around her with nary a look in her direction, that she'll always be isolated at the bottom of a hole of silence – Isola the isolated, that thought comes to her twenty times a week – disconnected from everything, crazy from loneliness. The stupid old woman with nothing to say.

She hasn't ever been fascinating, that, too, she knows. She has no gift for conversation, or very little, she couldn't care less what goes on outside her immediate world, her family, her own little bits and pieces, her banal problems. Her husband resembled her, they spent decades not needing anyone else, brought up children who soon turned away from them because of their lack of curiosity, while at Ernest's death – her Ernest, the love of her life, her man – she came up against a wall of silence, all alone in her house with nothing to say. And no one to say it to. Then she started talking nonsense to just about anyone to remind people that she still exists, to avoid being thought dull because she's too discreet or too shy. Or else … She has long since chosen not to think about it. Maybe madness. In any case, despair.

She is looking at the little girl sitting opposite her now that night has fallen, she knows that she's pestering the child with her constant chattering, but someone is looking at her, or at least pretending! It's better than nothing. If she didn't talk to this little girl she would feel as if she didn't exist all the way from Winnipeg to Toronto, so almost without catching her breath she says whatever springs to mind about whoever springs to mind, she gets dizzy, she jumps from one subject to another, laughs at jokes that she knows are laboured, she drowns the poor child in a flood of names and anecdotes of no interest to convince herself that she's still alive, to avoid being in her own eyes the most boring person in Creation.

She is worse than boring, she's unbearable, but at least someone knows that she exists!

Devon brought her something to eat. Which she put aside as soon as his back was turned to dig into the final sandwich – lettuce, ham, mustard – from Bebette. The meat is chopped fine and tastes of cloves, the crustless bread is saturated with mustard, there's even a hint of butter; it's luscious. After all those hours of pointless chit-chat, Rhéauna has finally managed to disregard the old woman, and while she chews she looks out as the lit-up farms – some even have electricity – speed by in her field of vision. Pinpricks of yellow light on a black silk curtain. The night is moonless so it's possible to see millions of stars through the barrier of fir trees that come very close to the railway. The milk that Devon brought her is just a tiny bit too warm for her liking but she doesn't get upset and takes long gulps, being very careful not to let any of it run onto her chin or her cheeks. The last serving of the pink-and-green cake is down – more icing was left than cake, which made her very happy – she stuffs into the now-empty bag the greasy paper, the crumbs of bread and cake, the paper napkin on which she has just wiped her mouth and she gets up to look for a bigger wastebasket than the one hanging under the window.

At that very moment, Madame Robillard leans over, places one hand above her eyes and presses her nose against the window.

"We're arriving in Toronto. See how beautiful it is!"

Rhéauna places the bag on the seat, comes back to the window.

Something that looks like a huge yellow boat stands out in the distance. A long ribbon of light, like the reflection of the starry sky but in shades of gold and copper. Soon it covers the horizon, comes closer, then disappears because the train is turning south. The pitch-black night comes back, the sky falls again, swooping over everything. Rhéauna has the impression that she's just experienced a hallucination, that she didn't really see a yellow ribbon of light, that it was a remote reflection, maybe the northern lights in the middle of the summer ... Northern lights on the ground instead of in the sky? No, impossible. It was Toronto, all right. Then it comes back, even closer, so dazzling that it's nearly disturbing. She has never seen so many electric lights in one place; it's more than beautiful, it's sublime. And so imposing that it's frightening. The train – a foolhardy butterfly in front of an oil lamp – is quickly swallowed up by the shimmering golden light. And for the first time, it is lit from outside: the lighting coming from outside is stronger than that which it projects into the night. It is now drowned in light, it passes quickly, it runs along every side, houses go by at full speed, streets are lit up, too, and viaducts that straddle the railroad. Three prolonged whistle blasts, the train starts to slow down. Brand-new warehouses come closer, a station even more imposing, more gigantic than the one in Regina, than the one in Winnipeg, a lantern of unimaginable proportions, swallows up the train that's now surrounded by hundreds and hundreds of parallel tracks forming an inextricable network of intersecting roads that run in every direction before they end up at an incalculable number of concrete platforms.

Madame Robillard has of course been holding forth non-stop but this time, Rhéauna doesn't hear her, plunged as she is in the bath of light.

The platform is packed with people waiting to board the train. The stretch between Toronto and Ottawa is a very busy one and the train is a little late. Impatient travellers holding suitcases are already craning their necks in search of cars that aren't too full.

Madame Robillard puts on her coat, her crows' nest, her gloves, all the while commenting on what's going on outside. She describes to Rhéauna what they can both see perfectly well, the idiot! Then she concludes as she places herself right in front of the little girl.

"I want you to know, you won't be on your own to Ottawa, poor child ... I hope that Devon will take good care of you ... At night there aren't the same people as in daytime, you never know who you're travelling with … In any case, good luck. Say hello to your mother for me. I've never met her but I've heard a lot about her …"

No hug and no kiss, not even a handshake, she turns her back, walks away, erect as a fence picket painted black.

Devon appears, looking busy, and gestures to Rhéauna to stay where she is, most likely to let her know that she's not in Ottawa yet. As if she didn't know. Then he disappears with the bag she wanted to throw out.

The new passengers are noisier than those who've just left the train. Some, crimson-faced and out of breath, reek of alcohol, and Rhéauna hopes that she won't have to deal with a bunch of drunken uncles who will shout and tell stories she won't understand while they keep sucking at their forty ounces of gin on the sly. But Devon arrives with what seems to be a family: a father, a mother, two children – boys – people who speak French as well and who sit down beside her. The boys give her a look, frowning, a funny look; she chooses to ignore them and pretends to be asleep.

She falls asleep for real even before the train leaves the platform in Toronto.

DREAM ON THE TRAIN TO OTTAWA

This time she dares.

She jumps into the water. A standing jump.

It's cold. Not too cold, though. The water makes the light ripple around her but to her astonishment she's not surrounded by waterweeds or fish. At the bottom of the water fish live and weeds grow, everyone knows that, and a multitude of creatures move about that aren't even fish, so they say – the whale, for example, an animal that lives underwater though it's a mammal. Here, no. The ocean, or Lake Superior, or that mere pond she's just jumped into that's empty.

And she can breathe there!

She brings one hand to her neck, checks to see if gills have sprouted without her knowledge. She remembers enjoying the class about gill structures at the local school in Sainte-Maria-de-Saskatchewan. She laughs, she imagines being able to breathe underwater, not having to keep coming up to the surface, spend hours, days, her lifetime under water. Swim between the sunbeams. Filter oxygen with the help of her gills. Play with her sisters, who've also become mammals that live underwater though they aren't fish.

So now that it is possible, she is alone in the midst of the sunbeams, without her sisters, without fish, without waterweeds, without air …

She lacks air! She must go back to the surface! She lacks air! No, it's all right, she can breathe. Something that isn't air. Water from deep in the ocean. Or the lake. Or the pond.

But what will become of her, all alone in the empty water? It's liable to be long, isn't it? She's not going to stay like that, hands sketching a little waltz ahead of her in the undulating sunbeams, with nothing to do and no one to talk to, is she?

The world is at one and the same time empty and filled with liquid. And she can't even manage to drown ... Because she can breathe the water. In spite of herself.

Then, in the distance, a silhouette takes shape.

She liked very much the story of the little mermaid in love with a human, who grows two beautiful legs that let her move around on terra firma, to the great displeasure of her father, king of the Tritons. Maybe she's the one that's arriving. The Little Mermaid in Andersen's story comes to meet her opposite, the little human girl without gills but able to breathe under water. She looks at her feet. No, and no fish tail either. She hasn't turned into a mermaid.

But the silhouette that's approaching is not that of a delicate redhaired girl with a robe of seashells and a fish tail covered with shiny emerald-green scales. It's that of a woman. Staggeringly beautiful. With an irresistible smile. And who gestures to her as if they knew one another, as if they were reunited after a long separation. A friend, a close friend, who might replace her sisters, with whom she could chatter away as much as she wanted, confide her child's secrets in the middle of the empty water. No, no one can replace Béa and Alice, and no one is to know about the sorrow and bad luck she's suffering now. Especially not a stranger, no matter how beautiful, how friendly, how much of a mermaid she may be!

The little mermaid who is now an adult opens her mouth, speaks. But what she says is incomprehensible.

The new mermaid tries to turn around, to move away, but her feet are caught in the mud. She flaps her arms, she can't breathe, can't breathe underwater without gills ... The fish-woman approaches her, touches her shoulder, shakes her.

Rhéauna wakes with a start. Devon is bending over her. He tells her something, pointing to the window. She understands that they must have arrived in Ottawa while she was asleep. He's probably telling her that she has to get off the train. She's soaking wet, cold sweat is running down her forehead as far as her neck. She's afraid she has a fever. No, her forehead is cool. It's just a remnant of fear. Of dying. It will pass. It passes. It's over.

She thanks Devon in her version of English.

4

TI-LOU

✖

Never in her life has she seen a woman so beautiful. Or so elegant. Leafing through the Eaton's catalogue, she often admired the drawings of fashionable ladies in flattering poses, with their unbelievably elaborate and varicoloured hats, holding a parasol, their waist squeezed by corsets too small for them (those are Grandma Joséphine's words), perfect women who – again according to Grandma Joséphine – didn't really exist. Rhéauna admired them with a smile, ran her index finger over the drawings, dreamed of one day wearing birds on her head or gloves as long as that, though suspecting it was most unlikely. Grandma Joséphine had also explained to her that those women were only used to sell products, dresses, hats, shoes, accessories, undergarments, that you couldn't look like that and walk down the street:

"Can you just see yourself, sweetheart, trying to walk on our wooden sidewalk in the middle of winter dressed like that? With boots as thin as those? Or to cross the road in April? Through the horse buns? Even on the church steps after Sunday Mass, you'd be a laughing stock! Or at the height of summer when the earth is dry because it hasn't rained for weeks! No, no, no, those women are just catalogue people!"

She has one in front of her, though, dressed even better than in the ads, not so slender, it's true, more plump, but beautiful like it isn't possible to be so beautiful, with a radiant smile that's barely concealed by a little black veil dotted with tiny mauve silk butterflies, her eyes shining, her waist – nearly as slim as Rhéauna's – in a lilac cotton dress that drags just a little along the platform. And perfume that brings tears to your eyes. It smells of flowers from exotic lands that are new to Rhéauna, that grow in tropical forests where it's hot and rainy all year long. Flowers from novels that don't exist in real life either.

The sight of her so radiant beside the train, you might think she was getting ready to travel around the world. Or is coming back from it.

As soon as she spots Rhéauna, the beautiful woman heads for her confidently, then leans over to speak to her.

"You're Rhéauna, aren't you? Maria's girl? I knew you right away because you look just like her ... I haven't seen Maria for years but I'd recognize those eyes anywhere! They aren't eyes that you've got, they're two pieces of coal! And me, I'm Ti-Lou."

Too impressed to speak, or even to hold out her hand the way you're supposed to when you meet a stranger, Rhéauna blushes to the roots of her hair and looks down.

This time, the lady practically bends double to talk to her.

"You aren't afraid of me, are you? I'm your mother's cousin, daughter of her aunt Gertrude who's the sister of her mother, your grandmother Joséphine ... But maybe that's a bit complicated for a tired little girl like you? You'll spend the night at my place. A short night because it's now practically midnight!"

She thanks Devon in English, holds out some money. Now it's his turn to blush. He stammers, trembles a little as he pockets the bill. Ti-Lou merely smiles as if she were used to provoking this kind of reaction in men.

A gentleman arrives with a kind of metal wheelbarrow that makes a deafening noise, loads Rhéauna's suitcase into it and sets off without a word. Before the little girl's look of panic, Ti-Lou lays a hand on her shoulder.

"He's a porter ... he's going to carry your suitcase for you; don't worry, he won't run away with it! Say good night to the gentleman who looked after you on the train, thank him, too, then we'll go ..."

Rhéauna thanks Devon. In English. He looks thrilled, says something that's incomprehensible because he talks so fast, and waddles away.

The little girl doesn't have time to gaze at all the wonders of Ottawa's magnificent railroad station. Ti-Lou and Rhéauna cross it in less than thirty seconds, following close on the heels of the porter whose wheelbarrow is creaking louder than ever.

They go out into the sticky night. Not much traffic now. And no battle between streetcars and automobiles. A small square, empty. Lit by electricity. Rhéauna hesitates between surprise and disappointment.

"You've come a long way. You must be tired to death!"

Rhéauna can barely get out something that resembles a little protest. Ti-Lou stops short in the middle of the entrance to the station.

"Now listen. You're going to have to talk to me! Are you always mute like that? Are you?"

Rhéauna has just one thing in her head, to ask Madame Ti-Lou for the name of her perfume or at least the names of the flowers that it's made from. There might be some names that she knows, that she thinks are beautiful, like gardenia, or jasmine. But she's too overawed.

Ti-Lou sighs, takes her hand, pulls her along. At the bottom of the steps she holds up her right arm with deliberate carelessness. And the most beautiful carriage in the world stops in front of them: small, all black, very high, square, incredibly elegant. The horses drawing it, black as well, have been so well curried, they gleam in the night. Even Bebette's carriage, though it's exceptional, would look like a poor person's next to this one!

Rhéauna can finally exclaim:

"That carriage is so beautiful, *ma tante* Ti-Lou!"

Ti-Lou looks at her as if she's just said something extremely stupid.

"It's just a carriage you know! A phaeton."

She gives her a little shove to make her get into the phaeton.

"And in just a little while I'll be getting around in an automobile!"

It smells of new leather, fresh paint, it's comfortable, the night is mild; Rhéauna forgets how tired she is. Drowned in Ti-Lou's perfume she rests her head on the back of her seat and envies this distant relation who has the means to buy ... a what is it, a fa- something, how do you say it, in fact, and how on earth do you write it? She knows that in the future it will be one of her favourite words. Not so much because of how it sounds – nearly funny – but how it smells. New leather and gardenia. They cross a small city, sleeping and silent. Rhéauna can't believe that it is the capital of her country, one of the biggest in the world, one of the most beautiful, most influential. According to her grandfather anyway. Few lights, deserted streets, the sound of horses' hooves echoing off stately dwellings that seem abandoned. A big Sainte-Maria-de-Saskatchewan after midnight. She nearly expects to see Monsieur Connells's general store loom up at some street corner or to hear the voice of old man Lacasse, the village drunk who only sings at night so he'll be sure that he disturbs everybody.

She finally undoes her new coat that she put on before getting off the train, despite the heat, to make a good impression. She feels relaxed, she wants to know more about Ti-Lou. You can't be as beautiful as she is and not have an interesting life!

"You're lucky you can go around in this! Is your husband rich?"

Ti-Lou breaks out in a lovely rippling laugh that rises up in the night to get lost somewhere in the stars.

"I'm not even married, Rhéauna … Do you think you absolutely need a rich husband to be able to pay for a phaeton?"

"Umm … yes."

"Well, you're wrong! I'll have you know, I don't have the slightest need for a husband to pay for everything I buy myself!"

"So who pays for it?"

"I just told you. I do. Me, myself and I!"

Rhéauna runs her hand over the leather seat, enjoys its suppleness, its softness.

"You must work hard! Do you work here, in the city? What do you do?"

Ti-Lou's laugh rings out again, longer this time, with a final snort that's not nearly as pretty as the cascade of trills before.

"How old are you, Rhéauna?"

"I'll be eleven next week …"

"You should be old enough to understand this ... Have you ever heard the word *guidoune?*"

Yes, Rhéauna has heard it. Many times. Especially about Madame Cantin who lives in a house that stands on its own just outside Maria, of whom it's said that she only earns her living after sunset. And on her back. But her grandparents have always refused to explain what that means. And she can't imagine how a person can earn their living after nightfall. Lying down in bed.

"Yes, I've heard that word. There's one of them in Maria. But I don't know what exactly it is that she does ..."

This time, Ti-Lou doesn't laugh. She lays her hand on Rhéauna's, squeezes it very gently.

"A *guidoune*, Rhéauna, is an independent woman."

Rhéauna can't imagine just what that means but she nods so that her cousin won't think she's too stupid.

"And an independent woman isn't somebody people approve of ... You still don't understand, do you?"

Why hide it? Rhéauna shakes her head.

Ti-Lou heaves a sigh, looks at the little river on their left, which seems to cut the city in two.

"Well, it's not up to me to explain. Especially not tonight. One day you'll understand and you'll be able to boast that you've met a real one, one of the best, one of the most professional, one of the most conscientious – the great Ti-Lou, the she-wolf of Ottawa."

The she-wolf of Ottawa? Rhéauna is wide-eyed. A she-wolf! She's just compared herself to a wild animal!

Ti-Lou runs her hand through Rhéauna's hair.

"It's just a way of speaking, Rhéauna. That's something else you'll understand someday."

She bends down, kisses her on the cheek.

"Meanwhile, I don't know what I'd give to have those eyes of yours ..."

The phaeton turns left, goes up a road made of big rounded bricks of a kind that Rhéauna has never seen ... and stops in front of a palace that's right across from the station!

Rhéauna raises her arm, points.

"We just had to cross the street!"

Ti-Lou hides her confusion, shaking her little veil.

"That's right!"

"Why didn't you come and get me on foot?"

Ti-Lou starts as if Rhéauna had slapped her.

"You'll learn, little girl, that the she-wolf of Ottawa never goes out on foot! Not even to cross the street! I wanted to show you a little of Ottawa before you go to bed."

Rhéauna turns toward the building in front of which the phaeton has just come to a halt. The structure is so immense that even the illustrations in her fairy-tale books pale in comparison. It's a gigantic edifice of stone and brick with towers, dormers, countless windows all lit up. It's the only building in this part of town or maybe in the entire city that displays a little life at this late hour. A great stone ship plunked down on a hill. Unmoving in the night. A gentleman in a costume, standing at the main door, approaches their carriage, opens the door, extends his hand to help her out. Welcomes her. In English of course.

Ti-Lou slips him a banknote as she'd done earlier with Devon, leans across to Rhéauna.

"Welcome to the Château Laurier, Rhéauna."

So it is a castle! She's going to spend the night in a real castle!

"Is this where you live?"

Ti-Lou smiles, stands very upright, raises her head defiantly.

"Since last year. Since it opened. I was there for the inauguration. In the presence of Monsieur Sir Wilfrid Laurier in person!"

"It isn't an old castle?"

"It's brand new! It still smells of paint and carpet cement!"

"But it looks like something from a fairy tale ..."

"That's the idea, child. The Château Laurier was built to make people dream. For those in power – the corridors are full of them going back and forth at every hour of the day and night, plotting, arguing, deciding; see, this is where most cabinet ministers have their headquarters – so that those in power think they've arrived for good, that it will never end, that they've moved into a castle, a real castle and nobody will ever throw them out! And me, well I'm the *damsel in distress* that has to be saved, Sleeping Beauty who has to be wakened, the Little Match Girl who has to be protected – or the she-wolf who has to be tamed. The jackpot, you might say. They're so naive!"

In the hotel's lobby – almost bigger than the Ottawa train station – everybody greets them. Rhéauna wonders what they're all doing here in the middle of the night. They're fashionable, busy, some as stiff as chair rungs behind their marble counters that in fact resemble the ticket wickets in all the train stations she's visited over the past three days. With nothing to sell, though. She imagines that they're too polite to be sincere and all, without exception, greet Ti-Lou with low bows and by her first name preceded by *Madame*: "Good evening again, Madame Ti-Lou," "You weren't gone very long, Madame Ti-Lou," "Your cousin is very cute, Madame Ti-Lou."

Rhéauna thinks that her second cousin must be a really important woman if everybody greets her like that. Ti-Lou pulls off her gloves with studied nonchalance, stops at an enormous mirror after lifting her veil, seems to like what she sees.

"Before you ask, Rhéauna, no, I don't own the Château Laurier. I just rent a suite on the top floor."

Rhéauna looks up.

"A *sweet*? What's a *sweet*?"

Ti-Lou shrugs.

"A *suite*, a *suite*, I meant a *suite*, Rhéauna, if you absolutely insist on speaking French."

"So what is it?"

Ti-Lou explains, pushing her toward the elevator. Rhéauna, who didn't know that elevators existed, is flabbergasted when Ti-Lou explains that the metal cage replaces stairs, that it climbs up by itself and will take them in a matter of seconds to the top floor of the Château Laurier, where her *sweet* is lodged. The royal *sweet*.

So this is a hotel. In some of the novels she's read there are descriptions of hotels far away, in Europe; she has also seen reproductions in old magazines but never would she have imagined that one could be so imposing. A genuine castle where you can rent rooms! And *sweets*!

An old gentleman in gloves opens the door for them and, bowing slightly, ushers them into the square compartment decorated in the same style as the train that Rhéauna has just left: shining metal and carved wood. Ti-Lou gives the man a big smile.

"You're still here, Monsieur Lapointe? You haven't gone to bed? It's past midnight, there's no elevator attendant at night ..."

The old gentleman flushes, coughs into his fist.

"You told me you wouldn't be gone very long, Madame Ti-Lou ... I waited for you to make your last trip of the day ... I wish you a good night, Madame Ti-Lou."

Ti-Lou places her hand on his shoulder. He blushes even more. Rhéauna has the impression that he's liable to pass out between floors. Just because Ti-Lou touched him? The man is sick ...

The corridor they turn onto when they leave the elevator is wide, silent, dimly lit. Ti-Lou takes a very ornate key from her purse. They stop at a door; it smells good already.

The suite in question – it's number 809 – is a cave with thick carpets, richly coloured silk, spotless lace placed here and there with skilful negligence, heavy brocade curtains and pictures that depict ladies scantily clad or frankly naked dancing before beaming men, themselves dressed from head to toe, or serving them drinks.

And everything smells so good – the same scent that follows Ti-Lou everywhere of course, that Rhéauna has decided is gardenia, but all sorts of other things, too, heavier, that go to your head, that tickle your nose in the strangest way – that the little girl stops on the doorstep, wondering if she will be able to put up with it all night without suffocating.

"C'mon in, don't be scared, I won't eat you!"

Ti-Lou tosses her purse, hat and gloves onto the first sofa she encounters, takes off her shoes – little soft leather boots in a colour that's neither black nor brown – sinks into a wing chair covered in pale-green satin.

"You don't know how much you're costing me, little girl ... My evening cut in two, my night cancelled ... But I shouldn't tell you that, it's not very nice of me ... I'm sorry ..."

Rhéauna doesn't know what she is talking about and answers her with a shrug.

"I'm glad to see you, Rhéauna, and I'm glad to do Maria a favour ..."

Rhéauna has put her suitcase in a corner and is still standing in front of the closed door.

"People call me Nana ... Nobody calls me by my whole first name."

Ti-Lou beckons her to come closer, helps her take off her coat.

"Why, don't you like your name? It's one you don't often hear, you should be proud of it ..."

"No, it isn't that ... Nana's just easier ..."

"All right, Nana, okay, just step back a little so I can look at you properly ..."

She examines her from head to toe. It's an embarrassing look, inquisitive, the look of someone who knows all about what she's seeing and doesn't let anything pass. It lingers on her face which it itemizes attentively.

"You're going to be awfully pretty, Nana. But you mustn't eat things that make you put on weight ..."

How does she know that? Rhéauna tilts her head, looks at her arms, her legs.

"It doesn't show yet. But you have to watch out."

"I know, Grandma's always telling me that."

"How is *ma tante* Joséphine? I haven't seen her since I was a tiny child ..."

The next few minutes are filled with news about Maria, Regina, Winnipeg, about distant relatives in the prairies, people Ti-Lou has long since done her best to forget and that this very lovely little girl is reviving with her pretty western accent and her colourful language. Perfumes of childhood come back to her and Ti-Lou sees herself visiting Bebette or Joséphine at a time when her mother, Gertrude, made it her duty to take the train at least once a year to visit her sisters and brother and their families. Or to get away from the tyranny of her lawyer husband, Wilson. Simplicity. The simplicity of it all. The stupidity, too. Ignorance. Of the outside world. Wealth. Power. A comfortable little life with no real need to know anything else. Everything her cousin Maria, for instance, has rejected to launch herself into the whole wide world. Early in her career, when things weren't moving as quickly as she wanted, she surprised herself envying the family of wanderers scattered across the continent, with their discreet little lives made up of humble deeds infinitely repeated with one goal – to get something to eat and clothes to put on their backs. Why not adopt that lethargic and carefree peace in the midst of the wheat fields? But she quickly took herself in hand, shook herself off, refused to let herself drift into pointless daydreaming – how can you choose poverty when you're born into the bourgeoisie of Ottawa like her, when you've always known money, luxury, when you've tasted champagne and caviar? – and dove back with false breeziness into the mass of men in rut who were always hanging around her and could well make her fortune.

Timid at first, Rhéauna relaxes as she speaks. Inflamed by the details she brings to her descriptions of Maria and its inhabitants, she gradually approaches her cousin and sits carefully on a lemon-yellow sofa that looks almost shiny in the semi-darkness. She takes off her shoes, too, rubs her feet like Ti-Lou. Her movements are graceful, her vocabulary amazing for her age; Ti-Lou listens to her with delight. When she has finished, Rhéauna crosses her hands on her knees, tilts her head.

"That's all. And I'm really tired. I'd like to go to bed ..."

Ti-Lou has made ready sheets, a pillow, a blanket which they place on the lemon-yellow sofa. Rhéauna takes her nightgown out of her suitcase.

"Where's the bathroom? I have to brush my teeth ..."

The bathroom is even more impressive than the rest of the suite: white porcelain everywhere, faucets that look like gold, mirrors on all four walls, electric sconces that imitate candelabra, towels – rose, lilac, mauve, crushed raspberry – as big as sheets. Alas, she doesn't have time to linger there ...

Once she has finished washing she comes back to the living room, slips under the sheet – satin, a little too cold for her liking but so soft! – and says good night to Ti-Lou, who has come to sit next to her on the sofa.

"Thank you for letting me stay here, *ma tante* Ti-Lou, and excuse me if I'm bothering you."

Ti-Lou runs her hand through the little girl's hair, leans over to kiss her forehead. The gardenia smell is nearly suffocating.

"You aren't bothering me, Nana. Not one bit. And please, don't call me *ma tante*! We're cousins! Distant cousins but cousins anyway! But don't call me cousin either, that sounds like an old maid, call me just Ti-Lou. Ti-Lou, period."

She seems hesitant to leave. Now it's her turn to cross her hands on her knees and tilt her head. She makes up her mind, looks Rhéauna straight in the eyes.

"You're leaving the country and moving to a big city ... Keep your eyes open, Nana. I know that your grandmother must have warned you but *ma tante* Joséphine has never lived in a big city, she doesn't know what it's really like ..."

She hesitates again, gropes for her words, starts to get up, changes her mind.

"What I mean is ... You look like a bright little girl, Nana, and all I can tell you is watch out and don't let anyone get the better of you. I know it's not up to me to tell you about those things, it's up to your mother, but she can be rough and it could come out the wrong way and frighten you. I don't want to scare you, just warn you ..."

Rhéauna, who was about to fall asleep, opens her eyes.

"Warn me about what?"

Ti-Lou gives her a big smile in which Rhéauna would like to lose herself, to find herself every night before she falls asleep, to dream about, to feed on to help her get through difficult moments that she will probably experience in the big city, to make it her refuge. Forever.

"When you grow up, you'll realize that we live in a world made by men, for men ... and often against women ... It's been like that since the beginning of time, it can't be changed and women who try get laughed at ... They walk around with banners demanding the right to vote, for instance, and everybody laughs at them – even other women ... You see we have just three choices: old maid or nun – to me it's the same thing; wife and mother; or *guidoune*. I'm not saying those are bad choices, I'm just saying those three are all we've got. The rest belong to men ... And when the time comes to make your choice ... I don't know why I'm telling you all this, you're too young to understand everything ... I just want ... I just want ..."

She wipes a tear with a handkerchief she's just pulled out of the sleeve of her beautiful lilac cotton dress. Rhéauna reaches out, puts her hand on her cousin's knee, who continues her monologue.

"For heaven's sake, what's got into me? I ought to let you sleep, you're dead tired ... But you're just beginning your life, Nana, and somebody has to tell you those things ... When you think about me again later on, when you understand what I do to earn my living, I want you to know that I've chosen to be what I am, that I'm proud of it because the other two choices don't interest me and it's my way to fight ... to fight men. By manipulating them. But here I am talking about myself and I ought to be talking about your future ... Look, here's what I want to tell you: when the time comes to make your choice, Nana, think about it. Think about it properly. Reflect, don't let yourself be led around by life, don't let them all influence you, just become what you want to become ... A nun? No problem, as long as you know what lies ahead and it's *your* choice. Same for wife and mother. If you choose to be a wife and mother, then become a model wife and mother. But only if that's what you want. Don't let anybody impose it on you if it's not what you want. And the third choice, well … If you're ever interested come and see me, I've got connections and I've got experience. And if you grow into the beauty that I think you will, you'll be able to wreak havoc in Ottawa. Like me … Or find a fourth way for yourself, you seem intelligent enough for that … In any case, give it a try …"

Rhéauna is beginning to suspect the meaning of *guidoune*. It's vague but she suspects it has something to do with the things her grandmother hasn't told her about that involve relations between men and women, about the weird and vaguely disgusting behaviour she's often seen in animals that apparently has something to do with making babies. Animal babies or human babies. Is her cousin's job to make babies with men?

She looks around her.

"Is that how you pay for all this?"

"Yes."

"Is it hard?"

"Sometimes."

"Would I like it?"

Ti-Lou can't help laughing. This time, though, her laughter doesn't get lost in the starry sky but in the wainscoting on the ceiling and the folds in the curtains.

"You won't know that for a good long while. Meanwhile, it's nearly two o'clock in the morning and you leave early tomorrow afternoon. Sleep now, don't think about all that, I shouldn't have brought it up, I should have let you sleep."

Rhéauna yawns hard enough to dislocate her jaws, closes her eyes.

Ti-Lou pulls up the sheet, bends down again to give her a kiss.

Ah! Gardenia! Rhéauna falls asleep intoxicated by gardenias.

✕

The telephone rings several times in the course of the night. Rhéauna vaguely hears Ti-Lou's voice that at first sounds stern, then threatening, but it's all mixed in with her own dreams about gardens of creamy white gardenias with a heady perfume and brand-new castles that give themselves airs of great age when they've barely been open for business. Later on, someone knocks at the door of the suite, a voice, pleading, whining, drunk, rises up in the corridor: "Ti-Lou! Ti-Lou! You can't do this to me! We had a date!" Rhéauna thinks she can hear furtive footsteps on the living-room floor, the sound of a door being opened a crack, a woman whispering: "You're really being unreasonable, Minister, my young cousin's asleep in the parlour …" The footsteps go toward the bedroom, the smell of alcohol and cigars blends with that of gardenia. Rhéauna's cousin is no longer alone. She's going to make babies with this minister Rhéauna hears say, laughing in a very strange way, this time she is fully awake: "Is your cousin old enough? Could she join us?" The crack of a slap. A man's laughter. The rest she couldn't interpret. It lasts for a certain time, the man seems to be puffing as if he's just run two miles, he squeals like a stuck pig. He is crying and laughing at the same time. Rhéauna closes her eyes, tries to get back to sleep. It's hard because the minister's shriek is getting louder. But her sleep ends up taking her away and the crazy gentleman's voice mingles with the scent of exotic flowers and the vision of the Château Laurier, the refuge, one might think for peculiar heroes from a very strange fairy tale.

X

Louise Desrosiers, known as Ti-Lou, the she-wolf of Ottawa, balked very early at bearing her father's name, Wilson. Already in elementary school she wanted to be considered a Desrosiers, her mother's name – a bold move on the part of a child at the end of the nineteenth century brought up in a strict and oh-so-provincial society. But she was adventurous, had always been what her father called pig-headed, which allowed her in fact as an adolescent to escape from her family's clutches and the laws of polite Ottawa society thanks to a near-diabolical strategy.

When asked why she wanted to change her name, she replied that Wilson was English, that she was proud of her French roots and of the beauty of her mother's language. But certain nuns, less naive than the others, had quickly guessed that something fishy was going on in that rich and influential family – Wilson was one of the most respected lawyers in Ottawa – but they did not intervene: out of propriety, a legacy of the Catholic religion where everything is always hidden; or out of cowardice, their three vows – poverty, chastity, obedience – exempting them from any intervention while leaving them with a clear conscience.

Louise tolerated her father's cruelty without a word – she wasn't his only victim, everyone in the family had to suffer law-yer Wilson's insults and blows, their mother most of all – she contented herself with renouncing his name and taking her mother's. When he found out through an indiscretion by one of her classmates, Louise had got the thrashing of her life. With the buckle of a leather belt, James Wilson's favourite weapon when he'd drunk too much or someone angered him. Emergency, doc-tor, stitches. But no one in Ottawa would have risked exposing James Wilson and matters stayed there: a stupid accident, a fall downstairs, a reckless little girl running too fast in a house where the floors are too well waxed. And Louise, against her will, had to agree once and for all to use the name Wilson. And the stigmas that go with it.

That law of silence within her family and even inside Ottawa's high society was one of the things that shocked her most. Hypocrisy, spinelessness, fear. Despite her great love for Gertrude, her mother, and for her brothers and sisters, she couldn't understand why no one rebelled against her father's behaviour – she herself, as the youngest in the family, discovered she was helpless to intervene – and had decided very early that she would make him pay. Not violently, no, leather belts with metal buckles didn't hold the slightest interest for her. Another way. How? Fate would look after finding a solution.

But she'd chomped at the bit for years and never saw any way out taking shape on the horizon. Everything stayed as it was. James W. Wilson was still reigning by terror and violence toward his family, the whole city, or at least its elite, knew that, and no one dared to do anything. At home, he was the lord and master. He had all the rights and he abused them all shamelessly. Louise had finally thought, to her great despair, that Ottawa might be full of James Wilsons, amoral torturers exonerated by a society they had invented according to their own sadistic needs, that life was made that way, life was like that, unfair to the point of cruelty and that she herself, a poor little girl, couldn't change a thing.

Then at the age of sixteen, she read *La dame aux camélias*, a scandalous novel from France that a friend had given her, saying that she mustn't show it to anyone because it's a forbidden book, a book *on the Index*, a shocking story set among Paris courtesans, the most depraved women in the world. And the most beautiful.

Reading about a dissolute life, about the poignant ordeals and the tragic death of Marguerite Gautier had left Louise dumbfounded. Everything in the book had moved her deeply, the story of a young girl who was allowed nothing and knew nothing of liberty: mid-nineteenth-century Paris, its splendour, its immorality, its exaggerated romanticism that had never managed to make its way to Ottawa, a dead city preserved in its hypocrisy. She wished she belonged to a world of powerful demimondaines, of idealized whores, of women who are powerful because they're beautiful and sassy, who are respected, adulated, decorated and carried on a man's arm instead of being looked down on; to know to its innermost recesses that antithesis to life imposed on an entire country by two religions based on humiliation and the denial of any sensuality; to see finally an open-mindedness, a happy-go-lucky attitude, an existence with no barriers, made up of unbelievably rich parties drowned in champagne or manic nights that ended in vast fragrant beds, of the impossible love between a penniless young man and a courtesan ready to do anything to keep him at her side, all crowned by a sense of duty that no one in her circle had to her knowledge ever shown, especially her father. In that book she found everything she was forbidden and she revelled in it.

She wanted to be Marguerite Gautier, to live like her, and if necessary, to die like her, young but experienced. And above all, avenged. She thought that she'd found her way out, found her revenge. Unthinkable for a girl of her position who shouldn't even have known about her, the fate of Marguerite Gautier became for her the example to follow, the goal to reach: nothing indeed would offend her father as much as learning that his daughter had lost her virtue, that she even used her body in her work.

But how to go about it, especially in a city as secretive as Ottawa where never, or hardly ever, was the word *prostitute* pronounced, reluctantly, on very rare occasions, expressions like "woman of ill repute" or "fallen woman," with wrinkled nose and hand on heart?

Was that really what she wanted to become, a "woman of ill repute"? Too young to weigh all the consequences, she wouldn't let herself think, concentrating on the thirst for revenge that she wanted to quench, the shame of her father in the face of the fait accompli and the indelible stain that would make him pay for his unwarranted invective and for the leather belt with its metal tip. She refused to see beyond revenge, most likely for fear of lacking courage or of having to pay the price: the everyday life of an

Ottawa prostitute, very different no doubt from that of the heroine of a novel.

No, she preferred to wallow in the most syrupy romanticism and drown in it rather than risk the predictable melodrama that her life was liable to become if she risked doing some irrevocable deed.

And so one sticky night in 1892, she did something that couldn't be undone, with bravery she'd never suspected she possessed. It was behaviour at once planned – she had long dreamed about it – and impulsive – the deed was done on a whim, it was brave and suicidal and, as she had hoped, it turned her life upside down.

As far as sexuality was concerned, Louise was pretty well ignorant, like most young girls from good families at the time. She'd had the necessary conversation with her mother when she was fifteen or so, but it hadn't really taught her much. A few references to the mechanics, the precautions to take before and after, the repeated trauma that had to be put up with because it was her duty ... Nothing clear – allusions, incomplete sentences, all delivered with eyes lowered and face red. Gertrude Wilson as much as her daughter would have preferred to be elsewhere, that was obvious. Louise had concluded that sex was a most disagreeable occupation and decided that she would try to avoid it as much as she could. She certainly had no idea that she would soon make a profession of it and that it would become the source of a rather impressive fortune.

On the night in question her father hit her once too often, without the leather belt, though, a simple slap because she'd dared once again to stand up to him. She slammed her bedroom door, threw herself onto her bed and, in the midst of her tears, decided that it was now or never: the time to pay her father back in kind, to humiliate him without his ever being able to recover, had come. Why then in particular? She could never explain precisely but she'd always been grateful for that moment of sheer madness that was going to throw her into what her circle claimed to abhor most, sensuality – it was true for women, false for men, Louise suspected and she intended to take advantage of it, even if she didn't know exactly what it meant – and that would turn her into the most adulated woman in the city and at the same time the one most held in contempt.

A young girl from her background would never go out alone after dark, it wasn't done, even though Ottawa was a fairly peaceful city, where danger didn't roam the streets. Reputations were quickly undone, gossip sprang up like weeds, engagements were broken over trivia: the rules were that much stricter as there were few families who mattered in this piddling little capital of a vast country, the fortunes significant and the stakes nearly always tinged with the corrupt hypocrisy that marks everything politics touches. Young girls served as currency in this provincial Victorian society and that currency had to shine.

What she did on that hot, humid night in July then was mad and bold.

She had noticed that Captain McDonald, the chief of police, ogled young girls at official receptions or balls given on the occasion of an engagement announcement; the birthday of some head of a family; the election of some notable to a position he didn't deserve. The more he drank the cheekier he became, being careful though to drop his libidinous innuendo into young ladies' ears or to run his hand around their waists in distant corners of over-furnished salons where it was easy to hide, or behind the doors of dimly lit offices.

Did the heads of families suspect, did the mothers keep a close watch? Of course. But he was the chief of police, he was feared, and nothing very serious had ever happened, so they let him go on in the hope that he would disappear after the next election. But mayors of Ottawa succeed one another and Captain McDonald, who incidentally did a very good job as a hunter of criminals of all kinds, kept his job. In any event, he wasn't the only one who fondled young ladies at receptions and the mothers spent long evenings looking for their daughters or on the lookout for their husbands' tactics. They attributed it all to drink, pretended that it was unimportant – men will be men – and the receptions ended with smiles – fulfilled on the men, forced on their wives.

Louise knew the location of the private club where Captain McDonald went nearly every night. As had his father. And all the important men in Ottawa. Women were not admitted, it was the refuge – inspired by London, most civilized and most hypocritical city in the world – where the men withdrew to drink and smoke cigars while they bragged, boasted of escapades that couldn't always be checked and pranks that were often imaginary. For a few hours, men would think that they were the driving force of a great city, they'd snap their suspenders, get drunk and go home content.

She also knew of the existence of what her father called "the anteroom," a parlour fixed up in a discreet corner of the Saint James Club where women, legitimate and others, especially the others, the legitimate would rather die than be seen in that cursèd place, could come discreetly and wait for their men while sipping tea. (Another open secret: everyone knew that what was served in the tea cups wasn't tea.) As rooms were available upstairs for the tired old gentlemen who were in no shape to go home, the tea drinkers had just one staircase to climb to dispense the services expected of them. That, though, Louise did not know.

After she'd dried her tears, she left the house with everyone thinking she was asleep in bed, humiliated and remorseful, and she made her way straight to the Saint James Club. You could almost hear her heart pounding: she was about to rub shoulders with women of ill repute, take tea that wasn't tea, offer herself, yes, offer herself, to the chief of police without revealing to him who she was, from a simple need for revenge! And hoping that he wouldn't recognize her because they had met on numerous occasions. The enormity of what she was getting ready to do made her tremble while she climbed the few steps that led to the colonnaded balcony of the Saint James Club. The two religions practised in the Wilson household, that of her father, that of her mother, would condemn her once and for all, she would be marked for life, the future that was being planned for her destroyed forever ... No husband, no future. But never mind, too bad for her, too bad for the others, they were going to see, all of them, who she was and what she could do!

What happened next was so fast that she didn't have time to think or to change her mind. She met Captain McDonald accompanied by an Anglican minister, Mister Glassco, who were getting ready to go home after an evening with plenty of wine. She didn't have to wait in the anteroom with the tea drinkers, she didn't even see them, and she approached the chief of police right in the lobby of the private club, with a look of alarm.

The story she'd prepared was implausible, ridiculous, a muddle of details from her forbidden reading – Marguerite Gautier wasn't far away – but for the two intoxicated men with overactive libidos the unexpected arrival of this magnificent young girl in tears who was throwing herself at them to tell them of her woes – the violent father, the escape by night (that's where the truth stopped), the bus chosen out of the blue, the arrival in Ottawa in the middle of the night, the reputation of the Saint James, its anteroom, its tea drinkers – was an amazing bargain not to be missed. Through the alcohol fumes they didn't see the holes, though huge and plentiful, in her melodramatic account, nor her clothes that were too elegant for a poor girl from Alexandria, nor did they notice her carefully chosen language or her extensive vocabulary. They took in only the easy prey they'd make short work of, drooling at the possibility being offered them, treated her kindly in a way that was soon transformed into thinly disguised propositions. Two men, intelligent and seasoned though they were, fell into the enormous trap set by an inexperienced young girl, from the sheer lust of intoxicated males. They behaved like profiteering boors without even a hint of guilt: they were powerful, they knew they were immune and they acted accordingly. As was their wont.

They talked to her about the rooms available upstairs, offered to provide her with one for the night, long enough for her to get over her emotions, even to accompany her if she felt that she needed protection …

Louise Wilson lost her virginity twice that night. First, through assaults aggressive but brief by the Ottawa chief of police, then in the quivering arms of a man of the Church. Both in fact would become regular visitors to the apartments, then to the houses she would keep, thoughtful protectors, mainstays of her clientele, but that night they allowed themselves shameful acts and she planned to make them pay.

She submitted to the act itself – painful, but not as sharp as she'd have thought, the actual lovemaking, the sweat, the odours – by concentrating on the advantage she could take from them, already the mistress of herself, controlling her emotions, lost in her need for revenge. She would amuse herself later, claiming that she'd become a professional whore in a few hours.

She went back to her father's home at dawn, sat down in front of him, very calmly, and told him everything. She hoped that she'd see him die of apoplexy but found herself facing the very image of offended Victorian virtue: forefinger pointing, the other hand on his heart, he called her an unworthy daughter and showed her to the door of his office, telling her that he never wanted to see her again. He was very effective at outraged indignation, he was used to it as a corrupt lawyer who owed part of his fortune to more or less dubious cases. He could have killed her, he would have had the right, or buried her in a convent or shut her up in her room for good, he contented himself with ordering her to disappear from his sight. He knew he was helpless before the chief of police who had fairly often helped him out of tricky situations – mostly having to do with women – to whom he thought of himself as debtor; as for the Anglican priest, she didn't mention his name. But he knew very well who it was, having himself taken advantage many times of the naivety of young girls along with his minister, Mister Glassco. He wasn't going to demand compensation from his companions in debauchery! And so Louise was no longer his daughter, she had never existed, she could make a new life for herself somewhere else.

But Ottawa was a small town and Louise would have many opportunities to remember her father. Especially because she often went to the same places he did.

She took her small suitcase, her copy of *La dame aux camélias*, and went back to knock on the door of the Saint James Club. She joined the ranks of tea drinkers awaiting her turn to climb upstairs to honour those gentlemen, but not for long. Because her ascent was meteoric: beautiful, bright, funny, she made for herself with dazzling speed a most flattering reputation across the capital and even beyond. Her taste for extravagant outfits, her scathing humour, the professionalism she displayed in plying her trade made her within a short time the queen of the secrets of the chaste capital of Canada. And she went from Louise to Ti-Lou. The she-wolf of Ottawa would come later, when her pecuniary requirements became exorbitant and her whims famous.

At first her family claimed that she had gone to Europe, to Switzerland more precisely, then that she had found a husband, a fortune and happiness. A false trip was even organized around her false marriage and the Wilsons disappeared for several months. In fact, they spent the summer at the seaside, in Cape Cod, Massachusetts. No one was fooled, though no one dared to say a word: you could see the supposed newlywed travelling the streets of Ottawa in a carriage every afternoon, but no one would have dared to contradict Mr. Wilson, even when he wasn't there. They treated her as if she'd just arrived in town and no one knew who she was.

But if someone who really didn't know her asked her where she came from – visiting foreigners were numerous and often partial to fresh meat in this tiny government town where opportunities for fun were rare – she started with her famous powerful throaty laugh and said:

"I'm the daughter of the lawyer James W. Wilson here in Ottawa.

Do you know him? If you don't, stay away; if you do, watch out, he's the biggest crook in town!"

They'd all been there: Catholic priests and Protestant ministers, dignitaries from far-off lands as well as local worthies, crowned heads, phoney nobility, real mafiosi, one or two gents with no money or brilliant positions but dangerously handsome: those, she kept for the end, as a treat. A cardinal. But no pope despite hints by the authors of hot gossip who never knew where to stop. And all, without exception, had fallen for her charms. Her cultivation matched her expertise, her conversation and her style. She held sway over balls, reigned supreme in bed. She made men laugh after making them moan. She dressed wounds to self-esteem when a client turned out to be not up to it – alcohol could take the blame and she had the sensitivity to accuse it – and she knew how to congratulate those whose performance found favour in her eyes. Never did she disappoint. Anyone. She was the barely hidden gem of Ottawa and people came from far afield to honour her. Not from Rome, though. No, a pope wouldn't have been so reckless as to cross the Atlantic twice for an encounter with a simple *guidoune*! Although …

Legends, each more unlikely than the others, were then created around her personality, like the pope's, actually, and she allowed it because she knew that it was excellent for her reputation.

She had but one regret and she thought about it for the rest of her life: she had aimed at her father but it was her mother she'd killed. In fact, Gertrude had died of sorrow after several months of pleading with her husband, in vain, to retract his censure of their daughter, and trying for reconciliation with Louise. Both refused. Of course, Louise didn't dare show up at her funeral and mourned all alone. And never forgave herself for what she would see as the single bad deed she'd committed.

In 1912, when the Château Laurier had become the new Saint James Club, its corridors travelled by all of Ottawa's influential political riff-raff, from the most serious senators to the new members of Parliament, ambitious but still green, the she-wolf of

Ottawa settled there into a suite that would soon become the most popular salon in town. Outstanding *salonnière*, idolized as much by artists as by the political community, she was finally able to play Marguerite Gautier as she pleased. And like her, every month she placed a bouquet of red camellias in the doorway to her *sweet*. The perfume they spread around her then was not that of gardenias.

Today, when she happens to run into her father – retired, bitter, sick – she always makes it a point of honour to greet him with a great big "Bonjour, Papa!" that every time he receives as a knife to his heart.

Rhéauna didn't know that it was possible to have your breakfast in bed, unless you were sick of course.

In Maria, breakfast is a joyous ceremony around the big kitchen table: bread is toasted on the wood stove, summer and winter; eggs are fresh – Méo has just collected them in the henhouse; coffee is fragrant; bacon sizzles; everyone talks at the same time; everyone hurries because they're late for school or for the day's work. But it would never occur to anyone in the house to have it in bed. Meals have to be eaten together, not separately!

After she has finished explaining, Ti-Lou grabs the telephone majestically and orders all kinds of things in English. A little later, a lady in uniform – different from the one who'd come earlier to change the sheets – delivers it all on a metal cart. Now the two of them are sitting up in the big cream satin bed, trays between them, breadcrumbs all over, empty little jam jars on the plates, remains of eggs solidifying in a sauce that Rhéauna doesn't know and decides is exquisite. The little girl is even allowed to drink her first cup of coffee. It smells better than it tastes.

She hasn't mentioned the sounds she heard during the night and Ti-Lou hasn't taken the trouble to explain them. The conversation is trivial, about this and that, Ti-Lou repeats the same questions as the day before about her mother's relatives scattered all over Canada, life in Maria out in the middle of the prairies, school. At first Rhéauna appears to be reserved, simply replying to the questions as she had the day before and not really presenting her own ideas. She bites into a piece of bread, chews slowly, seems to think it over before replying to the question she's just been asked. Her reactions are serious, overly polite. Gradually, though, more personal thoughts slip in, then some confidences, discreet at first, then more and more intimate. She deals with the same subjects but in a way that's more thoughtful, less automatic. And she can't help herself, she needs to confide in someone and finally bares her heart to her cousin Ti-Lou: her life in Maria, which she'll miss; how she found out that she had to leave Saskatchewan, no doubt forever; her desire to see her mother again combined with her fear of living alone with her, after all she doesn't know the woman, in a big city unlike anything she has experienced so far; her uncertain future with or without her sisters because she doesn't even know when she'll see them again; the loss of her grandparents who provoke her first sobs.

Ti-Lou takes her in her arms, wipes her tears with a big lace handkerchief on which Rhéauna smells again the scent that overcomes her soul.

"I don't want that life, Ti-Lou, I want my other life back!"

Ti-Lou holds her even closer. The scent of gardenia explodes around Rhéauna, who wishes she could drown in it, wishes she could die there, between satin sheets, in the arms of the most beautiful woman in the world.

"Your mother has a heart of gold, Nana. I don't know her very well but you could already tell when we were little girls that she was a good person, even though she could be difficult sometimes. We only saw each other at Christmas but I always looked forward to it because she was my favourite cousin. You have to think about how brave she was, Nana, to move all the way to Providence, to bring up a family on her own because her husband was at sea, to separate from them when she realized that she couldn't bear that life ... She separated from all of you because she loved you, and now if she's called you back ... You'll have to be brave, too, Nana, probably it'll be hard at first, but she's your mother, you have a mother who loves you! You mustn't ever forget that you've got a mother who loves you!"

It's time to get ready to leave. Rhéauna calms down, repeats again that she understands, that she'll be sensible, that she'll do everything she can to accept her new life. She told her grandmother, her two aunts, now she repeats it to her distant cousin. But she's far from convinced. Anyway, she's nearly there, in a few hours she will be in Montreal. The outpourings are over, the messages delivered, her move to Montreal is settled, she'll see what's going to happen. Her instinct reminds her, however, that it won't be all that simple, that she must be prepared for surprises and difficulties of a kind she can't imagine, and her anxiety comes back, more oppressive than ever.

Ti-Lou tells her to take her bath, that they'll leave the hotel a little earlier to enjoy the beautiful morning.

"We'll take the phaeton again. And put the top down. We'll show ourselves like two queens through the streets of Ottawa. Ti-Lou and Nana, friends for life."

Bathed and dressed, Rhéauna folds her nightgown, closes her suitcase for the last time. When she opens it again her journey will be over, she'll have settled in with her mother. She bids a silent farewell to Ti-Lou's beautiful suite, thinking it will be a long time before she sees such a gorgeous apartment again. Another wonderful memory. But one that she'll keep for herself.

The ride in the phaeton, even though shortened because it took Ti-Lou forever to get ready, is wonderful. The weather is glorious, Ottawa is a very pretty city with all its flowers; peaceful; inhabited it seems by stylish people who stroll the streets without hurrying as if they have nothing else to do and seem to be part of a never-ending procession. Even this early in the morning. Some of them, all men, greet Ti-Lou as she goes by; others, all women, turn away with contempt when they spot her perched in her carriage, barely protected by a small transparent parasol that only veils the light from the sun without hiding her beautiful she-wolf face. She smiles at the men, laughs behind the backs of the women.

"I always see women from behind. I prefer that."

From outside, the station looks like the Château Laurier in miniature: the same turrets, the same ogival windows, even the entrance, which suggests a pretentious grand hotel. Ti-Lou is welcomed like royalty on a state visit; gentlemen who aren't obliged to rush to open the door of her phaeton, pull down the small metal step, extend a gloved hand to help her descend, open the main door of the station. She hands out smiles while giving the impression that she's giving candy to children.

A tall boy, redheaded and freckle-faced, rushes toward them as soon as he spots them on the platform. Rhéauna thinks to herself that it's probably another Anglo and she won't understand a word he says; he surprises her with his excellent French, broken of course, seasoned with a pronounced accent, but clear and perfectly comprehensible.

Their farewells are exchanged in a breath of gardenia that brings tears to the little girl's eyes. The hugging and kissing stretch out, there are more and more resounding kisses, promises to see one another again are exaggerated and made without illusion because they both know that the chances of that are slight and it saddens them.

Michael – that's the redhead's name – picks up Rhéauna's suitcase.

"You looks tired. You has big circles under the eye. You sleep bad? Me find quiet place where to sleep good."

He chooses an empty bench, tells her she can lie down if she wants, that the trip to Montreal will take just a few hours.

"You goes to meet mamma not see since long time ... You must happy now, yes?"

She nods, presses her nose against the window after thanking him as politely as she can. Ti-Lou is still on the platform, a sad smile on her lips, a big white handkerchief in her hand and she waves it as soon as she sees Rhéauna. Ti-Lou approaches when Rhéauna lowers the window.

"I don't like separations, departures, all those things, which means that I'm going to say my goodbyes right now. If you don't mind I'm leaving before the train goes ... It's too sad. Bye now, sweetie ... Everything's going to be fine, you'll see ... Say hello to Maria for me ... And tell her I said to take good care of you, otherwise she'll have me to answer to!"

She blows one last kiss, a white lace skirt rustles as she turns onto the concrete platform, a huge straw hat moves away. Ti-Lou is now out of her life. Rhéauna shuts her eyes, breathes in the last whiff of exotic flowers.

She takes off her coat, folds it, lays it on the suitcase as a headrest. Her neck is bent slightly but she falls asleep at once, exhausted by the agitated night that kept her awake off and on, though she's used to sleeping for eight solid hours.

DREAM ON THE TRAIN TO MONTREAL

They have taken refuge in the tall grass around the pond behind the house. It's the third brush fire this summer, the worst they've ever witnessed. The smell of smoke has intensified in the past few minutes, the fire is now very close. Grandpa said that it was time to take shelter. They are crouched in the water, even Alice who is disgusted by the mud and afraid of bloodsuckers, even though she doesn't know what they are. Bulrushes block their view but they can hear the crackling of the fire, which according to Grandpa advances at the speed of a galloping horse when there's a wind like there is tonight. And a powerful wind has been blowing in their direction since sunset.

Grandpa Méo tries to make them laugh to turn their attention away from the danger that surrounds them:

"The corn's going to pop tonight! We won't hear it grow, we'll hear it burst!"

No one laughs, his wife pats his arm.

"Silly fool! Making jokes at a time like this!"

He replies in the same tone.

"Do you think I'm in the mood for jokes? It's for the girls! I'm doing it for the girls, silly yourself!"

Then all at once, flames higher than the others shoot up in the night. Grandma cries:

"The house! The house! The house is on fire!"

Rhéauna stands up under her two sisters' protests and looks at their house, which really is in flames.

The sight is terrifying but it's also overwhelmingly beautiful. The big white building has become an enormous wood stove and burns with sounds of crackling and a happy roar. As if it were happy to be burning! That is making its farewells while laughing like a loon! The so-beautiful veranda forms a ring of fire, a wild and devastating circle around the main fireplace, the smoke swirls, sending up sheaves of sparks that are coming toward her, that will burn her hair, devour her body, to kill the whole family! Fire fairies and murderous sprites pounce on her to devour her! Her sisters cry, her grandmother pulls her by her dress to make her lie down in the mud, her grandfather shouts orders that she doesn't understand. A spark touches down on her arm, then another, followed by hundreds, by thousands of biting insects. It hurts, it pinches, it stings … Oh, her dress is on fire!

All of a sudden, her grandmother is standing beside her and screaming as she points to the house:

"Somebody's missing! Somebody's missing!"

Rhéauna doesn't understand what she means, they are all there – her two sisters, her grandmother, her grandfather and she herself, the whole family, no one is missing … She cries into her dress which is ablaze.

"Nobody's missing, Grandma! We're all here! Look, we're all here, nobody's missing …"

"Yes, yes, there is someone missing! I have to find her! I can't let her burn like that, I have to save her!"

Grandma Joséphine marches into the mud, she tries to get out of the pond, her clothes are plastered against her body, she has trouble advancing in the mud, she staggers, everyone protests.

"I can't leave her there. I can't leave her there …"

Rhéauna wants to follow her but her grandfather holds her back.

"Is it Mama that's missing, Grandma? But Mama isn't here! Mama's in Montreal!"

Grandma has come out of the pond and is heading with

outstretched arms toward the house, which is spitting thousands of
fairies and sprites.

"It's not your mother! It's not your mother, but there's a person
missing!"

She climbs up the burning staircase, crosses the veranda, she
disappears into the flames, she will burn trying to save someone who
doesn't exist!

"Grandma! Grandma! There's nobody! There's nobody, Grandma,
there's no use looking, nobody's there!"

The house collapses with a grim crackling sound.

It's over, they have both died, Grandma Joséphine and the person
who doesn't exist.

She opens her mouth, she cries out, she weeps. She is frozen in a
horrified grimace and she howls silently in the sputtering night.

Grandpa puts a hand on her shoulder.

"That's why you're going to Montreal, Nana. So the Desrosiers line
will carry on.

She wakes with a start. Cold sweat dampens her back, she's afraid
she has wet her pants. No, she checks, all is well. She looks up. The
train has stopped moving. They're in the station. Surely she hadn't
been dreaming about a fire all that time!

Then the thought that her mother is waiting for her nearby
strikes her and she leaps to her feet.

LAST STOP

✗

She didn't see Montreal emerge on the horizon, then come nearer, or the Victoria Bridge that stretched across the very impressive Saint Lawrence River, Windsor Station – another fake castle put up to the greater glory of the Canadian Pacific Railway – most of all she didn't check that there really was a mountain in the middle of the city, because she was sleeping. She's mad at herself for missing it all.

Michael – she hasn't said a word to him since they left Ottawa – brings her a glass of water. He seems worried.

"Are you okay? Youse all red! I thought you to be cold so I spread out your coat on top. Maybe he's too warm ..."

Glancing out at the platform in the hope of seeing her mother, she gulps the water, which cools her throat. She sees only the passengers who've just got off the train and are moving away from it as fast as they can, as if no one is there to meet them ...

"Your mother will be back of the barriers over there ... Nobody is allowed to get so close to the train ..."

Reassured, she picks up her belongings, puts her coat back on despite the rather unhealthy heat in the car. Michael grabs her suitcase, gets down from the train, sets it all on the platform, then turns back to Rhéauna and holds out his hand.

"This is bad time for fall just when you are to meet together ..."

As soon as she sets foot on the concrete platform, she hears someone call out her name. It's her! She turns around and sees the woman beckoning her, very far away, behind the big metal grilles, in the middle of a crowd of people who are embracing and patting each other's backs.

Her heart takes a leap. She's there! She is in the presence of her mother! She's going to be able to kiss her! She races through the travellers, followed by Michael who tells her that it's pointless to run like that, he'll lose sight of her …

She stops abruptly a few steps from the grilles and stands there frozen in place in her coat that's too big for her.

Her mother, seeming on edge, waves frantically, and this is weird, she's holding a package in her other arm. It's pale blue and it looks like clothes, tiny little clothes … Diapers. Her mother is holding pale-blue diapers in her arms!

All at once, Rhéauna understands why her mother wanted her to come to Montreal from so far away. And everything crumbles.

Maria gives her a magnificent smile and shouts:

"Nana! You're so pretty! You've grown so much! And I'm so glad to see you! Here, come and meet your new baby brother! Come and give him a kiss! You'll love him! His name is Théo, Théo Desrosiers. I'm using my maiden name again! Come give me a kiss, Nana, give both of us a kiss! I've missed you so badly!"

ABOUT THE AUTHOR

Born in a working-class family in Quebec, novelist and playwright Michel Tremblay was raised in Montreal's Plateau neighbourhood. An ardent reader from a young age, Tremblay began to write, in hiding, as a teenager. Because of their charismatic originality, their vibrant character portrayals and the profound vision they embody, Tremblay's dramatic, literary and autobiographical works have long enjoyed remarkable international popularity; his plays have been adapted and translated into dozens of languages and have achieved huge success throughout Europe, the Americas and the Middle East.

A seven-time recipient of grants from the Canada Council for the Arts, during his career Tremblay has received more than sixty prizes, citations and honours, including nine Chalmers Awards and five *Prix du Grand public*, presented during Montreal's annual book fair, *Salon du Livre*. Tremblay has also received six honorary doctorates.

The French Government, in 1984, honoured Tremblay's complete body of work when it made him *Chevalier de l'Ordre des Arts et des Lettres de France*. Thereafter, in 1991, he was raised to Officer of the Order. In 2008, he was created *Chevalier de la Légion d'Honneur de France*. Tremblay was appointed, in 1991, *Chevalier de l'Ordre National du Québec*. In 1999, he received the Governor General's Performing Arts Award. In 2011, he was honoured with the *Révolution Tranquille* medal, given by the Ministry of Culture of Quebec, awarded to artists, creators and artisans who began their careers between 1960 and 1970 and who still have an influence in their field of practice.

ABOUT THE TRANSLATOR

Born in Moose Jaw, Saskatchewan, Sheila Fischman is a graduate of the University of Toronto. A co-founder of the periodical *Ellipse: Œuvres en traduction / Writers in Translation*, she has also been a columnist for the *Globe and Mail* and the *Montreal Gazette*, a broadcaster with CBC Radio and literary editor of the *Montreal Star*. She now devotes herself full time to literary translation, specializing in contemporary Quebec fiction, and has translated more than 125 Quebec novels by, among others, Michel Tremblay, Jacques Poulin, Anne Hébert, François Gravel, Marie-Claire Blais and Roch Carrier.

Sheila Fischman has received numerous honours, including the 1998 Governor General's Award (for her translation of Michel Tremblay's *Bambi and Me*, Talonbooks); she has been a finalist fourteen times for this award. She has received two Canada Council Translation Prizes, two Félix-Antoine Savard Awards from Columbia University and, in 2008, she received the Canada Council for the Arts Molson Prize. She holds honorary doctorates from the Universities of Ottawa and Waterloo.